The Killers of Cimarron

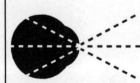

This Large Print Book carries the
Seal of Approval of N.A.V.H.

THE KILLERS OF CIMARRON

FRANK LESLIE

WHEELER PUBLISHING

A part of Gale, Cengage Learning

GALE
CENGAGE Learning

Detroit • New York • San Francisco • New Haven, Conn • Waterville, Maine • London

GALE
CENGAGE Learning

LIBRARY OF CONGRESS CATALOGING-IN-PUBLICATION DATA

Leslie, Frank, 1963–
    The killers of Cimarron / by Frank Leslie.
        p. cm. — (Wheeler Publishing large print Western)
    ISBN-13: 978-1-4104-3481-4 (softcover)
    ISBN-10: 1-4104-3481-8 (softcover)
    1. Large type books. I. Title.
PS3552.R3236K53 2011
813'.54—dc22   2010045049

Published in 2011 by arrangement with NAL Signet, a member of Penguin Group (USA) Inc.

Printed in the United States of America
1 2 3 4 5 6 7 15 14 13 12 11

To Kit Prate,
for her friendship, first and foremost,
but also for her wonderful Western yarns
and for reintroducing me to the
Lancer *TV series*
and right tasty deer jerky.

CHAPTER 1

Colter Farrow hooked a leg over his saddle horn, nudged his floppy-brimmed, coffee brown hat back off his sunburned forehead, and raised his spyglass so that it touched the upper end of the letter S that had been burned into his left cheek.

He could no longer feel the brand's searing burn. The nights of agony and torment in the aftermath of the savage branding — the glowing iron had been rammed against his cheek until his nose had filled with the stench of his own burning flesh — had gradually diminished, so that now he could touch his hand, or a spyglass, to his face, and become only vaguely aware of the hard, knotted tissue that would mark him forever.

But he was never, ever only vaguely aware of the horrified looks, pitying glances, and incredulous stares that the S brand constantly won him.

Nor was he unaware that the scar would

prevent him from acquiring the handsomeness that he, at vain moments in his youthful past, had expected to gain once the boyish softness of his features had been tempered by a few judicious swipes of manhood's chisel. He would never be a handsome man. And no girl would ever marry him, because — and of this he'd become certain over his year of riding branded, a disfigured wandering man who'd ridden up to Wyoming from southern Colorado on a mountain-bred coyote dun — not only did he wear the hideous scar, but the scar wore him, so that it had become him. Him, the scar.

It was the first and last thing anyone ever saw.

Colter Farrow adjusted the spyglass's focus until the three riders washed up from the wind-buffeted brome and buffalo grass and over a low knoll, moving toward him at easy lopes, the brushy cut of Little Gooseberry Creek falling away behind them. The three riders — sunburned and ragged-looking but well armed — rode through a stand of aspens, the leaves beginning to turn now at the bittersweet end of a short high-country summer. Several crows alighted from the crooked limbs of the gnarled trees and winged raucously back toward the chokecherries and willows lining the stream.

One of the men, wearing a long wolf coat and a felt sombrero with a bent brim, turned his head to one side to spit chaw. He wore two cartridge belts around the outside of his coat, and the pistol-filled holsters attached to the belts were thonged on his checked wool–clad thighs.

Sitting his white-stockinged black to Colter's right, Griff Shanley said, "You recognize 'em?"

"Nope." Colter lowered the spyglass to frown across the bending grass and silver-green sage at the three men loping toward him, Shanley, and their partner, Stretch Dawson.

All three rode for Cimarron Padilla's Diamond Bar brand in the shadow of the snowcapped Cheyennes, and they were looking for herd-quitting steers and un-branded calves, mavericks that they'd missed in the fall gather a month ago, getting ready to settle down in the Diamond Bar bunkhouse for the long Cheyenne Mountain winter.

"But, then," Colter added, handing the spyglass over to Shanley, "I don't know anyone up here but you fellas and the few I met passing through the Diamond Bar headquarters."

Shanley held the spyglass to his eye for a time, his wind-blistered lips stretched back from his chipped, tobacco-stained teeth and framed by a three-day growth of stubble, then handed the glass to Stretch Dawson, a lanky, good-natured rider from Dakota.

"Nah," Dawson said as the riders drew to within sixty yards and checked their mounts down to trots. "I never seen them rannies out here. Saddle tramps by the look of 'em. Regulators, maybe, judgin' by the hardware they're packin'. The Pool mighta hired 'em to keep nesters out of the mountains this winter."

"I don't know," Shanley replied, keeping his voice low as the riders approached, their hoof thuds and tack squawks growing louder beneath the humming wind. "They look a might ringy to me. 'Specially if they've got a passel of Diamond Bar beef boxed up in a canyon nearby. Might reward us to sit watchful, fellers."

"Out here, you're always watchful among strangers, you old mossy horn."

"Ah, shut up about that mossy-horn shit," Shanley snapped at Dawson. "I ain't all that much older than you, Stretch. The difference is, I've learned more in my time above-ground, and" — he shaped a sneering grin — "had a helluva lot more women than you,

10

my friend."

"Bull-sheeeit!" scoffed Dawson.

The two men — lifelong thirty-and-found ranch hands — had been partnered up so long, mostly in remote line shacks around Wyoming and Dakota, that they could hardly exchange a civil word to each other. Colter knew, though, from having known many other men of the same breed, that they'd die for each other at the drop of a hat.

Colter hoped it didn't come to that here. Judging by the old pistols each wore in soft leather holsters that were cracked and yellowed with age and weather, neither was very practiced with a shooting iron. If it came to a lead swap here, with the three obviously gun-handy hardcases closing on them fast, they'd likely give up their ghosts, and Colter would be left to shoot it out alone.

The three strangers reined their sweat-lathered mounts to a halt twenty yards away. Shanley's horse whinnied shrilly, and Stretch Dawson's old steeldust mare jerked up her head with a start. The horse of the rider straight ahead of Colter returned the greeting by chomping its bit. The riders merely stared, hard eyed, over their horses' heads at Colter and the other two drovers,

11

coolly taking the stockmen's measure.

The one on the left — a dark-haired, blue-eyed gent with a black soup-strainer mustache and a calico shirt under a black cowhide vest — said with a stern air, "What're you three doin' out here?"

From age more than any formally assigned hierarchy, Griff Shanley usually acted as unofficial *segundo* of the Diamond Bar crew. He cocked his head to one side and narrowed an eye. "I was about to ask you the same thing, amigo." He softened the statement with a grin that made his soft gray eyes flash in the crisp afternoon sunlight.

The three strangers studied him with stony faces. Keeping a tight rein on his blaze-faced coyote dun, Colter appraised the strangers in return. They looked harried and ornery. The middle one had his hand on the big Schofield jutting from the holster on his left hip, not as though he was about to use it but as though he was always ready to use it.

Obviously they didn't like Shanley's question. The eldest drover flushed and glanced from Colter to Stretch Dawson as the pregnant silence grew increasingly tense, the only sounds being the breeze and the raspy blows of the tired horses.

Finally the man on the right parted his

lips, chaw juice streaming down over his red spade beard. "We're lookin' for the trail to the Lone Pine Stage Station. We was told we'd cut it just after we crossed Devil's Creek, but we didn't see no trail, and here we are, a good five miles beyond the Devil's."

He and the other two men shifted their eyes among Colter, Shanley, and Dawson. *That's it,* Colter thought. *They're lost. And they're in a hurry.* The information did nothing to quell the uneasiness he felt with these three obvious gun hands sitting twenty yards away from him, and looking owly as coons trapped in a privy, but it explained their restless, impatient demeanors.

Stretch Dawson shook his head. "You won't find the trail to Lone Pine anywheres near Devil's Creek. From here, you'd pick it up over yonder." He canted his head toward a large rocky-topped bluff about two miles to the southwest, off his own right shoulder. "Wagon Mound Bluff's where you'll find it. This side but before Wagon Mound Canyon. Nasty country in there. That's why they done closed the Lone Pine Station. Trail kept washin' out or burnin' out by wildfires. The new station's farther east."

"We ain't askin' about the new station,

mister," said the black-haired rider, who was perpetually squinting his eyes. "We done rode through the new station, and that's where they told us we'd pick up the trail to the old station by Devil's Creek."

"Well, that's a pity," said Shanley. As usual, Colter couldn't tell whether the old drover was merely being sarcastic. He doubted many people ever knew when Shanley was being serious and not funning around. "And what explains that bit of lousy information is the fact that the stationmaster at Rock Creek Station is new around here. Howard Rigsby. The company shipped him in from Kansas. Don't know shit from Cheyenne, and he'd probably send you to Cheyenne if you was lookin' for Laramie."

Shanley smiled at his humor. Stretch Dawson did, as well. Colter felt his own mouth corners rise, not so much because he found Shanley humorous but because he wanted as much as his partners did to lighten the mood and keep the minds as well as the hands of these three long coulee riders off their guns.

His lopsided grin wasn't catching, however. The faces of the strangers remained as hard as the granite faces of the Cheyennes looming in the west.

"How long will it take for us to ride to

Lone Pine from here?" asked the dark-haired man.

"Oh," Shanley said, closing one eye and thinking about it. "The rest of today, a few hours in the mornin'."

"Say," Stretch Dawson said, pitching his tall frame forward and resting his forearms on his saddle horn, "what you boys wanna waste your time ridin' all the way to that old abandoned station for, anyhow? Folks say Injuns use it for a camp now and then, and . . ."

Colter's gut had tightened as the overly chatty Dawson, too curious for his own good, had leaned his head out to his right to inspect the saddle of the man sitting straight in front of him. Whatever Dawson had seen there, apparently draped over the hindquarters of the rider's claybank stallion, wasn't what he'd expected.

Or had wanted to see.

Stretch had a big V-shaped face with a silver-brown mustache colored like a summer sunset, and the smile he tried to fashion only gave him a frightened, constipated look.

The rider in the gray sombrero scowled. "Now, why did you have to go and do that?"

"Do what?" Stretch said.

"Look at them saddlebags behind me."

15

"I didn't look —"

"Oh, don't try to hornswoggle me, you old saddle tramp!" the man in the gray sombrero fairly shouted. "You ever hear the sayin' 'curiosity killed the cat'?"

Colter looked from Dawson to the three hardcases. Now, suddenly, they were all three smiling. The smiles weren't fun or humorous. They were dark smiles. The smiles of men who knew something bad was about to happen and they weren't all that unhappy about it.

Because they were used to bad things happening. More to the point, they were used to doing bad things, and even rather enjoyed it.

Colter became aware of the Remington riding in the cross-draw position in the soft leather holster angled back away from his right hip. The fingers of his left hand tingled the way they often did when he rode to high altitudes . . . or when he was about to kill a man.

The black-haired man must have noticed the movement. He switched his dark gaze to Colter. His lips shaped a sneer. "Good Lord, boy, who in the hell laid that brand on your cheek?"

The others looked at Colter then, too, revulsion and mockery mixing in their expressions.

Colter said evenly, "Ain't you ever heard about curiosity killin' the cat, mister?"

The sneer died on the black-haired gent's lips. The others let their evil smiles grow, sliding their eyes toward the dark-haired man, wondering what he'd do about the smart retort he'd just taken from the branded kid.

Shanley tried to ease the tension.

"Look," the old puncher said, dipping his chin and holding up his gloved hands chest high, "Stretch didn't mean nothin' by that. He was just curious, that's all. We three . . . we don't care what the hell you boys are up to. All we care about is our herd. We're movin' it down closer to the headquarters, ya know?"

He paused and stared at the three hardcases, who stared back at him, their lips curled beneath their mustaches.

"Okay?" Shanley said. "Can we all live with that and just ride on out o' here real peaceful-like?"

"Well, I don't know," said the middle hardcase, his hand still on his pistol grips. He had green eyes under a shelf of straight-cut, corn yellow bangs, with deep smallpox scars on his cheeks. "I don't really see how we can, old man. You see, any deputy

17

marshal who rides through here lookin' for us and stumbles across you — well, he's gonna get the full story, now, ain't he? How you seen us right where you see us now, and how we told you where we was headed . . . with twenty-six thousand dollars in stolen army gold."

The green-eyed hombre kept his gaze on Shanley. The black-haired man looked at Colter, Shanley, and Dawson in turn from beneath his shaggy eyebrows. The man in the gray sombrero worked his cud, his eyes bright with mockery.

Colter's heart tattooed an even rhythm against his breastbone. His left hand, splayed across his thigh, itched. He kept his gaze forward on the cutthroats, but in the corner of his right eye he could see sweat glinting on Shanley's and Dawson's chiseled, weathered cheeks.

Colter waited.

The cutthroats expected their main opposition to come from the two older gents to Colter's right, not from the branded kid in the shapeless hat, ragged trail clothes, and suspenders, and wearing an old, rusty Remington in an even older holster on his hip.

But they were wrong.

No sooner had the green-eyed hombre

jerked his revolver from its holster, the other two following suit, than they were all three screaming and tumbling back off their horses' rumps as the animals lurched and bucked and whinnied and arched their tails at the three quick explosions.

The black-haired gent cursed loudly when his horse kicked him inadvertently as it wheeled and galloped after the others.

The man reached for the gun he'd dropped, and Colter's Remy roared once more.

The .44 slug plunked through the man's left temple, exiting the back of his head in a spray of brains, bones, and blood. The man's head jerked back and forward, and then followed his shoulders to the ground, where he lay, kicking himself in a semicircle as the life fled him quickly.

The others, both shot through their briskets, were finished. They lay slumped and twisted, hats off, bloody, dusty, and crumpled by their horse's trampling hooves.

Colter held his reins tight in his right fist as his coyote dun skitter-stepped, nickering. Shanley's and Dawson's mounts both did likewise as the two aging drovers looked around, jaws hanging, right hands clamped over the handles of the hoglegs that were still in their holsters.

They looked from the dead men to Colter, and then to the smoking pistol in the kid's hand.

Shanley glanced at Dawson, then back to Colter, and said, *"Ho-leee sheeeit!"*

CHAPTER 2

Colter stepped down from his saddle, dropped his dun's reins, and went around to each of the dead men, kicking their dropped revolvers well out of range of a possible grab and ripping their spares from their holsters and tossing those, too, into the sage and buck brush.

Not that the three hardcases weren't dead. But he'd learned after surviving several ambushes in Colorado before being driven out of the territory by bounty hunters and lawmen looking for the killer of a prominent rancher and the deputy sheriff of Sapinero to always kick the guns away from his attackers whether they looked dead or not. It was a precaution he'd learned the hard way, having ignored the guns of a bounty hunter north of Denver who'd looked dead after Colter had shot him three times in the chest and belly but who'd resurrected himself with both fists filled with roaring Smith &

Wessons.

When the cutthroats' guns had been disposed of, a few chosen ones to be retrieved later, he turned to Griff Shanley and Stretch Dawson, who were still sitting their jittery cow ponies and regarding him skeptically. Their faces were blanched behind their leathery tans, and their eyes were wide and glassy.

"Didn't see no other way," Colter told them, canting his head toward the dead men lying in growing pools of red sand.

He felt sick to his stomach and weak in the knees. He had not been born a killer, as some of the men he'd had to kill over the past year had. Killing nauseated him for days, filled him with a leadlike depression and such a grim outlook that he sometimes wished he'd simply let the hunters have him.

But then, too, he'd have to let them stretch his neck or shoot him and cut off his head and send it back to Bill Rondo — sheriff of Sapinero, Colorado Territory, the man Colter had left branded with his own iron and in a wheelchair, and who'd put out the two-thousand-dollar bounty on Colter's head.

Colter fingered the gruesome brand on his cheek. It always burned a little after he'd killed.

"I didn't wanna do it," he heard himself muttering, stamping around the dead men — the men who would have killed him and Shanley and Dawson as easily as they'd have shot coiled diamondbacks off their trail.

They'd been alive and breathing and heading toward the rest of their lives — their next meal, next drink, next woman — a few seconds ago. Now, in the wake of Colter's belching Remington, they lay limp, dead, and ugly against the ground, their hearts stopped, futures wiped out, blood seeping into the earth beneath their slumped and twisted carcasses.

They were nothing now but cooling, rotting flesh. Food for the coyotes and vultures.

"Look there."

Dawson removed his hand from his old Schofield to point out the saddlebags that the horse of the man in the gray sombrero had bucked off its back. The twin bags lay with one pouch on its side and leaking bright gold coins into the sage and sand.

The pouch's flap was stamped U.S. ARMY.

Dawson dropped his lean, tall frame to the ground. Shanley, considerably bulkier than Dawson, as well as seven years older, grunted with the effort of leaving the back of his own horse. Looking grimly around at the dead men, he followed Dawson over to the saddlebags.

Dawson dropped to a knee, bit a glove off his big red hand, and scooped up a handful of the coins. The slanting afternoon light shone brightly off the gold, tingeing Dawson's gray-blue gaze above his wisping mustache as he shuttled it to Shanley.

"What do you think about that?"

"How much you think is there?"

"I don't know." Dawson looked at the bags, both pouches of which bulged like the bellies of pregnant women. "Didn't they say twenty-six thousand?"

"Oh, yeah," Shanley said. "I could barely hear him above my old, hammerin' ticker."

Colter stood staring down at the men, saw the hesitation in both their faces, even felt the same hitch he knew was in their chests. He'd known both men for a little over a month, since signing on with the Diamond Bar brand when he'd heard in Casper they were looking for line riders, but he'd come to know what each was made of.

"Reckon Cimarron'll know what to do with it?" Dawson said finally, his voice raspy.

Shanley rubbed his gloved hands on his thighs. He straightened, stared off to the southwest, in the direction of the Lone Pine stage station, nibbled his thick gray mustache thoughtfully. "Yeah, ole Cimarron'll know what to do with it. What I'm wonderin' is . . . what about the fellas these fellas here was to meet at Lone Pine?"

Colter cleared his throat. "We'd best bury 'em."

It was the first he'd spoken in several minutes, and both Shanley and Dawson snapped their heads toward him as though half expecting to see his Remy in his fist once more. They appraised him for a moment silently, warily, taking his measure all over again, the way they'd done when he'd first shown up in the bunkhouse back at the Diamond Bar, his sougan, war bag, and saddle — all he owned — on his shoulder.

Only now they were thinking they'd sized him up all wrong.

But they hadn't.

He was the same kid they'd seen in that bunkhouse doorway — narrow of hip and shoulder, big of hand and foot. Arms and legs a little long for the rest of him. Long dark red hair and a long, angular face peeling from too many miles under a hot western sun and marked by that grisly S no one had asked him about and about which he'd offered nothing. Just a young, raggedyheeled saddle tramp raised on a ranch high up in Colorado's Lunatic Range and now looking for a place to throw down and bury

25

a picket pin for a time until he could figure out what to do with his young life.

He was that same kid. Only a run of awful luck back in Sapinero had turned him into a killer and a kid on the run toward what he hoped would eventually be a life consisting of something more than bloodshed.

"Yeah," Shanley said finally, continuing to rub his hands on his cracked bull-hide chaps. "We'd best bury 'em where they won't be found. And we'd best catch their horses. If them other owl hoots find their mounts, they'll likely track 'em back here, find the graves, then backtrack us to Diamond Bar."

"Shit," Dawson said, on one knee and looking up at Shanley, anxiously pinching his earlobe. "Maybe we oughta just leave this here gold right where we found it. Packin' it back to the ranch might just be packin' a whole lotta trouble back. Cimarron might not like it. I can just hear him now. 'Well, what in the name of Jehosophat's cat did you bring it back here for?' "

Shanley glanced at Colter, as if looking for help in making his decision. The boy didn't care what they did with the gold. It was a temptation to keep it. Money caused a lot of troubles to go away. It attracted as many more. Stolen money attracted the most troubles of all. And once you'd taken it, you'd always taken it, and it was a hard thing to live down, especially to yourself.

Of course, this was all speculation on Colter's part. He was only eighteen years old, and he'd never stolen so much as a horseshoe or a forkful of hay for his horse. But in the past year of his short life, he'd lived as much as most men lived in twice that time.

And he'd come to recognize trouble from a long ways down his back trail.

"It's up to you fellas," Colter said, spitting to one side and looking off toward where the outlaws' horses had fled. "I'm green here but I'll back you, whatever you decide."

Dawson shoveled the spilled coins back into the pouch and latched the flap closed. He stood slowly, staring down at the two swollen bags, then looked at Shanley. "I reckon we'd best take it back to the ranch. That'd be the right thing. Likely, soldiers died when these men stole it from 'em."

Shanley nodded. "Yeah, that's about how I see it, too. Cimarron'll likely see it that way — he was a cavalry grunt himself once — though this here gold could be trouble for all of us."

"Maybe not if we cover our tracks, take that Jackrabbit Canyon trail back to the

Diamond Bar. It's rocky in there, and our tracks won't show on the slide rock."

"Okay." Shanley nodded, looking down at the saddlebags before glancing again at Dawson. "Let's fetch their horses and then bury these sons o' bitches in a dry fork of the creek back yonder."

"Sounds fine by me," Stretch said. "No one'll find 'em in there. Afterwards, maybe we oughta just unsaddle their horses and turn 'em loose. Wouldn't want the wrong fellas seein' 'em in the Diamond Bar corral."

Shanley thought it over, shook his head. "If them other owl hoots found 'em out here, they'd know their partners' trail ended around here somewhere. The way I figure it, if they don't find the horses and they don't find *them* — the dead sons o' bitches — the other robbers might think these three lit a shuck with it."

"A double cross?" Stretch said, and laughed his high-pitched, almost feminine laugh. "Hot damn — I like it. You know, Griff, your thinker box sometimes works better than I give it credit for."

"Well, then," Griff said, "let's get a move on. We're burnin' up daylight a pound a minute!"

Colter saw that as the older puncher

climbed into his saddle, he was staring down at the Remington on Colter's hip. An old, harmless-looking weapon. One that most cowhands would use only on snakes and calf-thieving coyotes.

Colter would tell his old partners how he'd come to use it so well, better than a gun like that deserved to be used. He'd tell them about his murdered foster father, Trace Cassidy, and the men who'd killed him, the men whom Colter in turn had killed or maimed after learning how to shoot the old Remy, which he'd grown so attached to that he'd never considered replacing it, no matter how many other better, newer weapons he stumbled upon.

But first they'd get their chores done here, and get the gold back to the Diamond Bar. It was getting on in the afternoon, and the sun fell fast this high in the mountains this late in the year.

And they didn't want to be caught out here after dark with those other cutthroats catting around, looking for their gold.

CHAPTER 3

"Gravels me — turning men down in unmarked graves," Stretch Dawson said when, two hours later, they'd buried the three cutthroats at the bottom of a dry wash forking off the cut of Devil's Creek, about half a mile from where Colter had dropped them. The two older drovers had each taken one of the guns that Colter had tossed into the brush, and they'd buried the rest of the weapons with the men themselves.

"Don't bother me at all," said Shanley, resting his folding shovel on his shoulder and puffing a loosely rolled quirley. "Sons o' bitches like that don't deserve to be buried at all. They deserve to have their bones picked and licked clean by turkey buzzards and porcupines."

Colter was running a cedar branch over the shallow graves to make the ground blend with the rest of the gravelly wash, disguising the cutthroats' final resting place.

Their brethren would have to be damn good trackers, or come searching with bloodhounds, to find the dead men here.

"Yeah, well, they were still men. They mighta come to no good, but they were men nonetheless. My pa said even the worst of us deserved to be buried proper-like and have words read over us."

"Your pa was a preacher."

"That's right — he was."

"Sky pilot." Shanley drew deep on his quirley and turned to his horse cropping needlegrass on the bank of the shallow wash. "Never cared for the breed. No better'n rock-worshippin' Injuns with tom-toms."

"Better'n a goddamn farmer like your old rebel pa!" retorted Dawson as he, too, climbed the bank to his horse. He glanced over his shoulder. "Come on, Colter. Don't leave me too long alone with this ornery old son of a bitch. I might back-shoot him!"

Colter dropped the cedar branch, hitched his Remington and cartridge belt higher on his hips, and climbed the bank to his coyote dun. He had the reins of one of the cutthroats' mounts tied to his saddle horn. Shanley and Dawson had each done likewise, so that they each would lead a horse back to the Diamond Bar.

Now as Colter stepped into his saddle, he saw that the other two waddies had stopped bedeviling each other, as each tended to do when he was nervous — and Colter could tell they were both plenty nervous now — to cast dark, speculative looks along their back trail. He did the same.

Nothing back there but the flour white trail twisting back through the steep-walled canyon from Devil's Creek, strewn with boulders and spotted with wind-gnarled cedars. The sun was falling fast, cool purple shadows bleeding out from the canyon's western slope. An unseen hawk screeched, the cry echoing eerily in the canyon's stillness and silence.

"Well, we ain't makin' any time like this," Shanley said, turning forward in his saddle and batting his spurred boots against his piebald's flanks. "Hell, them owl hoots is probably still waiting for these dead three to show at Lone Pine."

Following Shanley, Dawson said, "They won't start lookin' for 'em until dawn tomorrow, most like." He glanced at Colter, his eyes holding more curiosity and meaning than they had before. Maybe a tad of caution. "You think so, Colter?"

"That's how I figure it," Colter said, jerking the claybank stallion along behind him.

He'd saved their lives, but he was a dangerous killer in the eyes of his old partners. It
was in their quick, probing gazes and in the
way they spoke to him. He felt even odder
now than he had before, with only the grisly
S blazed into his face.

Hell, for all they knew he could be some
cold-blooded pistoleer on the dodge from
Texas or Oklahoma, an owl hoot run out of
the Indian Nations by marshals or Pinkerton
agents. Maybe with a passel of dead lawmen on his trail. He wanted to tell them
right now how he'd come to handle a hogleg like that — that, yeah, he was on the
dodge but he was no cold-blooded killer —
but Shanley and Dawson had their minds
on the trail and getting back to the Diamond
Bar before nightfall.

They rode up out of the cut of Devil's
Creek and through a badlands area, a maze
of shallow, rocky gorges cut by an ancient
river and in which springs, all that remained
of the long-ago stream, still bubbled and
flowed in muddy rivulets. As they left the
badlands, following a game path, they
spooked a passel of coyotes feeding on a
dead mule deer fawn, and crossed a short
tableland before climbing a steep slope up
through fragrant pines and then dropping
down through the cut of Charlie's Creek.

The sun was hovering low over the western ridges, an enormous rose in full bloom, when they rode out of the mouth of Charlie's Creek Canyon and into a broad valley in which the Diamond Bar crouched against the valley's southern, pine- and fir-clad wall. The valley shone silver green with its carpet of low, wind-twisted mountain sage. There wasn't a single tree on the valley floor, which was sandy and rocky and fit for only sage, needlegrass clumps, fescue, and tough but bright wildflowers, a different batch every week, it seemed. Willows lined the creeks.

The ranch headquarters wasn't much more than a two-story, shake-roofed log cabin flanking several unskinned pole corrals, and a low bunkhouse twice as long as the cabin but consisting of only one story and a brush roof. There was a windmill and a springhouse for keeping the dairy provided by the single milk cow fresh. The chicken coop in which Cimarron's adopted daughter, Pearl, kept her barred rocks and leghorns was set off in the wolf willows near the creek that ran along the base of the canyon wall.

The headquarters was buried in the shadow of the ridge now at nearly six thirty in the late-summer evening. Gray smoke from the cabin's broad, fieldstone hearth unraveled against the deep, cool green of the pines rising steeply above.

Shanley, Dawson, and Colter crossed Diamond Creek and rode under the portal in which Cimarron Padilla had burned the Diamond Bar brand and surrounded it with now-rusty horseshoes and had capped it with the rack of a giant bull moose, which Cimarron had found along the creek late one fall. The regular, solid thuds of someone chopping wood grew louder as the trio passed the corrals in which the stock ponies and Cimarron's two mules stood, dolorous after their suppers of oats, hay, and the chill, fresh water from the windmill.

The horses' hooves clomped. The finely churned dust of the trail past the corrals rose, smelling cool and floury in the quickly chilling air. There was the piney smell of the corral poles as well as those from the broad, sloping ridge, and the smell of dung, piss, tack, hemp, and freshly cut hay. Interwoven was the mockingly intermittent aroma of the beef that Pearl was cooking for supper on the black iron range inside the cabin.

Ranch smells.

To Colter, they were homey smells. He had grown up on a ranch, and, until a year ago, had figured on marrying his sweetheart, chestnut-haired Marianna Claymore, and settling on a place of their own in the Lunatics, not far from his foster father's, Trace Cassidy's, place, and raising a passel of horses, his own cattle herd, and children.

On a place very much like the Diamond Bar.

As they rode up to the cabin, Colter saw that the front door was open to let out the hot air from the range. Pearl was walking out just then, glancing toward the three riders leading the three horses. Moving toward Cimarron, who was splitting wood on the chopping block fronting the cabin, she stopped suddenly to look back toward the Diamond Bar riders and the unfamiliar horses they were leading.

Colter felt uneasy around Pearl, who was close to his age, and he had a feeling he was going to feel all the more uneasy around her now.

Cimarron Padilla was looking at the riders, too, as he swung his long-handled mallet down through a chunk of aspen, cleaving it into two clean pieces before leaving the mallet wedged in the beat-up chopping block. He straightened, wincing a little and pressing a hand to the small of his back — a thin, slightly potbellied man, somewhere in his fifties or sixties, Colter thought. His mother was said to have been from Sonora, Mexico, his father an Irish soldier. But he'd taken his mother's family name when he'd lit off on his own when only twelve years old.

Cimarron, as he liked to be called — and not Mr. Padilla, as most ranchers would have demanded from their help — had long, dark red hair, almost the same color as Colter's, and a hawkish face whose severity was relieved by philosophical coffee brown eyes. His face was as dark as a well-aged saddle, his nose broad and long as a splitting wedge, with an old knife scar on one side. His eyes were spoked with deep black wrinkles.

He wore a threadbare undershirt, open halfway down his flat chest that was padded with long, dark red hair and mottled with light red freckles. Snakeskin suspenders held his buckskin trousers on his lean hips, and the cuffs of the trousers were stuffed into the high tops of mule-eared boots whose fancy, Mexican-style stitching was so badly worn as to be barely noticeable.

He wore a Colt Peacemaker on his right thigh, thonged down like a pistoleer's. The hide-wrapped handle of a broad bowie knife jutted from a beaded sheath on his other hip. Something about the way old Cimarron wore his weapons, or maybe because of how sharply the well-tended weapons contrasted his otherwise ratty attire, suggested to Colter that the rancher might have been a wild-eyed border tough in his day. Twenty, thirty years ago, say. Shanley had hinted at it. Maybe it was out of habit that he still wore the gun and the knife even around his quiet, carefully maintained headquarters here in Wyoming's Cheyenne Mountains, far away from the deadly border country he'd haunted in his youth.

Cimarron walked over, blinking against the dust catching up to the riders, and Shanley leaned back in his saddle, hooked a leg over his saddle horn.

"Guess what, Cimarron?"

Cimarron stopped at the horse that Shanley had led by a lead rope, ran his hand down the bay's fine neck. The rancher had only the slightest trace of a Mexican accent, which told he'd been north of the border a good ten years or more. "Where'd you find him . . . these other two hosses?"

Just then his eyes found the bulging saddlebags draped over the rear of Shanley's extra mount.

"You ain't gonna like this, Cimarron," Dawson said, sitting his horse behind Shanley.

Pearl walked up, her waist-length, straight black hair blowing in the evening breeze. Colter's breath caught in his throat. The round, full-bodied Pearl . . . She was a full-blood Hunkpapa Sioux, with a wild, sensual air about her. Colter had no idea how she'd come to live here with Cimarron and Shanley and Dawson, because he'd never asked anyone and no one had offered the information. No one seemed to want to talk about Pearl, as though she was a mystery to all of them and words just couldn't explain her.

All Colter knew was that the girl hardly ever looked at him, but he looked at her plenty — the way she swung her hips when hauling water from the well, or how she often wore doeskin skirts cut above her knees, showing most of her long, tan legs. And sometimes it was painfully, heart-twistingly obvious that she wasn't wearing the usual underclothes that most girls wore.

The girl, with whom Colter had never had a conversation in the month he'd been there, stayed a little ways away from the horses, crossing her arms on her full breasts, which pushed out her red calico blouse as she regarded the riders warily, darkly, as though she'd sensed the trouble before it had even come riding into the yard. Her full lips were pursed, and her black eyes looked even blacker than usual.

Cimarron looked askance at Dawson as he opened the saddlebag flap and dipped a hand into the pouch, jingling the coins in his fingers.

"Let's see," he said in his quiet, philosophical way, narrowing one dark eye at the old drover.

CHAPTER 4

"While you fellas explain how it was to Cimarron," Colter said, reaching up to take the reins of one of the spare horses from Shanley, "I'll tend the mounts."

Shanley stepped out of his saddle with a grunt, and Colter took the reins of both his horses. Shanley removed the heavy saddlebags from the back of his buckskin. No one said anything as Colter took Dawson's reins.

Cimarron stood staring, quiet as an Indian, at the men and horses. Pearl quietly gathered split wood from the small stack beside the chopping block, her eyes looking haunted. She hardly ever said anything, and when she did, her words were almost always directed at Cimarron. Even when addressing someone else, if Cimarron was there, she addressed him through Cimarron.

Dawson shucked his rifle from his saddle boot as Colter turned his two horses around and led all six droopy-headed mounts toward the main corral, where the stock ponies stood regarding them with ear-twitching curiosity. Behind him, Colter heard the men begin to speak, their voices soft and quiet with grim importance. As the young drover lifted the wire hoop that latched the corral gate, and shoved the gate back away from the corral, he glanced at the cabin.

Cimarron was following Shanley and Dawson inside, the men pausing to scrub their boots on Pearl's rope rug just inside the door. Miss Pearl herself continued to gather an armload of wood, and in the quiet gloaming he could hear her labored raspy breaths, hear the split sticks knocking together in her slender, tan arms.

Her simple black skirt, likely made by her own hands, and held around her waist with a rawhide riata to which she'd fasted a leather buckle, buffeted about her slender legs and the tops of the dark brown stockman's boots she wore when she wasn't barefoot or wearing beaded moccasins. White flour showed on her thighs, stamped there in the shapes of her small, strong hands.

When she straightened, she turned toward the corral. She stood by the low pile of split wood, looking toward Colter. Her V-shaped, black-eyed face was tanned a dark cherry. Her eyes under soft brows were expressionless, and her long hair slid about her slender shoulders. She could look so severe at times that Colter felt himself wanting to cower around her, like a whipped dog. Other times, when something amused her, the corners of her mouth rose warmly, and her eyes sparkled beguilingly, thrillingly, before she'd toss her head away in embarrassment of having shown such emotion.

Feeling his face warm, Colter turned away from the girl and began leading two of the horses into the corral, the other mounts following obediently and nickering and working their snouts at the smell of hay and oats and likely at the fresh water in the stock trough on the surface of which bits of hay and oats floated. When he'd gotten all the mounts inside, he looped the wire over the post to latch the gate, and glanced once more across the yard.

Miss Pearl's long, dancing hair, buffeting skirt, and clomping heels disappeared inside the cabin. The door closed with a dull bark.

Colter methodically worked on the horses. He tied them to the corral to keep them from the water until they'd cooled down. Then he stripped each horse of its tack, setting the gear in the tack room lean-to addition off the corral side of the barn. He brought out a couple of old gunnysacks, cut them up, and used the pieces to rub each horse down carefully.

While he worked, he thought about the men he'd killed, and about his job here. He knew instinctively that Cimarron Padilla was a fair man, but he wouldn't blame the rancher for firing him when he'd heard what he'd done. Few ranchers wanted a pistoleer on their rolls. It was sort of like having a rattlesnake around the place — you never knew when or at whom it would strike. You never knew what trouble such a rider would bring.

A land-grabbing rancher might want a gunman in his bunkhouse and out riding his range. But Cimarrom seemed satisfied with his modest holdings, and none of the other ranchers around seemed to be crowding him. The Diamond Bar had no use for a pistoleer. Colter had to be prepared to gather his gear and ride out of here in the morning, unless he could convince Cimarron he was not a cold-steel artist but only a young man who'd had to learn to use his old Remy to survive a patch of hard luck.

Several times, he glanced toward the cabin, wondering what the three men were discussing. Wondering what they'd decided about the gold, and about him . . .

He'd just finished rubbing the six horses down when he heard the cabin door open. Pearl poked her head out and rang the iron triangle hanging beneath the eaves — four quick ringing whacks with an iron mallet that sat out on the rickety wooden washstand just right of the door.

No sooner had the girl rung the supper bell than Shanley and Dawson stepped out to the washstand, dippering water into the chipped enamel basin from the wooden bucket beneath the stand, and taking turns scrubbing the trail dust from their faces, hands, and arms, then combing their damp hair in the cracked mirror that dangled from a nail in the cabin wall.

By the time they were both finished and had gone back into the cabin, Colter had finished rubbing down the horses and turned them loose to drink at the stock tank and to eat hay from the crib and the oats he'd poured into the feeding troughs, hazing back a couple of the cow ponies that had figured on ferreting a second helping of oats.

The young puncher heaved a weary sigh as he studied the cabin, the windows of which now glowed with wan lamplight. The sun had fallen, the air had turned crisp and almost eerily still. Stars had sparked to life over the velvety, pine-clad ridge, a couple flickering like near lamps.

Colter glanced back out across the valley toward the main trail.

Spying no riders who might have had their own ideas for the gold, he doffed his hat, slapping dust from his brush-scarred chaps and faded denim trousers, and ducked through the corral poles. He crossed the yard and rolled up his shirtsleeves before setting to work making himself presentable for the Padilla supper table.

When he'd combed his damp hair and run his fingers through his ears one more time, making sure he'd scoured out as much grime as he could, he opened the door and went into the cabin, a wary, tentative expression on his scarred, sunburned face. He doffed his hat quickly, hung it on the antler tree beside the door, which sported four others, then closed the door behind him.

Shanley and Dawson sat at the long, split-log eating table, their backs to Colter. Cimarron was seated at the table's right end, his back to the small, rough-hewn but cozy living room that glowed with a low fire in the fieldstone hearth. Colter's place was on the other side of the table from the older waddies, while Pearl always sat at the left end to be near the range and kitchen shelves.

At the moment, she was dishing up smoking beef stew, standing between Shanley and Dawson. She did not look at Colter, who made his slow, tentative way around the table toward his own place. Cimarron sat with his hands folded, steam from his filled plate obscuring his dark, stony face. He seemed to be staring at the middle of the table. Shanley and Dawson said nothing, only sat waiting for the girl to finish filling their plates, their hair and mustaches slick with the recent combing.

As Colter took his seat across from them, he saw the saddlebags sitting on the floor about four feet from the door, under the heavy winter coats and rain slickers that hung from square pegs. He slid his gaze from the gold to Shanley and Dawson, who sat idly, politely looking down at their plates, hands in their laps, and then to Cimarron, who was looking at Colter with faint speculation in his brown eyes.

Colter looked away.

He placed his hands in his lap and waited, as he did every mealtime, for Pearl to load up his plate and then to fill her own. She returned the big kettle to the range, and then she took her own place at the table, reaching back with one hand to flatten her skirt against her legs as she sat down in the hide-bottomed chair, drawing one leg under her, as was her way, and keeping her expressionless eyes on the table.

She did not look at Colter and he did not look at her. At least, not directly, but only out of the corner of his eye. Because she had not spoken to him since he'd come here, and hardly ever looked at him, he was convinced she had no use for him.

But then, he thought, what pretty girl would have use for a young man with a face as hideously scarred as his own? The brand probably repelled her so badly she couldn't even bring herself to look at it.

Cimarron said grace in perfect Spanish. It was always the same, short prayer, and now he crossed himself as he always did upon finishing, and picked up his knife and fork.

He held the silver above his plate as he turned to Colter, and spoke in English in which both Spanish and Texas accents were obvious. "Son, we're gonna have you ride into town tomorrow, leave a message with the constable there. Tell him to have the sheriff over in Buffaloville ride out for the gold, if he wants it. It's up to him to get it back to the army. I'll have nothin' to do with the goddamn army," he added with a curt edge.

Shanley and Dawson paused in their hungrily devouring of the succulent stew to give him incredulous looks. Colter did the same.

Not elaborating, Cimarron began cutting into one of the large chunks of stew meat on his battered tin plate. "Till then, we'll keep it here, safe and sound, though I might have to sit up of a night with my shotgun to keep old Stretch from filling his pockets."

Dawson and Shanley chuckled. Pearl hardly ever reacted to the men's conversation, but now she smiled, eyes flashing as she regarded her adoptive father on the other end of the table from her. It seemed that only Cimarron could make her smile.

Cimarron returned her smile, chuckling, and then she put her head back down, busily cutting into her meat and gritting her teeth a little with the effort. She had perfect white teeth, and Colter was always taken by how her rich upper lip curled back slightly toward her nose, which was long and fine and ever so slightly, alluringly crooked.

"We gonna keep an eye out for them owl hoots?" Shanley said after everyone had gotten well into their meal, the tick of silverware on the tin plates and the other sounds of eating filling the cabin. The fire popped along, the two candles on the table sputtering and hissing.

Cimarron hiked up a shoulder. "I doubt they'd be able to follow you through Lost Canyon. Chances are, they won't even find the graves. Like you said, they'll figure they was double-crossed. I'll bury the gold in the old cellar out back. They'd never find it there even if they did come callin' . . . not that we'd give 'em a chance to."

Cimarron's eyes were darkly resolute as he gazed at Shanley. "Anyway," he added over the rim of his steaming coffee cup, "we're all light sleepers. And the horses'll warn us of riders."

He sipped pensively from his cup and resumed eating. Colter fidgeted, watching Cimarron out the corner of his eye, glancing occasionally across the table at Shanley and Dawson, then at Pearl sitting to his right, hunkered down over her plate as busily, hungrily as the men.

Pearl was not a dainty eater. In fact, she wasn't dainty about much of anything she did — from milking cows to sweeping floors to helping shoe horses or branding calves.

Although she was obviously shy, she had an earthy, forthright, no-nonsense quality. A tomboy, some would say, who approached the grueling work of everyday frontier life head-on and without complaint. In that way, she was like the chestnut-haired girl, Marianna Claymore, Colter had left back in the Lunatic Mountains of southern Colorado.

With only a little chagrin, he often found himself wondering whether Pearl would approach her natural pleasures that way, as well. Marianna had been a no-nonsense lover. Ravenous, at times. Wild as any she-cat with the springtime craze. He sensed Pearl would be that way, and his young loins often ached with the thought of it, of seeing what she looked like behind her loose blouses and skirts, which almost always offered a liberal view of her smooth, ripe, Indian-tan flesh.

His discomfort over the gold situation scoured his young man's natural curiosity about Pearl from his mind, and he finally set his fork and knife down, adjusted his suspenders with his thumbs, and entwined his hands on the edge of the table. He looked at Cimarron.

Because these men had become, in the month he'd been here at the Diamond Bar, practically like family to him — the only family he had left — he wanted them to understand him. He didn't want them to wonder about him or have any reason to distrust him or be wary of him.

"I ain't no pistoleer, Cimarron." He'd almost spat it out, like a bone he'd hacked up from his throat.

Cimarron raised his candlelit brown eyes to him calmly, but said nothing.

Shanley narrowed an eye at him from over one of the two sputtering candles dripping beeswax over the sides of the Delaney's Tomato tin propping it up. "You don't owe us no explanation, Colter Farrow. If it wasn't for your handiwork with that old six-shooter of your'n, we'd all be havin' our dead flesh gnawed by coyotes about now. In the mornin', the buzzards'd be pickin' our bones clean."

"Never seen the like of shootin' like that," Stretch added, swabbing gravy from his plate with a baking powder biscuit, and popping the biscuit into his mouth. "But like Griff says, without it we'd be goners."

"Just the same," Colter said, "I want you to know I ain't no ring-tailed catamount. I had to learn how to shoot after my foster pa was killed in Sapinero, Colorado Territory. He had some secrets down there in that town I found out about after someone sent his body home nailed to the back of his own supply wagon. Them secrets I won't go into.

I still ain't quite sure I believe 'em all myself.

"But I will tell you straight and clear and without no shame at all that I wrought vengeance upon his killers. His wife, Ruth — my foster ma — wanted me to find 'em and kill 'em, and I did. All but one. Bill Rondo, the county sheriff. I burned the same brand into his face as he burned into mine — the S for Sapinero — and I left him an invalid there in the town. A raving, drooling old invalid."

Colter settled himself back in his chair, feeling lighter from having gotten just that much off his chest. He looked at Cimarron. The rancher's normally placid eyes now appeared skeptical as he held a gravy-drenched chunk of meat and potato halfway to his open mouth. Both Shanley and Dawson, too, had turned to hang-jawed stone as they stared across the candles at Colter.

The young puncher turned to Pearl, and shock nearly threw him out of his chair. The girl faced him straight-on. Not askance. She did not turn away but continued to hold his stare with an incredulous one of her own, her black brows beetled slightly.

She was slowly chewing, studying him pensively. Swallowing, she kept her eyes on him.

Cimarron broke the silence with his slow

drawl pitched with bemused surprise. "I sorta figured you mighta learned to handle a six-shooter by pinkin' tin cans off rocks behind your daddy's barn or some such. . . ."

Stretch Dawson had a mouthful of food. Now he swallowed it. "Good Lord, boy — you been through it!"

Griff Shanley gave an ironic snort, but quickly regained his composure. "I gotta admit, I was naturally curious why a young man would venture so far from home. I just figured you was fiddle-footed, like I was at your age."

"I ain't fiddle-footed, Griff. I got a bounty on my head. Put there by Bill Rondo. Two thousand dollars to anyone who'll gun me, cut my head off, and send it back to him in a croaker sack."

The men continued to stare at Colter, their minds slow to absorb the shocking story. Pearl continued to stare at him, as well, but after a time she dropped her gaze to her plate, forked a chunk of meat, and smeared it around in her gravy.

"Well, then," Cimarron said. "I reckon —"

"I know what you're gonna say, Cimarron. And while I'm sorry to hear it, I understand your thinking. Decent folks like yourselves can't live peaceable with a snake in their

54

wood yard. I'll pack my things and pull out first thing in the morning."

"Boy, you didn't let me finish."

Colter frowned.

"I was gonna say I reckon we got just the help we need if them owl hoots come snoopin' around for their gold." A faint light flashed in Cimarron's eyes, and Colter imagined it was the remembered blaze of a six-shooter belching years ago in the Texas border country — the Brasada.

Colter looked at Dawson and Shanley. Pearl was still swabbing gravy with the meat chunk. Turning back to Cimarron, the young puncher said, "You mean, you're not gonna — ?"

"Boy, I'd never send a man packing who only sought justice for his own blood."

Shanley sighed, cleared his throat, and absently turned his coffee cup around on the table before him. "Don't sound to me like you did anything none of us wouldn't o' done."

Cimarron looked across the table at Pearl. "If I was turned toe-down without just cause, I can only hope my kin would seek the same reckoning."

Pearl lifted her eyes to him. Her lips rose slightly, wide black corneas reflecting the guttering gold light of the candles, and her voice was a husky purr. "Don't you worry none, Pa."

Colter felt an inexplicable tightening in his chest. "Rondo. That bounty on my head. I could have men hunting me even this far north."

The men only stared at him.

Pearl's hard, even voice said, "Let them come."

Colter turned to her, another bolt of shock leaving him dumbfounded as well as uncomfortably conscious of the brand burned into his cheek. Again, she stared at him directly, unwaveringly.

After a stretched moment, she dropped her bent leg to the floor and slid her chair back. She picked up her plate, then Colter's plate, and hauled both over to the washtub steaming on the range.

Cimarron said, "Best have you some o' Miss Pearl's chokecherry puddin', boy. Then you'd better tumble on into bed. You're lookin' at a full-day's ride tomorrow."

Colter nodded. He lifted his coffee cup to his lips, but he knew the cup was empty. He wanted only to cover the emotion he was sure his face betrayed, though he wasn't exactly sure where that emotion had come from.

All he knew was he felt like bawling like a damn baby.

CHAPTER 5

His name was Spurr Logan. Most people simply called him Spurr, though there were plenty who called him a son of a bitch and worse.

He was a deputy U.S. marshal out of Denver but not for very goddamn much longer, he thought, wincing at the tearing pain in his chest and left shoulder — an ache so raw that he leaned forward over his saddle horn as his big roan climbed up out of a dry wash in the Beaver Creek Hills northwest of Buffaloville, Wyoming Territory. He clamped a gloved hand over his left arm, and cursed, fighting nausea and a spinning sensation while clamping his left hand over his saddle horn, to keep from falling off his horse.

He sucked a breath through pinched lungs and managed to get the roan stopped at the edge of a pine forest.

Quickly, feeling as though a railroad spike

were being driven into his chest from beneath his left arm, he fumbled inside his wool-lined elk-skin vest, his fingers clawing across the badge he wore hidden beneath the vest, to the breast pocket of his hickory shirt, and pulled out his small, flat, hide-wrapped whiskey flask. He popped the stopper attached to the flask's lip with a slender strip of rawhide, and tipped the flask back hungrily, until the railroad spike began to ease back gradually.

He released his right hand from his left arm, loosened his grip on his saddle horn. He looked around, testing himself, grateful that the trees and rocks and Spanish bayonet had stopped swirling around him, then released the horn altogether.

He took one more long pull from the flask, almost draining it, then lowered the bottle and hammered the stopper into the mouth with the heel of his hand. He drew a deep breath, bunching up his craggy, horsey face with its patches of light red beard mottled gray, several moles from a searing frontier sun splotching his leathery cheeks just below his eyes, one on his right temple. He'd contracted the cursed heart condition over the long winters he spent in northern Colorado and Wyoming, chasing killers, rustlers, train robbers, mail thieves, crooked

Indian agents, and bronco Sioux and Cheyenne running roughshod off their reservations.

Twelve years' worth, riding for Chief Marshal Henry Brackett out of Denver's Third District Court, though Spurr himself holed up most of the time in Cheyenne.

With whores in Cheyenne.

He was, by his own admission, a whoremonger, but brothels and bedbug-infested flophouses were far from where he'd contracted the dreaded disease — "the colicky iron crab in his chest," as he called it. God knew, enough whores carried a plethora of other catching maladies from crib to crib and from one suds shop to the next, ready to pass them on to the next jake who paid his two silver dollars to bend her over a rain barrel or a pile of split cordwood for his two minutes of carnal bliss.

No, he hadn't caught the condition in the so-called pleasure parlors. His family had a penchant for the affliction, as both his ma and pa keeled over from heart strokes in their early fifties, Spurr's age now. The long, lonely trails in all sorts of harsh weather on mountain and plain had sealed the lawman's fate. The strain of tracking killers.

In fact, he'd never caught anything from a *nymph du pave* more severe than what a couple of physician-prescribed powder packets of silver nitrate hadn't cured quite handsomely. The whorehouses, however squalid, might even have staved off this grievous malady a few years, given him a longer life than he otherwise might have had if he'd been, say, married.

Marriage — now, that was a sure bringer of an early end!

The lawman called Spurr chuffed a laugh now, having dismounted his big roan and, leaning forward, pressed his forehead against his stirrup fender, regaining his wind. Suddenly, he lifted his head, his sudden giddiness from having parried one more jab from the iron crab fading like wood smoke on the wind. And that's just what he'd sniffed of a sudden — wood smoke on a breeze that whistled and clattered in the tops of the low pines and cedars. A branch broke off and fell, tumbling and crackling through lower limbs, before smashing to the ground with a soft thud.

The roan lifted its head sharply and sidestepped. It was about to nicker until Spurr closed his hand over the end of its snout, rendering the exclamation stillborn.

"Quiet, Cochise!" Spurr grated into the horse's ear, looking over the beast's neck and into the woods from which the occasional smell of burning pine touched his nostrils. "Hush up and hold your water."

When the horse seemed to relax a bit, Spurr slid his 1866, brass-framed Winchester repeater from its scabbard and tossed the reins over a cedar branch. Slowly, moving his moccasin-clad feet cautiously, he stole up to the edge of the woods, shouldered against a faintly creaking pine, and peered into the forest ahead of him.

Here the smoke smell tanged with pine resin was a tad stronger. Somewhere inside the copse, someone had built a fire.

Possibly drovers. Maybe teamsters; he'd seen a couple of bull teams on the trail a few hours ago.

On the other hand, they might be the cutthroats Spurr had been shadowing for the past week and a half, riding up from Gunnison in southwestern Colorado. But he'd lost the trail of those curly wolves in Saw Creek Canyon a little more than a day ago. Could he have just accidentally stumbled onto it again right here, while riding aimlessly, hoping for a bit of good luck until the old iron crab had closed its pinchers over his ticker?

If the men who built the fire were his quarry, they were also the ones who'd robbed the stage between Gunnison and

Montrose and taken three women hostage — a Mex girl and two Mormon ranch girls on their way to Moab to visit their grandparents. Spurr, who had been in Gunnison at the time looking into other sundry, federal-oriented dustups, had gone after the stage robbers because they'd drilled seven rounds through the head of the stage's shotgun messenger, who, as chance would have it, had been employed by the U.S. Postal Service, making his killing a government offense.

Gritting his teeth, Spurr slowly levered a round into his Winchester's breech. He glanced once more at the horse staring curiously, a bit anxiously at its rifle-wielding owner, then, holding two fingers to his lips, strode slowly forward, meandering through the trees.

Spurr followed the intermittent smoke smell stitching the breeze, glad that chance had placed him downwind of the fire. When he'd walked fifty or sixty yards, a creek angled toward him on his right, and the trees thinned out a bit. He rose on a low hummock and dropped to both knees suddenly, crouching and quickly doffing his broad-brimmed, weather-stained plainsman hat with its red-tailed hawk feather jutting from the braided leather band.

Holding his head low to the ground, he heard the distant murmur of men's voices. He was about to lift his head to peer over the hummock's crest when an object caught in the periphery of his vision. He turned his head to his right. Something white lay just on the other side of a deadfall log, visible from beneath the log that lay propped across two others.

Spurr crawled over and peered over the top of the deadfall.

"Sons o' bitches," he muttered.

The girl had been dead only a couple of hours, he judged from a past littered with strewn corpses of every age, shape, and size. The poor thing lay belly down, hands tied with rawhide behind her back. She was naked, scraped, and badly bruised. Her blond hair lay mussed and coarse as doll's hair around her head, sprinkled with dirt and pine needles.

Spurr had found the bodies of the other two girls along the killers' back trail, two days apart. They'd been in much the same condition as this one — naked, tied, beaten. Dead. Used and discarded, like swill from a farm kitchen.

"Sorry I didn't get here in time, little lady."

Spurr muttered a curse, feeling a raw

burning in his loins to go with the lingering heaviness in his chest. He ran his sleeve across his beard, then crabbed back away from the corpse to lift his head slowly, looking over the rim of the hummock.

The fire lay about forty yards away, at the base of the low hill and fronting the creek sheathed in aspens. The creek lifted a tinny sound that partly covered the voices of the three men sitting around the fire over which two small rabbits smoked and sputtered on a green willow spit.

The men were some of the most raggedy-healed saddle tramps Spurr had ever seen, all sporting beards of various lengths, all wearing battered hats and ratty fur coats or, in the case of the gent on the fire's left side, a vest of rawhide and wolf fur that appeared to have been badly singed, likely from an errant cook fire spark. He and another man faced each other across the fire while the third man had his back to Spurr.

This man reached forward frequently to turn the sizzling rabbits on the spit, speaking in a low, grumbling drawl and occasionally spitting to one side.

Rage was a bloodred rose blossoming in Spurr's eyes. He could hear his breath rasping as he stood and raised his Winchester to his shoulder, ratcheting the hammer back to full cock.

"Hold it there, murderin' bastards!"

Two of the killers froze. The one on the right side of the fire jerked his head toward the rifle-wielding lawman, eyes wide in shock.

"Name's Spurr. Deputy U.S. marshal, and you're all under arrest for murder, includin' the murder of that poor little flower over yonder."

The man on the left and the one on the right did just what Spurr hoped they'd do. They bolted up and clawed leather, bunching their bearded faces in fury.

Spurr's Winchester leaped and roared in his hands, and the man on the left went down spinning and triggering his pistol toward the pine tops. Spurr ejected the smoking cartridge and levered in a fresh one as he swung his Winchester right, past the gent still sitting with his back to the lawman, and pumped a round into the face of the man on the fire's right side, who was screaming savagely, showing his teeth through his beard, as he lifted an old Colt Dragoon revolver from the low-slung holster on his thigh.

The barrel of the ancient, heavy weapon had just cleared leather when Spurr's roaring Winchester blew the top of his head off

and sent him stumbling backward, dropping the Colt and throwing his arms out to
both sides as though in exasperation of his
sudden demise.

The second man hadn't hit the ground
before Spurr had ejected another smoking
cartridge over his right shoulder and planted
the sights of his Winchester '66 on the chest
of the third man.

The big hombre, with heavy-lidded eyes
and the tip of his broad nose missing,
stumbled to his feet and swung around
toward Spurr. He held his hands above a
heavy Smith & Wesson Russian .44 positioned for the cross draw on one hip, and a
smaller, ivory-gripped .32 pocket pistol jutting from a deerskin shoulder holster.

The cutthroat set his feet wide, staring at
Spurr with bright, anxious eyes.

"Oh, go ahead," Spurr said, gazing down
the Winchester's barrel. His weak heart was
beating a logy war rhythm in his chest.
"Look at me — I'm an old man. Old and
beat-up. Eyesight's bad. Ticker's bad.
Battled the gout last winter. Go ahead —
pull them pistols. You might just make it!
Hell, you're gonna hang, anyway!"

The third man stared at Spurr. The
scarred tip of his nose was bright red.
Finally, he spread his lips in a grim smile

and dropped his right hand over the grips of the big Russian.

Bam!

The report of the lawman's repeater flatted out over the pine tops, echoing.

The bullet plunked through the belly of the third man, who was so lumbering and slow that he hadn't even begun to lift the Russian from its scabbard before he was sent stumbling back through the fire. He kicked over the spitted rabbits and scattered the burning pine branches. He screamed as his pants caught fire, and spun around, gripping his bloody belly, then tripped over a small pile of firewood.

Dropping to the ground on the far side of the fire, he rolled around to extinguish the flames, sobbing and cursing as the pain bit him hard. He stopped rolling and kicked over onto his back, sobbing and smoking.

Spurr racked a fresh round into the Winchester's breech and looked at the first two men he'd taken down. Both lay dead in growing blood pools. Holding his Winchester straight out from his right hip, the stock pressed against his double cartridge belts, Spurr tramped around the fire and looked down at the third man.

The man had his eyes pinched shut, and he was wailing loudly as he pressed his hands to the gaping hole in his belly leaking liver-colored innards. He was a goner. Only a few, long minutes left, Spurr figured.

He gritted his teeth, and his big pitted nose blossomed as red as the rose in his vision as he yelled, "That, amigo, is called gettin' your just deserts! Die hard" — he swung his right boot back, then buried the pointed toe in the man's left side — "you *son of a bitch!*"

"Stop!" the dying man screamed. "You done kilt me already, ya mangy lawbringer!"

Spurr reached down and plucked the pocket pistol from the big man's shoulder holster, and tossed it off in the brush. He threw it too hard; his heart leaped and drew taut as a rope dallied around a saddle horn. Spurr rasped, slammed his fist to his chest, trying to jar the knot loose, and drew a deep, slow breath.

Goddamnit. Don't kill me, you son of a bitch. . . .

The rope slackened, and Spurr's breath made it to his lungs and back out again. With another curse, his face's red fury having been replaced by a gaunt pastiness, he turned away from the wailing, dying man and plucked his flask out of his shirt pocket once more, and drained it.

The raw liquor he'd bought from the army subtler at Fort Laramie seared his chest like flaming turpentine, but it brought the color back to his cheeks and quelled the ache in his brisket.

Returning the empty flask to his pocket, he lowered the Winchester and stepped around the smoldering fire to the dead girl.

He stared down at her for a time, and Spurr's bloodshot, lilac eyes acquired a sad cast. He dropped to a knee, set his rifle down against a log, and placed his hand on the dead girl's pale, slender back that was mottled with dirt and pine needles.

Spurr doffed his hat and ran a broad hand through his thick, sweat-matted salt-and-pepper hair. He'd seen a good many dead folks in his day — old as well as young. So many innocents taken long before their time.

In the past, he'd managed to turn and ride away, his soul intact. But for some reason now, in these later years with own horizon in sight, his heart had grown tender as a ripe tomato. Tears glazed his eyes, began to dribble down his mole-mottled cheeks.

"Oh, shit, little dear. Hellfire."

He placed his hands on the girl's shoulders and gently turned her over. Her eyes were half open, and she almost seemed to be

smiling up at him, as though she were trying to reassure him.

"Oh, why? For cryin' out loud — why?"
Spurr sobbed, lifting the girl's head higher
and brushing the dirt and sand from her
pretty, bruised cheeks. Tears streamed down
Spurr's own craggy face, leaching into his
scruffy beard, as he pressed his own cheek
to the girl's cool one, and held her tight in
his arms.

His heart felt as though it would burst
with sadness — his life, hers, the endless
calamities that befall everyone.

His shoulders jerked as he cried against
the dead girl's cold cheek.

CHAPTER 6

It was a long-faced, blown-out Spurr who rode into Buffaloville on the far eastern edge of the Cheyennes the next day, around ten o'clock in the morning. He'd dragged the three cutthroats he'd killed into a dry wash, a fitting resting place for such men, he figured. They were likely being torn apart at this moment by a hungry bobcat or lean coyotes.

A fitting funeral.

Spurr had wrapped the dead girl in one of the men's sougans and tied her over the back of one of their horses. He was leading all three horses into town, the girl riding belly down across the paint thudding along directly behind Spurr. With bleak eyes, the deputy U.S. marshal gave a cursory inspection of the town, a fair-sized ranch town grown up from a water stop and supply camp along the Bozeman Trail.

At nearly midday and in the middle of the

week, few people were out. Only a few saddle horses stood at hitch racks fronting saloons on either side of the wide, sun-blasted main drag. Ahead, a shaggy, burr-laden dog sat in the middle of the street, scratching its neck with a hind leg. The town was so quiet that Spurr could hear the cur groaning as it scratched at the tick or flea lodged behind its ear.

The air was September-crisp. Likely, snow would fall in the high country soon. Spurr shuddered at the thought of another winter coming on. But he appeased himself with the thought of Mexico.

In two days, when he got down to Denver, he would turn his badge over to his boss, Chief Marshal Henry Brackett, and head for the warm sands and voluptuous women residing along the shores of the Sea of Cortez. There he would spend the winter. Then, the good Lord willing and his ticker still ticking, he might venture into the Sierra Madres to look for gold.

Christ, the women he could buy in Mexico for just a few ounces of low-grade dust . . .

The sheriff's office sat along the street's left side, all alone on a dusty lot — just a rough log cabin little bigger than a spring-house but with a brush-shaded veranda on which a wicker rocker perched. A jar sat on the veranda floor beside the rocker, brown from Sheriff Bill Wilden's chaw, and Spurr was halfway surprised that Wilden wasn't in the rocker.

God knew there was little enough to do around this dust-beaten burg during the week when the punchers were out working the range, and since the Hunkpapa Sioux had been hazed onto their reservations.

Spurr turned the big roan toward the lone hitch rack fronting Wilden's office, then reined up and turned a glance at the blanketed lump of the dead girl. He made a sour face. One of her thin arms had dropped down from beneath the blanket, and the fingers of her small pale hand were brushing along the street's foot-deep dust and horse manure.

Spurr stepped down from his saddle, walked back to the paint horse, and knelt down by the delicate hand. He took the girl's hand in his own and pulled the blanket out a little so he could tuck the hand back inside.

A door latch clicked. Rusty hinges squawked. Spurr turned to see Sheriff Wilden amble out of his office building, leaning against a homemade cane with a handle carved in the shape of a ram's horn.

Wilden was an old Texan who'd followed

the herds northward and somehow — he couldn't even say how exactly — he'd ended up in Buffaloville and stayed, first as a saloon owner, then as sheriff of Grant County.

Wilden limped over to the edge of his veranda, gave a spit, and a long line of dark brown chaw landed with a plop in front of his hitch rack. "What you got there, Spurr? You run them wolves down, did ya?"

"Yep." Spurr tucked the girl's hand up under the blanket he'd wrapped her in, then straightened his popping knees and tightened the ropes he'd tied her with.

"And I see you found the third girl."

"That's right."

"Where's them jackals?"

"Feedin' coyotes up in the Beaver Creek Hills."

"Well, damn."

Spurr cursed as he tightened the ropes around the dead girl. "Have that funiture-makin' fella take the girl over to his ice-house," he told the sheriff. "Send a cable to the sheriff over to Gunnison. Tell him them cutthroats killed their hostages. I buried the other two girls — both brunettes, one young, one twenty or so — along the trail. I got the body of this blond girl here — I believe Katy was her name — and we'll keep her here for her family to fetch."

"What about the loot?"

"They either spent it already or buried it along the trail somewheres. I wasn't able to locate it."

"Well, shit."

Spurr, leaning against the paint's hindquarters, turned to Wilden; he'd grown a little weak-footed and dizzy after the long ride in the high-country sun. "Bill, after you send that cable, ask Squires over to the livery barn what he'd give me for these ponies, will ya? I'm gonna leave 'em here, and he can come over and look at 'em. They're worth thirty dollars each if they're worth a dime, so tell him not to short me or I'll shoot him."

Wilden limped down off the veranda, leaning hard on his cane. He'd been thrown from his horse several weeks ago, and the doctor had told him his knee might never be right again. Arthritis had set in, fouled the joint like sunbaked adobe.

Wilden had taken the information in stride. He was even older than Spurr, in his early sixties, and for years now he'd been ready to settle down in his cabin near Cutter's Gulch with his half-breed wife, tend his chickens, kill rattlesnakes, and watch the clouds float by. Only, Buffaloville's six-man city council hadn't been able to find a replacement for him yet, though they promised they were looking.

The dull-eyed Texan came around the hitch rack and studied Spurr, who was leaning against the paint as he removed his hat and sleeved sweat from his sun-reddened forehead. "You don't look good, Spurr. Fact, you look like you wrestled a bobcat in your saddlebags."

"Feel like it." Spurr tied the three spare horses, including the one packing the girl, to Wilden's hitch rack. "Believe I'll head on over to the Skinner House and have me a long soak in a hot tub, and a nap. Might just sleep till tomorrow."

He turned to Wilden. "We'll have us a last game of seven-up before I head out, Bill. 'Cause when I head out this time, I won't be back."

The stove-up sheriff frowned.

"Turnin' in my badge and headin' for Mexico."

"Well, shit, Spurr."

"Hell, Bill, I'm tired."

Wilden closed the gap between him and Spurr so he was standing only three feet away from the deputy marshal and was staring directly into his eyes. "You all right, Spurr? I'll be damned if you haven't lost weight since the last time you were through. And you look a might peaked."

Spurr scowled, turned to the roan, and toed a stirrup. "Hell, Bill, I just told you I was tired."

He put the roan into a spanking trot, angling across the street and past the burr-laden cur now sleeping with its snoot between its paws in the shade of the town's only tonsorial parlor and before which the barber, Melvin Anderson, sat in a Windsor chair, reading the *Cheyenne Ledger*. Since Anderson didn't like Spurr and Spurr didn't like Ledger — Spurr had put the man's son-in-law in the federal pen for selling whiskey to Ute Indians — neither man acknowledged the other.

The Skinner House was a narrow, three-story, unpainted frame building without frills, its name written in large, blocky, green letters across its nondescript, sun-blistered facade. Spurr pulled his horse up to the hotel's empty hitch rack, and a long minute later he tramped heavily up the front steps with his saddlebags draped over his left shoulder, his Winchester in his free hand.

The small, dusty lobby was dingy with wan sunlight pushing around the sides of cheap, dusty drapes drawn closed over the windows. Spurr kicked the door closed behind him, and a man said, "Jesus Christ!"

A girl giggled.

Spurr turned his head far enough to his left to see the bald-headed hotel proprietor, Lyle Kingman, sitting on a chair beside a potted palm, with a dusky-skinned girl on his lap, straddling him barelegged. Spurr recognized the girl without having to take a good look at her — Carmelita, the Mex whore some freighter had sold to the woman who ran one of Buffaloville's two whorehouses. Spurr also recognized what Kingman and the Mex whore were doing in that chair without having to take a good look at either one of them.

"Spurr, goddamnit, can't you knock?"

"Jumpin' Jehosophat, Lyle — ain't she a little young for you?"

Lyle grunted and groaned as he held the girl on his lap. "If you're lookin' for a room, leave your money on the counter and grab a key. Any one. You're my only business, Spurr, goddamn your mangy old hide, anyway. Shit, you're breakin' my concentration."

The girl made a sympathetic cooing sound. In the corner of his eye, Spurr saw her running a hand over Kingman's bald pate.

"Oh, keep your pants on, Lyle." The law-

79

man chuffed at his unintentioned irony as he moved around behind the short desk secluded beneath the stairs and plucked a key from the wall behind the desk at random.

Lyle had gone back to grunting. The girl had gone back to pretending the hotel proprietor was pleasing her.

Spurr stopped at the bottom of the stairs, looking up the dark well. "If all your rooms are free, why in the hell are you diddling that girl down here?"

"Didn't want to mess up a bed," Lyle panted. "Lilly just boiled all the sheets. Leave me now, damn it, Spurr!"

"When you're done there, if Lilly don't catch you and fill you with buckshot first," Spurr said, starting up the stairs, "I'd like a bath. A hot one."

Kingman only groaned and wheezed as Spurr continued up the stairs, turning on the landing and pausing to catch his breath before using the banister to pull himself up to the hotel's second floor. The place smelled of tobacco and whiskey and sour carpet runners and candlewax. As Spur made his way to room 5, he wondered how many times he'd smelled similar smells in his years wandering the frontier and overnighting in nearly every flophouse ever built west of the Mississippi.

Lyle Kingman's wasn't the worst stable he'd thrown down in. Hell, late one night in Montana he'd stumbled up dark stairs to a room already occupied by a dead man. Sure as hell, the man lay there in the bed Spurr had rented for fifty cents, with a big rusty knife sticking out of his brisket and his eyes wide and staring, his lowering jaw hanging to his chest.

The kicker was the man had been lying there for so long he'd swollen up like a giant tick and smelled like a privy.

Damn, Spurr thought, sticking his key in the lock, it was going to be nice to get down to Mexico and hole up in his own digs with the smell of the ocean lulling him to sleep every night and waking him up every morning. . . .

He fumbled the door open, stumbled into the room, casting a cautious glance at the bed, as had become his habit since finding the dead man. Deeming the room unoccupied, Spurr tossed his gear onto the bed, the frame of which had been covered in cheap enamel that had mostly flaked off.

There was a scuttling sound — little toenails ticking against the room's bare floor.

"Goddamnit!" Spurr yelled, whipping

around and drawing his Starr revolver from the cross-draw holster on his left hip.

A rat the size of a pocket gopher dashed out from behind the washstand, heading for the gopher-sized hole in the floor at the room's far corner.

Bam! Bam! Bam!

All three of Spurr's slugs plunked into the floor just shy of the critter's wiry tail. The rat gave a shriek as it scuttled down the hole and was gone.

Spurr stomped over to the door, threw it open, and poked his head into the hall. "You still got rats, Lyle, you son of a bitch!"

CHAPTER 7

When Colter Farrow had first ridden into the Cheyenne country, he'd given the little supply town of Crow Dance a wide berth. He'd been able to smell the place from a mile away and knew it to be a buffalo skinners' camp as well as a trading post and a meeting ground for men who sold contraband rifles and whiskey to the Sioux while staying several steps ahead of the boys in blue, who were almost constantly hunting the Indians themselves.

Nothing good could come from his visiting such a place. The only reason he was heading there now — so close to the place that he could see the shacks between the creek and a pine-clad mountainside — was to inform the constable of the stolen gold.

Cimarron had sent Colter because he needed his more experienced hands at the ranch. At least, that's what Cimarron had told Colter early that morning, when the rancher had sent the young drover off on the blaze-faced coyote dun, with a grub sack of Miss Pearl's bacon biscuits and some chicken sandwiches hanging from his saddle horn. Colter suspected the real reason he'd been sent, however, was that Cimarron trusted neither Griff Shanley nor Stretch Dawson not to linger in the camp, maybe get caught up in the trap of whiskey and painted women that perditions such as Crow Dance were known for.

Colter didn't like the assignment for obvious reasons — the main one being he had a price on his head. But it was doubtful anyone this far north of Sapinero would have heard of the bounty. Besides, he didn't intend to let any grass grow under his feet here. He'd inform the constable of the gold, turn Northwest around, and head straight back the way he'd come, likely returning to the Diamond Bar in the late afternoon.

Now as he forded a branch of the creek, the tent shacks and log cabins with either brush or corrugated tin roofs shoved up on both sides of him. The stench from the privy pits was overwhelming when the breeze was just right, but now it was tempered by the fragrance of burning pine and smoking meat — bacon and sausages he saw hanging in a smokehouse as he passed.

Crow Dance wasn't much over a block long, but all the tents and cabins and a few bona fide buildings were all wedged together as though for protection against the high-country weather. Most of the tents were saloons, he saw, with bushy-headed men in buckskins standing around in the open doorways holding soapy beer mugs in their fists.

Most bore the bloodstains of the buffalo skinner, though others wore the stamp of mule skinners, prospectors, and local businessmen. Those better armed were likely in the business of selling rifles or hooch or possibly slave women to the Indians. Slave trafficking was big business along the Bozeman Trail, and Colter's gut tightened at the thought of having a girl he loved — Marianna Claymore, say — sold into such a hellish albeit short life.

As he rode through the sloppy street — a large rainstorm had obviously hit overnight, as there were puddles as large as sloughs and in places the mud rose nearly to Northwest's knees — he looked for a shingle announcing the constable's office.

He was distracted when, midway through town, he saw a genuine wooden structure, two stories high and with a balcony with a scrolled railing wrapped around its second story. The balcony was teaming with girls dressed skimpily in every color of the rainbow and some in black. They looked like large beautiful birds preening and ruffling their feathers, some standing, some lounging on couches. Some were smoking cigars or quirleys as they leaned over the rail to give passersby on the street a good look down their camisoles or negligees billowing out from their chests, and cooing like doves or laughing like gandy dancers at the reactions they evoked from the men.

One of the girls leaning against the second-story wall smiled down at Colter, and stepped out to the balcony, swinging her hips coquettishly. Unlike most of the other girls, she was a real beauty with brown eyes and brown hair gathered in a French braid with a bone comb in it, and she was wearing more than just underwear, but a puffy-sleeved black and red dress with a plunging neckline and several necklaces. Long, bejeweled rings dangled from her ears.

She smiled saucily and said in a heavy European accent, "Hello there, stranger — take care to light and sit a spell?" The words so commonly heard on the frontier sounded new and fresh and intoxicating, spoken in that accent and shaped by those rosy, painted lips.

Colter stopped Northwest in front of the balcony and stared up at the girl. He had to admit to a warm flush in his cheeks, and a tug down in his lower regions. A tumble might do him some good. After all, he hadn't been with a girl in months — not since he and Jennifer Spurlock had gotten together down in Sapinero.

Jennifer had been his second girl, after Marianna. Truth was, he was as shy around girls as he was inexperienced, and as much as he needed to be with a girl again — once you'd been with one, you tended to think about it most all the time — he wasn't sure how to go about it.

But that wasn't why he was here.

"Ma'am," he said, clearing his voice and trying to keep his eyes off the girl's deep, dark cleavage, "I was wondering if you could tell me where I'd find the constable — George Nolan?"

The girl's smile suddenly faded. She turned her head slightly, looking down at Colter's left cheek, and her dark brows wrinkled with something akin to both sympathy and revulsion.

"Oh, don't mind the mark, miss," Colter said quickly, shaping the best smile he could. "That there's a birth mark. The S

87

stands for 'special.' I know that's true 'cause my mama said so." He broadened his smile, trying to put the girl at ease. Trying to put himself at ease, also. He found the worst thing about wearing the grisly tattoo was parrying other folks' automatic reactions to it, and the embarrassment that usually followed.

The girl straightened her head, and her smile returned, though the nettling sympathy did not leave her eyes. "On up the street," she said, tossing her head in that direction. "On this side of the Chinaman's laundry tent. You'll see the shingle." She smiled down at Colter once more, and hiked her shoulders as well as her breasts. "Wanna come up first? Take the stiffness out of your bones. I have a birthmark, too, and I'd be happy to show you."

She batted her lashes and sashayed around, swinging her shoulders playfully.

Colter pinched his hat brim to her. "I do appreciate that, miss. Maybe when I'm in town again. I'm afraid this visit's purely a business trip."

"Ask for Destel."

Colter kneed Northwest ahead, continuing to gaze up at the delectable beauty staring down at him. "Destel. Damn, I like that. What country you from?"

Destel laughed. "I'm from France. What's your handle, cowboy?"

"Colter," he said, clipping the end off it when he remembered the bounty. But, hell, no one around here likely knew about that money on his head. "Colter Farrow."

"Damn," the girl said, slowly following Colter along the rail, "I like that!"

And then Colter had ridden on past the building, and the girl had to stop because of a couple of other whores blocking her way. Colter glanced back over his shoulder at her, and she lifted her arm high above her head, smiling brightly and waving farewell.

The vision of the pretty girl atop the saloon balcony lingered with Colter until he saw the sign nailed to a post on the right side of the street and fronting a square-shaped tent with both flaps tied back. On the sign was burned CROW DANCE CONSTABLE — GEORGE NOLAN.

There was a single hitch rack fronting the tent, and a cat was sitting on the stock trough flanking the hitch rack. The tabby cat, grown fat off the Crow Dance trash piles, no doubt, was hunkered down with its head in the trough, lapping the muddy water. As Colter put Northwest up to the hitch rack, the cat jumped down with an angry meow and ran into the constable's tent.

"Hey!" someone inside the tent yelled. "You scared my cat!"

Colter dismounted and tossed North-west's reins over the hitch rack. Hitching his Remington high on his right hip, where he had it positioned for the cross draw, Colter peered through the open tent flaps. Inside the tent was a rolltop desk and a small sheet-iron stove, and not much else. A gun belt and a pair of muddy spurs hung from the tent's center post.

One man sat behind the desk, holding the tabby cat on his shoulder. Another man sat behind the first man, laying out a game of solitaire on an apple crate. He had a shotgun across his knees, and a bottle and a glass on the crate. He was a big gent with a broad, pugnacious face under a floppy-brimmed canvas hat.

The man behind the desk stared hard at Colter. He was younger than the man flanking him, and he wore a copper eagle-and-flag badge on his coat lapel. He appeared tall, though he was sitting down. He was impeccably dressed in a black suit complete with black foulard tie snugged against a white paper collar.

He was a dark, handsome man, but his

90

dark eyes owned a cold, arrogant cast. He stroked the back of the cat, who was facing away from Colter, with a long, pale hand on which he wore a gold pinky ring.

"Sorry about the cat," Colter said, taking a step into the office.

"Watch your boots," the man behind the desk growled. "I just cleaned this floor."

Colter glanced at the wooden floor, clean except for the faint mud tracks the cat had made. He looked at the young man who obviously enjoyed being the constable of Crow Dance. "You Mr. Nolan?"

"Constable Nolan — yes."

"Constable Nolan," Colter corrected himself. "I work for Cimarron Padilla out to the Diamond Bar, on Diamond Creek. Cimarron sent me into town to inform you of a little problem we have."

"Cimarron, huh?" Nolan said dully, letting one nostril flare a little.

The man behind him had stopped playing solitaire to turn toward Colter with mute interest. A badge was pinned to the lapel of his shabby brown coat, which he wore over a soiled linsey-woolsey tunic.

Colter looked behind him, making sure no one else was within hearing, then stepped farther into the tent. He glanced at the man flanking Nolan, who looked every bit as

91

hard and unscrupulous as the other men Colter had seen in the town so far. Colter wondered how well he could keep a gold secret. After his experience in Sapinero, the young puncher didn't trust lawmen as far as he could throw them into a stiff wind.

"So, what's the problem?" Nolan said.

The cat leaped down off his shoulder and disappeared somewhere behind him.

Colter hesitated, switching his gaze between the constable and his hard-nosed deputy, who stared at Colter with a faint mocking in his hazel gaze under shaggy red-blond brows. Cimarron must have trusted Nolan, however, so Colter told the two men about the gold. He glazed over the fact of his killing the three who'd been carrying the loot toward the rendezvous with their amigos.

"How much is there?" Nolan asked, leaning toward his rolltop desk with interest.

"Twenty-six thousand dollars."

The deputy constable whistled. He narrowed one eye as he gave a skeptical grin. "And Cimarron ain't gonna keep it for himself?"

Ignoring the question, Colter said, "He figured you'd summon the sheriff over to Buffaloville, and he'd come out and fetch it. Cimarron said he'd only turn the money over to the sheriff. Wilden — ain't that his name? Cimarron'll keep the gold safe until Wilden rides out for it."

The deputy constable continued giving Colter that faintly sneering, skeptical stare while Nolan looked vaguely perplexed and nettled.

"Well, don't that beat all?" said the deputy constable finally. "An honest Mex."

"He just don't want no trouble with the law," Nolan said. "Ole Cimarron probably had his fill of it down in Texas."

"I reckon," the constable said.

Both men had obviously speculated as much as Colter had on Cimarron's mysterious past.

"Well, I reckon that's the long and short of it." Colter pinched his hat brim and started back out the open tent flaps.

Nolan's commanding voice turned him back around: "Hey, kid — what the hell's your name, anyways?"

It was the one question Colter had hoped to avoid. His mind raced. Should he give these men an alias? But he'd already mentioned his name to the pretty whore. Giving an alias now might only draw more unwanted attention to himself.

He swallowed, cleared his throat. "Name's Colter Farrow, sir."

He lifted a foot, but again Nolan held him in place: "Where you from?"

"New Mexico."

"New Mexico, huh?"

Colter tried an affable grin, and then he nodded cordially and walked on out of the tent. He grabbed his reins off the hitch rack and stepped into his saddle, swinging Northwest out into the muddy street.

As he kneed the horse back the way he'd come, he glanced over his shoulder, and his gut tightened. The constable and his burly deputy were standing outside the office tent, giving him a skeptical twice-over, the tabby cat curling its tail and banding itself against the constable's trouser leg.

Colter swung his head forward and kept riding.

CHAPTER 8

Spurr snapped his eyes open. He was staring at the lye-yellowed pillow his cheek was pressed against, but in a waking dream he was up in Dakota Territory, Sioux country, and, sleeping against the wool underside of his saddle, he'd heard a horse nicker out by the creek.

"Damn!"

In a half second, his Starr .44 was in his hand, and rolling onto his back and extending the pistol in the direction of the creek, he rocked the hammer back loudly.

A woman's voice said, "Spurr!"

Spurr blinked.

He blinked again, and suddenly he wasn't lying in the tall wheatgrass by the Little Cannonball River with the horses picketed nearby, but in his rented bed at the Skinner House in Buffaloville, Wyoming Territory. His cocked pistol was not aimed at an Indian sneaking into his camp to cut his throat while he slept but at the side of a large bare breast of the dove he'd known for years — the brown-haired, brown-eyed Miss Abilene, who, like Spurr himself, never went by a last name but only Abilene or, sometimes just for fun, Texas.

She was sitting on the edge of the bed, naked as she'd been after Sheriff Wilden had sent her up to Spurr's room last night — Wilden's treat — and she and Spurr had made the mattress dance and swing for a sweet, long time. She glowered over her shoulder at him and absently folded her arms over her heavy, sloping breasts.

"I don't know where you are, Mr. Law-bringer, but that gun ain't aimed at no firebrand wanted in seven territories, but at ole Abilene's left tit!"

Spurr depressed the Starr's hammer, lifting the barrel. He ran his other hand down his craggy, patch-bearded face. "Sorry, there, gal. I musta been dreamin'."

"Musta been."

"Ah, shit." Spurr turned and slid the Starr back into the holster hanging from the bed's left front post. "Don't know what's gettin' into me. When I'm in town, I dream I'm on the trail. When I'm on the trail, I dream I'm in town."

Abilene leaned back and twisted around

to him, dropping an arm over his left leg that was bare beneath the covers they'd wrapped up in when they'd finished their frolic around midnight. It had gotten cold, and they'd huddled together like the old lovers they were to share body warmth.

Abilene smiled. "You dream about me, do you?"

Spurr looked at her. He didn't know how old she was — he guessed around thirty. Old for a whore. But she'd kept her delectably round and man-pleasing shape, and she hadn't lost any teeth. All in all, she was a fine-looking woman, with her thick, dark brown hair pinned messily atop her head. He wished he could tell her he dreamed about her, but the only woman he ever dreamed about was his mother, long dead even before the war and moldering in a grave back in Missouri.

"All the damn time." Spurr gritted his teeth. "Gravels me, it does."

"Who were you dreaming about last night?"

Spurr frowned.

"You were moaning and groaning and calling out for Dearie."

"I was? Dearie?"

"Don't try to hornswoggle an old horn-swoggler, you old coot. Who was she —

97

whore from Cheyenne?"

In his mind's eye, Spurr saw the dead girl's face peppered with sand and pine needles, the half-open eyes staring up at him almost dreamily. He ran a hand down his face again, clearing the vision before it soured his outlook on the new day that already had a good start, slanting buttery sunlight through the room's single window.

"Just one of many, Abilene. One of many. You know how they all run together for me — 'cept for you." He favored her with his best lusty grin, though whether because of the dead girl or his abrupt awakening, he felt his blood running thick and heavy in his aging veins.

She sensed something was wrong. She frowned at him, ran a concerned hand down his leg. "You feelin' all right, Spurr? You don't look like your old self somehow. And last night, you had me ridin' on top. You usually like to take command of the situation, at least for a time or two."

"Ah, hell, Abilene — I'm just tired. I been chasing three wolves all the way from Gunnison, and before that I ran stock thieves to ground over by Pagosa Springs. I just put too many miles behind me in too short a stretch."

"You need a breather."

"I do, at that."

"Stay here awhile." Abilene's dark eyes flashed. "If you're real nice and pay attention to me and none o' the other girls — make me feel special — we'll roll dice for free tussles."

"Hell, Abilene, you are special. Don't you know that?"

"Special enough to keep you away from them all-night card games of yours? They're just as hard on you as any long trail, Spurr. All that smokin' and whiskey drinkin' . . . and too many young whores."

"Now, see here," Spurr growled, gently pinching her dimpled chin between his thumb and index finger. "There ain't no gal that special. And there ain't no such thing as too many young whores. Good Lord, woman — what's got into you?"

Abilene gave her husky chuckle and brushed her lips across his, playfully pulling at his beard. He took the opportunity to cup her heavy, pendulous breasts in his hands, thumbing her nipples. She giggled and swatted his hands away as she stood, making the bed squawk and sigh, and began gathering her clothes.

"So, what's on your docket, Spurr? You headin' out after more owl hoots today?"

Spurr felt his mood improve as Abilene

bent down, shoving her plump, round rump in the air, to pluck her camisole up off the scarred floor puncheons. "How'm I supposed to head out, with you in town, Abilene? Hell, I thought you was still in Laramie."

"Had a run of bad luck in Laramie." Abilene gathered the rest of her frillies and tossed them all on the bed. "And don't ask me what it was about, 'cause it's none of your business, Spurr. Just know that son of a bitch had it comin'."

Spurr laughed and laced his hands behind his head. "Don't doubt it a bit."

His features acquired a pensive cast as he watched her sit down in the hide-bottom chair by the window, facing him, to pull her black silk stockings on and give him a long, luxurious look at her sitting naked before him, dressing slowly. There wasn't a whore on the frontier who could dress as slowly as Abilene, nor more gracefully. He wasn't sure whether it was a method she'd concocted for ensuring future business, or whether it was just her style.

He hoped it was the latter.

"Nah," he said. "I'm gonna hang around here for another day. Take me a long nap, have a couple good meals, then a good, long night's sleep. Head out first thing in the mornin'."

Abilene looked at him pensively as she slipped into her calfskin half boots with little bells over the insteps, and pulled her powder-pink, whalebone corset off the bed. "Where you going, Spurr?"

"Denver. I'm retiring, Abilene. I wasn't gonna tell you, but after what you and me been through together, I figure you deserve to know."

She stopped lacing up the corset, letting it fall open as she opened her mouth to speak. Spurr held up a hand, cutting her off.

"My mind's made up, and there won't be no talking me out of it. And there won't be no convincing me to stay around here. I'm heading to Mexico. I know we talked about gettin' together once I turned in my badge. But you know as well as I do that that was the tanglefoot talkin'. We've had our best times in Laramie — in the Lady's Hole Card. And last night wasn't half bad. If we tried to stretch the game any farther or longer, we'd ended up dealing from the bottom of the deck, and if I didn't shoot you, you'd shoot me and hire a couple of jakes to throw me down the nearest privy hole. Two weeks, I'd give us."

Abilene stared at him. Spurr held her gaze. She dropped her chin and quirked her lips

101

with a wry, woeful smile. "But they'd be a helluva two weeks — wouldn't they, you old bull buff?"

"That they would."

She canted her head to one side and seemed to stare right through him. "You ain't goin' off to die on me — are you, Spurr? If you did that, I'd never forgive you, you law-bringin' son of a btich. If you're sick, I'll nurse you back to health. No strings attached — apron strings or any other kind."

Damn, Spurr thought. She knew.

He narrowed his eyes and pointed a finger at her for emphasis. "I'll live to a hundred and twenty and gallop back up from Mexico to lay lilacs on your grave, Abilene."

He threw his covers back and dropped his feet to the floor, scratching his shaggy head with both hands. "Now, quit horsin' around over there. Get that beautiful body of yours covered up so we can go out like respectable folks and have us a good breakfast together. I'm hungrier'n a bull griz takin' his first stretch after a long winter's nap!"

Five miles from Crow Dance, Colter put Northwest up the side of a steep hogback in a sagey valley between piney ridges, and reined in the mount about ten feet from the hill's crest. Turning the horse half around, the young puncher reached back into his saddlebags for his spyglass, telescoped it, and held it up to his right eye.

They were still there — two men riding hard along his back trail and now just turning into the mouth of the valley from the southeast. As Colter tracked them with the glass's single sphere of magnified vision, they disappeared briefly in the willows and white-flowering cow parsnip lining one of the two creeks webbing the valley floor.

Water splashed in the sunlight, arcing high above the lime green brush, and then both horses — a claybank and a broad-chested blue roan — leaped up out of the creek and changed course slightly, both riders heading directly toward Colter.

Colter stretched his lips back from his teeth, dread and apprehension sawing at him. No doubt about it — they were on his trail. Two miles back, he'd left the main trail, an old army freight road, just to be sure. Both riders increased their speed now, too, hoping to overtake their quarry within another mile or two.

Colter had to believe they were bounty hunters who'd followed him out of Crow Dance. Likely, they'd seen the hard-to-miss *S* on his cheek, and had matched it to the wanted circulars sent out by Bill Rondo from Sapinero. It was hard to believe anyone would recognize him this far from the source of his trouble, but apparently two-thousand-dollar bounty notices spread fast.

Colter lowered the spyglass and returned it to his saddlebags. He was only a couple of miles from the Diamond Bar. He couldn't lead those two bounty killers — if that was what they were — back to the ranch. Cimarron had enough trouble with the stolen gold to have to fight Colter's bounty hunters now, too.

The young puncher booted Northwest up and over the top of the hogback. He dropped down the ridge's other side, loped across a broad flat and another creek, and then up a steep ridge upon which nothing but sage and clumps of needlegrass grew. At the top of the bench that he knew continued a long, slow rise to the base of the saw-toothed peaks of the Cheyennes, a pine forest started, the tall pines and firs and occasional tamaracks denser than the hair on a dog's back.

There, in those trees, the bounty hunters' trail would end.

Northwest was blowing hard when they gained the forest. Colter found a relatively wide gap and followed it into the forest about a hundred feet, then leaped out of the saddle, dropped his reins, and shucked his old Tyler Henry rifle from its scabbard.

He loosened Northwest's latigo strap, slipped the bit from his mouth, then tramped quickly back along the gap through the columnar pines that creaked in the afternoon breeze. The air was tinged with the smell of loam and pine resin. He hunkered down behind a large deadfall log about ten feet back from the forest's edge, and doffed his hat.

From here he had a good view of the valley floor — the sage and tufts of blond grass and the willow-sheathed creeks. He stared at the farthest creek, just beyond the hogback from which he'd glassed his shadowers.

No sign of them.

He looked around, stared at the hogback.

A cricket of apprehension hopscotched Colter's backbone. They should be crossing the hill by now, traversing the last flat before the hill dropping just below him. Unless they really hadn't been following him at all. They could've been meat hunters working one of the mines in the area, heading for the slopes of the Cheyenne searching for game.

No. They'd followed him too closely, leaving the old army road almost exactly where he'd left it.

Colter doffed his hat and hunkered low behind the log, waiting. They might have stopped where he'd stopped, on the other side of the hogback, resting their horses before making the climb up the steep ridge and into the pines.

Time yawned.

There was only the scuttling, faint whistling of the breeze. Cloud shadows swept the valley. In the south, ragged-edged, gray-bellied clouds floated.

Behind Colter, Northwest whinnied shrilly.

Colter's heart leaped in his chest. He'd just started to turn his head and swing his rifle around when a fist grabbed his hair and jerked his head straight back so that for a second he thought his neck would snap.

Another hand — a large, scarred, brick red hand — swept down over his right shoulder, pressing a razor-edged knife to his throat, sawing through the skin with a raking pain, drawing blood.

"Drop the rifle," a deep voice boomed.

Colter saw the large, brown, Indian-featured face grinning down at him from straight above.

"Or I cut your throat and bleed you dry, boy!"

CHAPTER 9

Spurr and Abilene had a long, leisurely breakfast in Jim Bowie Café on the banks of Howling Squaw Creek, just outside Buffaloville. After breakfast, Spurr went back to his hotel to read the relatively recent Casper newspaper that he found in the café, and to take a nap, while Abilene sashayed off to do whatever a whore did in the blazing light of a late-summer afternoon in Wyoming.

Spurr had intended to sleep until suppertime, but he was feeling better than he had before riding into town the day before, so he decided to head over to the Wyoming House Saloon for a boilermaker and maybe a sporting game of blackjack. Most of the men he found in the saloon were men he wouldn't trust at cards, however, so he bellied up to the bar and ordered a shot of rye and a tall glass of beer from the burly bartender, Rutter Johnson, a former army packer whom Spurr had had a few run-ins with but whose conversation the old lawman generally enjoyed.

He and Johnson were talking about the endless line of mule trains running up the Bozeman Trail, hauling supplies from the Northern Pacific line to the gold camps in Montana, when Spurr saw in the back-bar mirror behind Johnson a familiar face edging toward him from his own right flank.

The man met Spurr's gaze in the mirror. His dull eyes flashed angrily, and he stepped out from behind the thickset gent he'd been edging around sneakily as he made his way to the bar. His name was Willard T. Coates, and he looked much as he had when Spurr had last seen him stealing horses from the Pend d' Oreille Indians up along the Musselshell River in Montana.

"Spurr, you hissin' adder," Coates shouted, throwing an arm and pointing a finger at the federal lawman, "I swore the next time I laid eyes on you, I'd fill you so full of holes that even your poor old mother wouldn't recognize your mangy carcass!"

"Ease up, Willard." Spurr swung around, sliding his faded denim jacket back behind the horn grips of his Starr .44. "You have no beef with me. You spent two years in the federal lockup for horse thievery when you should've been hanged for killin' them two

Injun girls."

"Liar!" Coates shouted. "You're lying and tryin' to turn my friends here against me!"

As four or five men and two saloon girls scattered in all directions away from Coates, one man knocking over a chair and another dropping a half-filled beer schooner onto the floor, Spurr chuckled. He had one hand on his beer glass. "You're the one that started the name-callin', you squirrel-headed son of a bitch."

"Die, you bastard!" Coates reached for his old Remington.

Spurr wasn't as fast as he once was, but he was still faster than the drunken horse thief and girl-killer. He had his Starr out before Coates had even gotten his pistol clear of its holster.

The Starr barked once. In crowded confines, Spurr always liked to make the first shot count, and he did that here. The slug plunked squarely through the breastbone of Willard T. Coates, knocking him back against a table. He dropped his gun with a wooden bark, then twisted around and knocked over a chair before following the chair to the floor.

He didn't so much as grunt — that's how dead he was before he collapsed belly down over the overturned chair.

The saloon fell as silent as a held breath. Spurr waved his smoking pistol around, in case any of Coates's cohorts decided to buy chips in Coates's game.

Voices sounded outside and then boots thumped wood, growing louder, until Bill Wilden's head appeared over the top of the hotel/saloon's batwing doors, a fateful scowl on his sunburned face under the funneled brim of his cream Stetson.

"Yeah, it's him, all right — shoulda known."

Wilden began pushing through the batwings. Spurr had just glimpsed another man coming in behind the sheriff — a handsome, dark-haired man much younger than Wilden — when a searing pain flooded Spurr's left side, at once paralyzing his left arm and filling it with hot lead.

He gritted his teeth and dropped the Starr as he grabbed his left wrist with his right hand and stumbled back against the bar.

"Spurr, what on earth?" Wilden quickened his gimpy pace as he threaded a path between tables, heading for the federal lawman, the younger gent on his heels.

Spurr's knees weakened and bent. He dropped to the floor on his left hip, growling and snarling like a wounded wolf as he clutched his left hand as though trying to wring some life into it with his right. Wilden eased onto a knee beside him, leaning on his cane and grunting with the effort of such a maneuver in his own current beat-up state.

"What the hell is it? You hit?"

"I'd say his heart," said the dark-haired man behind Wilden, who was bending down with his hands on his knees, dark brown eyes cast with only mild concern.

"Whiskey!"

Spurr's cheeks were hot with humiliation. All eyes in the place were on him, some serious, some looking bemused or even amused to see the old badge-toting mossy-horn in such a weakened state.

He glanced at the edge of the bar above his head. "Hand me . . . the shot!"

The dark-haired young man reached up to grab Spurr's whiskey off the bar. He gave the drink to the federal lawman, who took it in his shaking right hand and threw back the entire shot. Spurr smashed the empty glass back against the front of the bar, shattering it. Looking up, his fuzzy vision clearing, he saw several rough-hewn sorts looking over the tables at him, eyes expectant, almost eager.

The drink helped take the sting out of the lawman's chest, replacing it with a soothing burn. He threw his arms out toward Wilden and the young man. "Get me up, god-damnit. Haul me over to a table!"

On the floor was no place for a man to kick off. If he was going to die, he'd die in a chair, holding the wolves at bay until the very last with his .44. He'd have preferred dying out in the country somewhere, lying back against the wall of a deep ravine where no one would find him — no one would come along to ogle him and pick over his carcass, finding only a few dollars in his pockets, a deck of pasteboards, a notebook in which outlaws' names and descriptions and last known whereabouts were scribbled, tack, cooking gear, a change of clothes, and his weapons.

When he died, he wanted only the bobcats and buzzards to know, so they could pick him clean before the human coyotes got wind of his passing.

Now he snarled and growled at death, snagging the .44 off the floor as Wilden and the young man hauled him to his feet. He glared at the human coyotes pondering him bright-eyed, like dogs at supper bones, and held the Starr tight in his right hand. The sheriff and the young man both draped one of his arms over their shoulders and dragged him over to the nearest table, Wilden ordering the men already sitting there to clear out.

As the men grabbed their drinks and quirleys and bounded off, Wilden and the young man tried to ease Spurr into a chair.

"No!" Spurr shook his head from side to side and indicated the chair with its back facing the bar. "That one."

He wanted his eyes on the room, where he could watch the coyotes circling the dying campfire.

"Someone fetch the doc," Wilden ordered.

"No," Spurr objected. "Just a bottle." He looked down at his left hand lying limp in his lap, like a bird that had flown into a wall. He grabbed it, shook it. He could feel the warmth in his other hand, felt the nerves slowly returning to life in his left.

"Go, Gavin!" Wilden shouted at the man who'd started through the batwings after the local sawbones.

Gavin slapped his bowler onto his head and hurried out the batwings.

"I don't need a pill roller," Spurr told him. "Just . . . need a minute to catch my breath."

"You're gonna see a doctor, Spurr, and that's that, so shut up about it."

Wilden sagged down in a chair to the federal lawman's right while the handsome young man with thick, dark brown hair tumbling down from a crisp bowler was fetching a whiskey bottle from Rutter Johnson, the only other man besides Wilden who seemed genuinely concerned about Spurr's condition.

Wilden leaned toward Spurr. "I thought you looked peaked when you rode into town yesterday. How long you been gettin' these seizures?"

Spurr leaned back in his chair. His chest was raw, his heart fluttery. He tried sucking down as much air as he could, but he couldn't seem to get enough. The room spun. Not as badly as before, but it was spinning just the same.

The young man plopped the whiskey bottle onto the table.

"On the house, Spurr," Johnson said, leaning over the bar with a wry cast to his blue eyes. "Don't die on me, now. You've always been one of my best customers."

"Much obliged, Rut." Spurr plucked the cork from the bottle, then looked around the room before leaning toward Wilden. "All right — I'd best see the medico. But not here. Help me get over to the old sot's office, and when he's got me on the mend, I'll buy you both a fresh bottle."

Wilden looked at the handsome young man, whom Spurr did not know from

Adam's off-ox but who he saw now was wearing a constable's copper badge on the lapel of his expensively cut suit coat. Turning back to Spurr, Wilden said, "All right, but if you die on the street on the way over there, we're leavin' you for the dogs to clean up."

"Ouch — goddamnit, Angus!" Spurr railed as the doctor pressed his stethoscope against Spurr's naked back. "What do you do — lay that consarned thing over some old dead whore's grave every night before you go to bed?"

Dr. Angus MacGregor pulled the stethoscope away from Spurr's back to favor the lawman sitting up on the doctor's leather-upholstered examining table with a hard, admonishing look in his faded-out brown eyes. His long, horsey face was framed by long wings of silver-blue hair that hung to the man's spindly shoulders. "Goddamnit, Spurr, if you continue to mewl like a damn pig in labor while I'm listening to your consarned inner workings, I'm gonna take the old hogleg I keep loaded in my desk for folks who don't pay their bills, and conk you over the head with it!"

"I'll arrest you for assaulting a federal lawman!"

MacGregor shuffled his moccasined feet over to his battered rolltop desk and plucked a big horse pistol out of a top drawer. He waved the rusty gun in Spurr's face. "Shut up!"

"All right, all right, you old bone-setter — get on with it!"

The doctor returned the gun to its drawer, slammed the drawer closed, and pressed the icy wand of his stethoscope against Spurr's back. He had Spurr take several deep breaths. They sounded like the wind fluttering heavy curtains over a splintered window ledge. Then he came around to Spurr's chest, which he'd listened to a half dozen times already, and had him take several more deep breaths until Spurr thought he'd pass out and fall off the examining table.

Spurr's chest was even sorer than when Wilden and the young constable of Crow Dance, George Nolan, had hauled Spurr up the medico's creaky outside stairs and into the small musty office atop a furniture shop in the back of which a baby was constantly crying.

Finally, MacGregor pulled the stethoscope away from Spurr's chest and, a pensive expression on his long, ugly face, dropped down into his squawky swivel chair. Still thoughtful, MacGregor pulled a small burlap pouch from one of the desk's over-stuffed cubbyholes, dragged from the sack a sheaf of brown rolling papers, and spread the single leaf expertly between the tobacco-stained index and forefingers of his right hand.

"Well?" Spurr said.

"Put your shirt on."

Glaring at the doctor, apprehension filling him like a gallon of bad milk, Spurr grabbed his buckskin tunic off the table behind him and shook it out. He dropped the smoke-stained garment over his head. MacGregor was slowly dribbling a line of chopped tobacco onto his rolling paper, staring down at the quirley he was building as though it were a long-lost plat to El Dorado.

Spurr sighed. His voice was tense, caustic, fearful. "How long have I got, or do you even know, seein' as how I didn't come in here with the clap or a broken leg?"

MacGregor leaned back in his chair, care-fully rolling the cigarette closed. "Can't tell you that."

"But it is my ticker."

"It is your ticker. You have an irregular heartbeat, and part of your heart is working too hard, which means it's trying to com-pensate for a part that may not be working at all. The problem is, Spurr, you've burned

118

the candle at both ends for too long."

"Hell, tell me something I don't know — will ya, Doc? For instance, can you cure this problem or am I destined to finish out my years with these spasms?"

"I believe what you're having are small heart seizures. Strokes to the heart. Your old ticker is protesting when it's overstressed."

"What can be done about it?"

MacGregor grabbed a stove match and scraped it to life on the desk, touched it to the quirley. "For one thing," he said through a swirling cloud of gray tobacco smoke, "you're gonna have to give up these."

"Quirleys?"

"Cigars, too. And don't push yourself so damn hard, and cut back on the whiskey. Red-eye is good in small amounts, but no more benders. In fact, no more than two or three shots a day."

"Pshaw! How can somethin' that makes you feel so good be bad for you?"

"And you might consider retiring."

Spurr looked around as if making sure no one was listening at one of the two doors opening off the doctor's cluttered office that smelled of camphor, tobacco smoke, and baby piss. But the only other creature in sight was a canary in a metal cage hanging in one of the two front windows.

He turned to MacGregor, who was sitting back in his chair, one moccasined foot hiked on a knee, smoking. "Don't tell no one. The news'll only sadden my friends and encourage my enemies, as few of the former there might be. I've done decided I'm retiring. Soon as I get to Denver, I'm turning in my badge and headin' for Mexico."

"That's a good idea. A warmer climate in the winters'll do you good. As well as prolonged rest and relaxation." MacGregor stuck a bony finger out at the lawman, and narrowed an admonishing eye. "When I say relaxation, I don't mean lay with every *puta* in sight, Spurr. Mattress dances for a man in your condition will kill you as surely as long rides shadowing brigands will."

Spurr stepped down off the table and headed over to where his hat, shell belt, and revolver hung from a wall peg. "Will I make it to Mexico? I figure on takin' the train most of the way, haulin' my roan, then ridin' the thirty, forty miles to this village I know on the Sea of Cortez."

MacGregor took another deep drag from his quirley, then heaved his bony body out of his chair and walked over to a glass-doored cabinet sitting beneath a watercolor of a green-throated hummingbird. He opened the cabinet, took out a tobacco tin, and reached inside.

Returning the tin to the cabinet, he walked back to his desk and produced a small brown envelope from a drawer. He dropped his handful of tablets into the envelope, closed the envelope's flap, and extended the package to Spurr.

"When you feel an attack comin' on, take one of these. Sorta like a dynamite blast to the heart muscle. They'll keep it pumpin', should buy you a few months. Hell, maybe even a few years if you don't get careless and overly randy down there with them Mex whores."

Spurr shoved the envelope into his shirt pocket. "What are they?"

"Nitroglycerin tablets."

Spurr dropped his lower jaw.

MacGregor shook his head. "They're only powerful enough to keep your ticker ticking. They won't blow you sky-high. It's them Mex girls that'll do that." Inside a thick smoke cloud, the doctor's horsey face brightened with a lusty grin. "Purty as Fourth of July sparklers they might be, but they're careless and more than just a might liberal with their virtue."

He extended a pale, vein-webbed hand and blew smoke out his broad, pitted nostrils. "That'll be two dollars for the examination and another dollar for the nitro tablets. The advice, invaluable as it is, is free."

Spurr paid the man, shrugged into his vest, and opened the office's outside door. He stopped and turned back to MacGregor, who'd gone over to talk to his canary. "Hey, when I fed old Willard Coates a pill he couldn't digest, Wilden and that young constable was headin' for me. Seemed like they had business in mind. You know what it was?"

"How the hell would I know?" MacGregor chuffed. "But I suggest a day or two of solid bed rest for you, my friend!"

"Good riddance, you old quack!"

Spurr went out and slammed the door.

CHAPTER 10

Colter could see the copper-colored hand in the corner of his right eye. It clasped the bowie's handle so tightly that the knuckles were white. The blade of the knife was cold and sharp against Colter's throat, and the young waddie could feel his own blood dribbling down his neck.

His temples throbbed and his heart hammered. The Indian pulled his head so far back on his shoulders he could feel the bones in his neck grinding.

He released the Henry repeater. It dropped against the deadfall log he'd been hunkered behind, at the edge of the forest, waiting for his shadowers. His humiliation at letting himself get snuck up on from behind by at least one of the two men he'd been lying for oozed into his sundry other discomforts, making him sick and terrified.

The knife cut still deeper into his throat as the Indian said, "The six-shooter!"

Footsteps sounded on Colter's left. As Colter shucked his Remington from his holster and tossed it out away from him, wanting only to get that razor-edged bowie away from his throat, he rolled his eyes around. The second man stepped out of the trees, breathing hard. He was a white man in a rat-hair coat and bowler hat, his ugly face with deep-set malicious eyes sporting a three-day growth of sandy beard.

He held a Spencer repeater on Colter, and he was breathing hard. "Christ, you move fast for a big son of a bitch, Red."

"You move slow and loud for such a little bastard."

The Indian took the knife away from Colter's throat. Colter lifted a hand to his neck, felt the thin gash and oily blood. His pulse still hammered.

"It him, you think?" the white man wanted to know.

"How many redheaded younkers you know with S brands on their faces?" The Indian grabbed Colter's shirt collar, jerked him easily to his feet. "You got any more guns, boy?"

Gasping for air, Colter shook his head.

"You better not, or I'll give you an even closer shave than I just give ya."

Colter turned to face the Indian — a big

man in a torn blue-and-red-checked coat. His long hair was mostly loose, but he wore two small hide-wrapped braids in it. One of the braids was decorated with a hawk's feather. He grinned slightly, showing gap-toothed jaws, as he tossed a two-foot length of cut riata to Colter.

"Tie your hands. Shinnick, bring the horses. His is straight back in the trees yonder."

Colter looked at the rope. These men intended to take him back to Bill Rondo in Sapinero. His heart was turning somersaults of desperation, and his knees were jerking inside his denim trousers. He looked at the rope again, dangling against his wrist. If he tied himself, as the big Indian had ordered, he was as good as dead. It would be a long, excruciating death.

He looked at the Indian. He was smiling at Colter, still holding the big bowie knife, the point aimed at Colter. He wore two mismatched pistols on his thighs, beneath the coat, but at the moment he only held the knife. The other man was walking back the way he'd come, apparently tramping off to where they'd left their horses.

"You see me in Crow Dance?" Colter asked, fidgeting around with the riata.

The Indian narrowed an eye and dipped

125

his chin.

"Well, I reckon, then . . ." Colter draped one end of the riata over his right wrist, then flung the rope away with both hands and wheeled to his left. "I reckon you ain't takin' me nowhere, you smelly bastard!"

He ran, leaping deadfalls and sucking breaths. His heart pounded harder, drumming right along with his boots thumping against the loamy forest floor. He was angling into the forest where he might be able to hole up in a snag and hide from these men, maybe slip away later when it got dark.

He'd run maybe twenty feet when he heard a whistling in the air behind him. There was a blur to his right, the twirling object so close he could feel the wind against his ear, feel it ruffle his hair. The knife plunged into a tree trunk just ahead with a solid thud and a reverberating clatter.

And then he was beyond the tree and the knife, running hard, hearing the Indian curse sharply behind him and starting to run after him. Two gun blasts. The slugs slammed into the trees around Colter. A third clipped a branch just over his head.

"Shinnick!" the Indian bellowed.

His running steps faded slightly behind

Colter. He might have been able to shadow up on someone, but the young puncher was faster on his feet.

The white man shouted something. There were two more gun blasts. The slugs curled the air on either side of Colter's head. He scissored his arms, pumped his legs, adrenaline flooding him so that he barely felt the ground and had no trouble weaving around the trees and ducking under branches.

He'd probably run a quarter mile when light shone ahead. A clearing. Shit. He'd hoped for even denser forest.

He stopped at the edge of the clearing, raking air in and out of his lungs. The clearing was a shallow draw, rocky at the bottom. There were more trees on the other side of the cut.

Colt turned. The Indian was a thick, copper-faced shadow weaving among the trees within fifty yards and closing. Saffron sunlight angling through the forest canopy glowed off the silver-chased six-shooter in his right fist.

Colter looked around. On both sides of him, the trees were too thin for adequate cover. He had no choice but to try the draw, and he had no time to stand here and think about it.

He sucked a breath and bolted forward,

letting his own wild momentum carry him down the side of the draw. Behind, branches snapped and pine needles crunched beneath pounding boots.

He gained the bottom of the draw. It was about fifteen feet wide and carpeted with slide rock carried by snowmelt and rainwater. His ankles twisted as he made his way across the gulley.

Behind and above him, a gun roared. He felt as though he'd been hit in the back of his right arm with a brick. The blow threw him forward and twisted him around so that he landed in a skidding, aching heap on the ravine's far side.

His upper right arm burned. He grabbed it, felt the warm blood seeping from the hole in his sleeve. On his belly, he turned to look behind him.

The Indian was halfway down the slope, throwing an arm out for balance as he lumbered toward Colter. The white man, Shinnick, had just started down the slope from the edge of the trees. He had a pistol in each hand. His feet suddenly came out from under him, and he slammed down hard on his ass.

Colter fought back the pain and burning nausea, and bolted off his heels. He started up the slope but had gained only a dozen feet before his boots slipped on the wiry grass. He cursed, grabbed at the grass to hold him but tore two fistfuls out of the ground. He slammed down on his belly with a grunt and slid straight back down the slope, piling up on the rocks below.

"I thought we could take you back to Colorado alive," the Indian said, bunching his lips as he took long strides, swinging his shoulders menacingly, toward Colter. "That's all right — just as easy this way!"

Colter tried to scramble away, but he was too weak. The Indian grabbed his hair and jerked his head back as he'd done before. He grinned down at Colter, showing the gaps between his teeth. Holstering his six-shooter, he grabbed the bowie knife from his beaded belt sheath, held it up so the sun reflected off the shiny silver blade.

"Just your head'll do fine!"

Colter grunted and tried to fight against the Indian's viselike grip. The Indian held him even tighter, nearly pulling his hair out of his scalp, and lowered the blade to Colter's throat.

Colter squeezed his eyes closed as he felt the razor-edged blade bite the tender flesh over his Adam's apple. He looked up at the Indian, who was gritting his teeth and chuckling evilly, when the top of the man's head suddenly exploded.

A half second later came the whip-crack of a rifle, echoing.

The knife dropped in the brush. The Indian sagged back and away from Colter, bending over backward and plopping down on his own heels, shivering as though deeply chilled.

Colter looked around, his mind slow to follow the sudden events. He heard the metallic rasp of a cocking mechanism, saw the white man who'd been bolting down the side of the ravine stop suddenly about six feet from the bottom and shuttle his shocked, horrified gaze from his still-flopping partner toward the source of the shot.

A familiar voice shouted, "Toss them pistols away, friend!"

Colter looked down the ravine.

About fifty yards away, Cimarron was hunkered behind a flat-topped boulder sheathed in red-leafed shrubs and buck brush. He wore his black felt sombrero with the eagle feather sticking up out of the snakeskin band. Resting on the rock in front of him was his silver-plated Henry military-style rifle with a leather shoulder sling. Miss Pearl lifted her head up behind Cimarron's right shoulder, her dark brown eyes wide with anxiety, black hair blowing like mares' tails in the wind.

Colter looked back at the white man, who stared toward Cimarron, his features tense. He still held both pistols in his hands, the barrels slanted toward the ground. Colter could read his mind, weighing his chances.

Cimarron pressed his cheek against his Henry's stock and said with his voiced pitched with warning, "You got two more seconds to make up your mind, friend."

Shinnick licked his lips and opened his eyes wider. Suddenly, he crouched, jerking up both pistols.

Cimarron's rifle puffed smoke and flames.

The slug took Shinnick through his chest. It exited his back in a spray of blood that painted the ground behind him. He screamed and triggered one of his pistols skyward as he flew up and straight back, hitting the ground with a hollow thud and a great *whush!* as the air hammered out of his lungs.

Then he rolled at an angle to the rocks at the bottom of the ravine, piling up about ten feet away from the Indian.

Colter pushed himself to his feet, fingering the knife gash across his throat and holding his wounded right arm straight down by his side. It throbbed and burned, blood running down his sleeve and over his gloved hand. He saw Cimarron rise from behind his boulder, Pearl flanking him. The rancher shouldered his rifle and walked toward him.

Cimarron and Pearl each wore deerskin leggings and a calico shirt, and Pearl also had a rifle, a Spencer repeater, resting across her shoulder in the same fashion as Cimarron. They might have been blood-related, the way they walked toward Colter, hard-eyed and calm but at the same time cautious and dressed in similar styles.

Cimarron stopped ten feet from Colter, looking at the two dead men. "You pick these rattlesnakes up in Crow Dance?"

Colter nodded.

Cimarron spat chaw to one side, adjusted the rest under his lip. "I didn't figure anyone would have heard about the bounty this far north."

"I didn't, either." Colter massaged the bloody line across his neck, shivering. "Reckon if you hadn't come along, they'd be droppin' my head in a tow sack about now."

Cimarron spat again. "Pearl and I were digging out springs near Red Mountain, just headin' back when we heard the shots. Christ, boy." The rancher had turned to

Colter, stretching his lips back from his tobacco-stained teeth as he saw the young drover's bloody arm. "How bad they pink you?"

Colter looked at the wound and sucked a sharp breath. "Judging by how bad it stings, pretty good. But I think it went all the way through without hitting the bone."

Cimarron turned to the girl. "Tend it, Pearly. I'll fetch the horses."

Colter looked at Pearl. She stood with one hip cocked, her rifle on her shoulder, looking back at him with that oblique Sioux gaze.

Colter didn't talk to Pearl and Pearl didn't talk to him as she cut the sleeve off his right arm and tended the ragged flesh wound.

He felt like an idiot for letting himself get run down by Shinnick and Red, and something in the Indian girl's demeanor told him she felt likewise. She was back to not meeting his gaze again, and by the time Cimarron returned with Colter's mount as well as the two bounty hunters' horses and his own and Pearl's, Colter was feeling knee-high to a grasshopper.

A true-blue tinhorn.

They took the weapons off the dead men and buried the bodies under rocks at the bottom of the wash. Afterward, Colter, Cimarron, and Pearl mounted up and, Cimarron trailing the hunters' two horses, started back toward the ranch.

During the entire six-mile ride, the only time anything was spoken was when Cimarron chuckled wryly and said, "Didn't realize when I hired a drover last month I was gettin' a whole new remuda right along in the bargain. . . ."

Colter wasn't sure how to take that, so he kept his head down and said nothing, tending the pain of his flesh-wounded arm in moody silence. Pearl had fashioned a sling out of one of the dead men's cartridge belts, and he rode with the arm suspended across his chest, lightning bolts of pain lancing it whenever Northwest trod rougher than usual terrain.

When they gained the ranch, it was early evening. Shanley and Dawson were playing horseshoes out behind the bunkhouse, awaiting supper, which Pearl started throwing together as soon as she slid down from her cream stallion and let Colter and Cimarron and the two older drovers lead her mount with the others into the main corral.

Of course Shanley and Dawson wanted to know what had happened to Colter's arm and how their remuda had come to grow by two more horses. Colter told them as quickly and as succinctly as he could about the ambush, while he helped one-handed with the horses.

He used the wounded arm as an excuse to leave the supper table as soon as he'd finished Pearl's elk steaks and roasted potatoes, forgoing the usual cobbler dessert, and retreated to the bunkhouse. He wanted to lick his wound as well as his injured pride in the evening silence, alone, while Shanley and Dawson stayed up with Cimarron, playing euchre, which they usually did until about eleven o'clock every night, none of the three seeming to require much sleep despite the amount of hard work they put in every day around the headquarters or out on the range.

Colter had just stripped down to his long-handles and crawled under his cotton sheets and Indian blankets for what, with the aching arm, was bound to be a restless night's sleep, when the bunkhouse door scraped open. Despite it being only around nine o'clock, he expected to see either Dawson or Shanley or both saunter in to turn in early.

When he didn't hear the two drovers' good-natured jeers, he looked toward the front of the bunkhouse, and instantly furled his brows with incredulity.

Pearl turned from the door she'd just closed. She looked over at the cot in which Colter lay, propped on his one good elbow. The girl had a cigarette in one hand, a bottle and two glasses in the other. She wore an old buffalo robe and mocassins. Her hair was shiny from a recent brushing as it flowed down over the robe's heavy collar.

Staring at him without expression, Pearl brought the cigarette to her lips, took a deep drag, then blew the smoke at the low rafters. She held up the bottle and the two shot glasses. "You like whiskey?"

Colter almost shook his head to clear it of any possible hallucinations that might have been brought on by the wound. He croaked, "I reckon." He didn't normally imbibe, but the whiskey would help dull the pain in his arm.

Pearl walked slowly toward him, kicking out of each moccasin in turn until she was walking to him barefoot, setting each long, delicate, copper-colored foot on the scarred puncheon floor.

"How 'bout girls?" she asked.

Then she flung the robe off her shoulders, let it fall to the floor at her feet. She was naked. Not wearing a stitch. Her breasts were heavy and upthrust, with dark brown nipples. Her hair hung down her slender shoulders, framing the firm, pointed orbs, displaying them.

Her eyes were smoky as she said, "You like girls, too?"

CHAPTER 11

Colter wasn't sure how long he and Pearl
had frolicked as if they were lusty forest
creatures, but he was sure that, when he
opened his eyes later, they'd been asleep a
lot longer than they had frolicked. He could
tell for two reasons — one, the shoulder he
found her head resting on when he awoke
felt as heavy as an anvil and nearly as sore
as his wounded arm. Two, all the bunkhouse's sashed, dusty, warped windows
were gray with what he feared was dirty
dawn light.

His suspicion was confirmed when he
looked out the bunkhouse's east window
and saw streaks of pink and salmon light
over the purple eastern buttes.

Pearl must have sensed his alarm. She
lifted her head suddenly with a grunt, and
looked around at the windows. Then she
swiveled her head toward the two other sets
of bunks, the bottoms of both of which were

usually occupied by Shanley and Dawson. Colter looked at those, as well, and couldn't figure out why neither bunk was occupied, nor, judging by their unwrinkled Indian blankets, had been occupied recently.

Pearl's voice was a half-whispered grunt. "It's morning."

Colter winced when she lifted her head from his shoulder and the blood rushed back into it. As she dropped her bare feet to the floor, he wasn't too anxious about what time it was to admire the vision of her striding naked to the window facing the cabin — a long-legged, dusky-skinned Indian queen whose straight, indigo hair hung down the length of her slender back to where her round hips curved and her taut, tan buttocks swelled.

The sharp edge of his anxiety returned, however, when she gave another startled grunt, wheeled, quickly plucked her buffalo robe off the floor, threw it around her shoulders, and, holding it closed across her breasts, dashed to the door, fumbled it open, and bolted outside.

As naked as Pearl, Colter crawled off the cot, wincing at the pain in his wounded right arm, and tramped over to the door she'd left standing wide. One hand on the door frame, the other on the door, he gazed across the yard toward the cabin as Pearl traversed the gap in a defiant, stiff-legged stride, hair buffeting out behind her.

Colter had thought he'd heard muffled chuckles, and now he realized where they were coming from. Cimarron, Shanley, and Dawson were all three sitting on the cabin's front veranda, lounging like soldiers on furlough, half dressed and wearing hats and boots and clutching steaming coffee mugs in their fists. All three were grinning as Pearl bounded barefoot up the veranda steps, dashed inside the cabin, and slammed the door behind her.

Stretch Dawson laid a hand against his mouth to yell at Colter, "You two get a good night's rest, didja?"

He and the other two laughed heartily.

Shanley said, "Cimarron said it wouldn't be polite to interrupt two young'uns in love's embrace, so we slept in the cabin. We'll come over there now and wash up, if that's all right with you, Casanova?"

Colter had thought that yesterday he'd been as uncomfortable as he could possibly get. Now he knew better. He just stared across the yard in disbelief at the three howling stockmen. Then he turned away from the door and tramped over to the washstand and poured nearly a whole pitcher of water over his head.

Later, when Shanley and Dawson had come over to the bunkhouse to wash and dress and ready themselves for another day, Shanley told Colter that Cimarron had noticed Pearl's growing interest in the young drover over the past week, and that Colter's knocking off the three bank robbers had seemed to cinch it for her.

"You see," Dawson said, stomping into a boot, "them Injun girls take a fancy to a young buck, they don't beat around the bush as much as white girls do. And they got stronger needs than white girls, too. Cimarron knows all about that. He done had him one 'Pache wife down in Arizona, and a Comanche squaw in Texas."

"Don't think you were Pearl's first, boy," Shanley chuckled as he shaved in the mirror hanging from a nail over the washstand.

Dawson lifted his boot up on the edge of his cot to tighten his spur strap. "Oh, no, sir. The girl's got needs, and she tends 'em. Trying to stand in her way would be like tryin' to stand in the way of a she-griz with the springtime craze. Cimarron's just glad she set her hat for you and not one of them fork-tailed owl hoots Graham Fletcher has ridin' for him over to the Box W."

"Damn," Colter said, running a short

141

willow branch soaked in crushed spearmint leaves across his teeth, "I'm just glad you didn't warn me beforehand and that you three got so damn much fun out of it." But he'd known from how adroitly the girl had performed in his cot last night — far more expertly than he, and with an astonishing lack of inhibitions — that she'd been no virgin whom Cimarron had kept locked in an iron maiden.

"Don't worry," Shanley said. "She might give you another tumble before she tires of you."

He and Dawson laughed. A horse's whinny from the main corral cut them both off abruptly.

"That was Hair Trigger," Dawson said.

Another horse whinnied. Colter dropped his toothbrush into the tin can he used for tooth care. "That was Northwest." The horse didn't normally get skittish unless strangers were near.

Colter rinsed his mouth out as Dawson stepped to a south-facing window, drawing his suspenders up his arms, and ducked his head to look out the low, sashed panes. "Six riders. None I recognize."

Shanley grabbed his shell belt and hogleg off a wall spike, wrapped the belt around his hips. Colter grabbed his own rig, and when he had it cinched, he heard the thud of hooves in the yard. He glimpsed through a window riders passing the bunkhouse's west end. He didn't get a good look at the visitors, but something in their straight-backed, square-shouldered bearing made him apprehensive.

Waddies visiting from other ranches usually rode loosely, with a casual air, and hailed the ranch as they passed under the wooden portal.

Colter donned his hat, grabbed his Henry, and followed the other two drovers to the front door. He stepped outside behind them as the six strangers pulled their horses up to the cabin on the other side of the yard — five men and a stubby, blond woman. Cimarron was already out there, standing on the cabin's veranda and holding his own Henry on his shoulder and wearing his broad-brimmed hat with its eagle feather, a quirley smoldering between his lips.

Movement drew Colter's attention to the cabin's right front corner, where Pearl stood, casually holding a Winchester in her crossed arms, one boot cocked out in front of her. She wore a calico blouse and a bright green skirt of some Indian material, and her floppy-brimmed black hat with a bullet-shaped crown. She must have gone out the cabin's back door to back Cimarron's play with her Winchester.

Knowing the girl's confidence and expertise in various situations, Colter had a feeling the girl knew her way around a rifle, as well as a bunkhouse cot.

"Howdy, there," the apparent lead rider said, his raspy voice clear in the quiet morning ranch yard. He gave a nod to Cimarron, who returned it cordially.

Colter could see only the riders' backs from his vantage fronting the bunkhouse, but he could tell the lead rider was a big man with long gray-streaked brown hair and wearing a knee-length wolf coat. The gang's lone woman wore men's checked trousers and long coat comprising several different animal skins, and with a brown bowler hat from which tufts of tight, yellow hair stuck out. There was a black man, a man in a long beaver coat, a broad-shouldered hombre in a blue bandanna, no hat, and with the teeth of some animal dangling from his ears. On the far right of the group facing the cabin, a lanky blond kid in a dusty top hat and tan duster straddled a brown and white pinto.

"Name's La Brie," the leader told Cimarron.

"How can I help you, La Brie?"

La Brie glanced at the man riding beside

him, and Colter could see the incredulous grin on the side of the man's long, stubbled jaw. Turning back to Cimarron, La Brie said, "Well, for starters, you could ask us to light and sit a spell. Offer feed and water for our horses. We come a long ways."

"I don't care how far you come," Cimarron said tightly. "I don't know you boys." He glanced at the bullet-shaped blond woman sitting beside La Brie, and added, "And lady. Nor your reputations. So you remain seated on your ponies while they drink at my stock troughs. There's plenty of feed along the creeks."

Shanley glanced warily at Colter, and then he and Dawson walked a little ways down the bunkhouse veranda, spreading out and holding their rifles up high across their chests. Dawson's boot made one of the porch's loose boards squawk. The drover winced and lifted his anxious gaze toward the strangers, all of whom jerked their heads around toward the bunkhouse.

Seeing Colter and the two older, rifle-wielding ranch hands, all six of the riders curveted their horses so they could keep both the cabin and bunkhouse in sight. A couple dropped gloved hands over holstered pistols. They'd all seen Pearl by now, as well, so they all looked as edgy as three-legged jackrabbits at a coyote picnic. One of the men — a husky black man in a brown corduroy coat and sporting two pistols and a big knife jutting above the coat flaps — clucked his disapproval as he looked at Pearl and the three rifle-wielding ranch hands behind him. The whites of his eyes beneath his cream Steton's down-canted brim looked as white as eggshells.

The kid in the top hat held his pinto's reins taut, and narrowed his eyes on either side of his long, broad, sunburned nose, one hand on a big Smith & Wesson holstered for the cross draw under his duster.

La Brie ran his gaze across Colter, Shanley, and Dawson, then turned his head toward Pearl standing calmly at the cabin's corner. He swung his gaze back to Cimarron and gave a tight laugh. "Now, this ain't no way to treat guests."

Cimarron said, "You ain't guests if you weren't invited. Name your business and git."

"You know why we're here." This from the man in the long beaver coat and sitting on the other side of the blond from La Brie. He straddled a long-legged, cream barb that sort of danced in place and chewed its bit, as edgy as its rider. The man himself was dull-eyed, long-faced, with a broad, flat

146

nose, and only a red knot appeared where his right ear should have been. Besides his long beaver coat, he wore a black derby hat, and a big bone-gripped Colt jutted from a holster strapped snug against his saddle horn.

Cimarron said, "I look like a mind reader?"

"Where's the money?" The blond woman had a mannish voice, but she pitched it shrill with exasperation, setting her jaw hard.

Cimarron stared at her dully, puffing the quirley wedged in a corner of his mouth. "If you're lookin' for money, you came to the wrong damn ranch. Now, I suggest you git before you overstay your welcome."

Shanley and Dawson shaped nervous grins and adjusted their grips on their rifles. Colter held his own Henry straight down by his right leg, ready to bring it up in that hand despite the wound in his arm, leaving his left free for the old Remington positioned for the cross draw on his right hip. His heart beat in steady, measured beats.

He'd been through this before. He didn't like it, but he was ready for it.

The woman gave a loud, caustic chuff. She rose in her saddle and thrust her head like a weapon toward Cimarron. "You know

147

what money, you greaser son of a bitch! Turn it over or we'll lay waste to this place!"

"Mercy!" La Brie chasted her, chuckling. "Sister, please, let me handle this."

Holding her jittery horse's reins up close to her chest, Mercy whipped her head toward La Brie and said tightly, "He knows what money we're talkin' about, brother. He's a lyin' Mex, is what he is!"

La Brie got his black-legged bay calmed down and turned it to face the cabin. The other horses calmed down somewhat then, as well, and La Brie leaned casually forward against his saddle horn. "My sister, while high-blooded, has a point, senor. We found the graves of our dead pards in a dry wash forking off Devil's Creek. Recognized the horses in your paddock when we rode into the yard. You see, our dark-skinned brother here, Tenbow Preston, was an army scout and tracker down in Arizona, and he can track a june bug across a storm-tossed mountain lake in the dead of night. Three riders led three horses right up to your doorstep about two nights ago."

The black man said in a grim, accusing tone, "One of the horses bein' led was carrying considerable extra weight than the other two."

"Yeah," said the one-eared man in the

beaver coat. "About twenty-six thousand in gold bullion extra."

"You see," La Brie said, "we split it up with our pards — one bein' my own brother, the other two bein' my true-blue cousins on my dear mama's side — when soldiers tried to run us down out of Camp Collins, down in the Colorado Territory. We was to meet at Lone Pine Station, but when our pards didn't show, we got worried, so we tracked 'em from Rock Creek Station, where they apparently stopped to get directions."

La Brie stared at Cimarron. Colter couldn't see the outlaw leader's expression from this angle, but he could see Cimarron staring back at the man with a bored air.

Colter couldn't fathom what was going through the rancher's mind. If it was anything like what was going through Colter's, it was shock and a keen and bitter amazement that these border toughs were so good at their business that they'd tracked the money straight to the Diamond Bar's front door.

There was a long, taut silence broken only by the occasional blows and snorts of the horses, and the peeps and chirps of the mud swallows, sparrows, and mountain jays flitting around in search of breakfast. The man in the blue bandanna and bear-tooth earrings swatted at a fly buzzing around his nose.

Cimarron glanced at Pearl, who turned her head to meet his gaze. Then he ran his dark, appraising stare across the rough-looking group before him before his eyes settled on La Brie once more. "The money was here but we hauled it off to town. It's probably right now on its ways back to whomever you stole it from."

"Doubt it," said the one-eared man in the buffalo coat.

La Brie said, "This here is Beaver Charlie, and Beaver Charlie's always had him a sound sense about folks. Beaver Charlie, you don't think Mr. Padilla here turned that money back to its rightful owners?"

The rangy kid in the top hat and duster snorted a laugh.

Beaver Charlie scratched the scarred knot where his right ear had been hacked off, and shook his head slowly. "Nah. Padilla here is a Mex, and he's got him a purty squaw. If there's one thing I know about Mescins and squaws, it's they're greedy bastards. Greedier even than me or you, La Brie, or even Mercy over here. No offense, Mercy. We won't even start talking about Preston's grade o' greed. Ain't fittin' even to mention it way out here amongst these damn tinhorn cow nurses with shit behind their ears."

The big man with the dark blue calico scarf sitting on the far side of the black man shook his head, sighing his sad dismay.

Colter was looking around at the group, most of whom sat sideways to him, and he was wondering which one would start the trouble, when a rifle cracked. He didn't know who'd fired the shot until he looked at Cimarron, who was racking a fresh round into the chamber of his smoking Henry. The spent casing hit the floor of the veranda with a ping and then rattled around the rancher's boots.

Beaver Charlie cupped a gloved hand to his left ear and stared straight ahead at Cimarron. His neck was as red as his knotted-up other ear.

The others were staring at Cimarron now, too, all frozen in the motion of pulling hoglegs, or, in the case of the big man with the bear-tooth earrings, a rifle jutting up in front of his right thigh. They all looked more shocked than angry — so shocked none of them seemed to know what to say.

In the growing morning light, Colter saw blood oozing out between two fingers of the hand that Beaver Charlie was holding over his lone good ear. At least, the lone ear that had been good until a few seconds ago.

"You best quit talkin' about what folks got behind their ears," Cimarron growled, aiming the Henry at Beaver Charlie, "when you only got one good ear yourself and the other looks like a bobcat been gnawin' on your head."

Beaver Charlie didn't say anything but only continued to keep his head pointed at Cimarron.

When La Brie got his horse settled down once more, he looked across the yard toward the bunkhouse, then at Pearl, who stood as before, casually holding her rifle in her arms, her face expressionless. As he turned to Beaver Charlie, the gang leader's eyes became cautious, and flinty with anger.

Softly, he said, "You all right, Charlie?"

Beaver Charlie said nothing. A single blood drop fell from a knuckle of the hand over his ear to the collar of his long beaver coat.

"Everyone get your hands off them shootin' irons," Cimarron said, glaring down the barrel of his Henry at Beaver Charlie, his smoldering quirley bobbing between his lips. "Or all them saddles of yours are gonna be mighty empty in about three jerks of a steer's tail."

Mercy turned her horse in a complete

circle, her mannish, pug-nosed face set with fury. "We gonna let him take the break on us like this, brother?"

Beaver Charlie finally lowered his hand from his ear. As he wiped the hand on his fringed buckskin trouser leg, he turned to La Brie. His voice quivered with barely contained fury as he said, "I say we do what we come here for. Ain't none of 'em better than any of us." He looked toward the bunkhouse. "They got position on us, so, sure, we might swallow a few pills, but . . ."

La Brie turned his horse out into the yard, his own jaw so taut it looked as if it might break, then swung the horse back to face the cabin. He rose in his stirrups and jutted his chin toward Cimarron staring down his Henry at him. "I'm gonna give you honyonkers till five o'clock tonight to turn over that gold you stole from us." His voice with its strange northern accent teemed with calm menace. "By five o'clock tonight it better be sittin' over there under that ranch portal in plain sight for one of us to ride in and pick up. Understand? *Five o'clock!* If it ain't there, we're gonna ride in here and we're gonna burn this headquarters to the ground and we're gonna shoot all your stock and kill all the men and hang your lyin', thievin' carcasses from trees for the vultures to pick clean!"

The outlaw leader glanced at Pearl, narrowed his eyes eyes between wings of his brown-silver hair, and poked an arm at her. "And I'm gonna take that squaw girl over there, and you know what I'll do to her — don't you, Padilla? And when I've had my fill I'm gonna give her to the rest of the boys, and when they're done and we've had enough of her squealin', I'm gonna cut her throat from ear to ear."

Cimarron bolted forward, slapping his cheek to his rifle stock. But La Brie's horse was prancing, making a clean shot at the outlaw impossible. Then La Brie's hand moved in a blur, and when it stopped there was a cocked Colt in it, aimed at Cimarron.

"Two can play your game, Mexican!" La Brie laughed. "There ain't no one faster'n me. Not even the sumbitch who shot my brother and cousins out of their saddles. I know how they was shot, 'cause we dug 'em up. And what I'm sayin' is, whoever shot 'em — whether it was you or her or that boy back there or one o' them two old men — don't go thinkin' you can take me. 'Cause you can't — understand?"

He turned his head slightly while keeping his revolver aimed at Cimarron, and yelled,

"And don't think I don't know you're drawin' a bead on my back, young man back there with the branded face. If you shoot me in the back like a damn sissy coward, I'll kill your boss before I hit the ground. I'm *that* goddamn good!"

Colter's heart was thudding as he aimed down the barrel of his old Tyler Henry, his finger taut against the trigger. The other outlaws, all pracing around now on their nervous mounts, looked at Colter with bright challenge in their hard eyes.

Shanley and Dawson turned to him, too, both men's eyes cast with apprehension. The blonde, Mercy, laughed mockingly as she ran a pudgy hand nervously up and down a thigh of her man's checked trousers. Colter slackened his trigger finger, depressed the Henry's hammer, and lowered the rifle.

"Five o'clock tonight!" La Brie shouted, swinging his horse in a broad circle and then booting it toward the portal. "Not a minute later or the fires here will light up the whole goddamn valley, and they'll hear your squaw's squeals all the way to Denver!"

The other cutthroats reined their mounts around, casting cautious, challenging looks at Cimarron, Pearl, Colter, and the older men standing beside him. The big man with the bear-tooth earrings and brown braid falling down from his bandanna had a hand on his rifle butt. He was cursing under his breath, red face bunched savagely. He, Mercy, the black man, Preston, and the lanky kid in the top hat galloped off after their leader.

Beaver Charlie was the last to go, pointing at Cimarron and gritting his teeth as he shouted, "You and me, you bean-eatin', squaw-screwin' son of a bitch — we's gonna dance the screamin'-lead two-step!"

And then he followed the others around the corrals and the springhouse and out under the ranch portal. Tan dust churning behind them, the outlaws splashed across the creek, put their horses into lopes through the aspens, and dwindled off across the sage flats until the thuds of their horses faded and there was only the sound of the horses stomping in the Diamond Bar's near corral, and the birds.

CHAPTER 12

Colter looked up from his work on the stock trough to peer off across the main corral to the gnarled aspens following the meandering line of the creek, and dropped his hammer to reach for his rifle. He racked a round into the chamber and walked slowly around the trough he'd been nailing new boards around, to the corral's back fence.

He'd seen movement out by the creek, which he'd been keeping an eye on all day while he'd done odd jobs around the ranch headquarters. All the men and Pearl had remained on the ranchstead in the aftermath of La Brie's departure, keeping a careful eye out for an ambush while working on various jobs, their rifles close to hand.

Very little had been said after the outlaws had left.

Over breakfast, Cimarron had given assignments. There'd been no discussion of turning over the money to the brigands.

Colter had thought of it, and he knew the others including Cimarron must have mulled it in passing, also. This really wasn't their fight, nor their money to save. They could have turned the loot back over to the men who'd stolen it, and let the law run the hardcases down, saving their own lives and the Diamond Bar in the bargain.

It would have made the day simpler and easier on the nerves, without the waiting and the wondering what would happen when five o'clock rolled around and La Brie sent someone to the portal only to find that the money wasn't there.

It would have made the day simpler.

But it would have made their lives tougher, knowing they'd backed down to La Brie and his gang. Because the Diamond Bar riders had the money now, and while it wasn't theirs, a queer arrangement of the moon and stars had made it theirs to fight for.

So, while likely everyone on the ranch had considered it, no mention was made of it, and all the men and Pearl had gone about their chores with their rifles easy to grab, waiting and keeping an eye on the valley beyond the creek and the aspens, knowing that sooner or later from that direction, hell was going to pop.

Colter laid the Tyler Henry across the corral's top unpeeled pole as he stared toward the creek and the spot at which he'd glimpsed movement. He stared, waiting, and then a shadow moved between two low trees not far from the portal, and Colter drew his index finger taut against the Henry's trigger.

The thud of a hammer sounded from the direction of the cabin, and the thing in the trees lifted its head suddenly to show itself as a young spike buck, brown eyes looking this way as it chewed the rich bluestem that grew along the willows and aspens at the creek's edge.

Colter eased the tension in his finger, and in all the rest of his body, and lowered the rifle.

He turned and began to jerk the barrel up once more, but it was Pearl standing there, leaning against the corral, one bare foot propped on the bottom pole. A red bandanna kept her jet-black hair pulled back from her forehead as she chewed an apple, her red and black skirt billowing around her shapely legs.

Colter felt his cheeks warm as he walked toward her, but if she felt any embarrassment over what had happened the previous night, she didn't show it. A Winchester carbine leaned against the corral only a foot away from her. Casually, she took another bite from the green apple that had come from the tree behind the cabin and which she'd built a small watering trench to, and sniffed as she ran her hand across her nose.

"See anything out there . . . other'n deer?"

"Not yet."

"They'll come."

"I don't doubt it."

"How'd you get that scar, again? I was thinking about something else when you told it."

"Must've really broken your heart."

"I told you I didn't hear it."

Colter leaned his rifle against the corral, put his back to the fence, crossed his boots, and stared off across the valley. "The details don't matter. In fact, they've grown kinda dim. The fella that marked me got his own mark right back, but I don't reckon it really changed anything except it got me chased all the way up here to Wyoming."

He glanced over his shoulder at Pearl, chewing her apple and staring off across the corral and the valley beyond. "Does it make you regret last night?"

She turned her placid dark eyes to him. "Why should it?"

" 'Cause it's ugly."

"It's no uglier now than it was last night.

Besides . . ." She gave a mischievous grin. "It wasn't your cheek I was after." She tossed the rest of her apple toward the horses clumped on the far side of the fence. As Northwest started toward it, shouldering a pinto colt out of the way, she picked up her rifle. "I'm gonna go weed my garden out back of the cabin. If you see anything, fire a couple shots so I hear."

She started to walk away, then stopped. "Oh . . . one more thing. Don't go counting on having what you got last night every night. It's not like I'm in love with you or anything and it has nothing to do with your brand or anything else."

Colter's brows beetled with an exasperated scowl.

She threw up her free hand, palm out. "I only say it so you don't go making a fool of yourself."

"Hey, look here!"

Pearl laughed and, walking away, cast him a parting, mocking glance over her shoulder, dark eyes flashing gold. "Keep your finger on your trigger and an eye on your back trail, Colter Farrow."

Colter's scowl deepened and his face reddened as he watched her stroll away, her rump swinging saucily behind her skirt. Even her ass seemed to mock him.

Then he turned his back to her and picked up his rifle, vexation aggravated by goatish lust washing through him in waves.

"What time is it, Griff?" Cimarron asked.

Shanley fished his tarnished silver turnip from his vest pocket, and pressing down on the dented lid with one thumb, tripped the latch with the other, until the cover of the old timepiece snapped wide.

"Six minutes yonder o' five."

As the late afternoon shadows tumbled down the western ridges, all the Diamond Bar men had gathered on the cabin porch with their rifles. Pearl leaned in the cabin's open doorway, and from behind her emanated the aromas of bean and chicken stew and fresh coffee as well as gun oil.

"Maybe they won't come," Dawson said, leaning forward in his hide-bottom chair, his Spencer rifle resting across his bony thighs. "Maybe they'll decide it'd be easier to rob another army payroll or a bank or, hell, a train, and just drift on out of the country."

Cimarron stood on the porch's middle step, staring out toward the ranch portal and the creek and then the valley that stretched dusty green under a silver blue sky. "They'll come."

162

Colter, with a hip resting on the rail and his rifle on his shoulder, knew it was true. For the same reason Cimarron wouldn't return the money to La Brie, the cutthroats would have to try to take it back. Likely, men would die. Maybe one or two of those around him. Maybe he himself would die. But his fear was nothing compared to the suspense of waiting and wondering when La Brie would come.

"Maybe one of us should've ridden over to the Box W or to Milt Kethum's place. Milt — he'd have sent some men to help out."

"It's our fight," Cimarron said. Then he lifted his head, staring hard into the distance, and Colter craned his head around to see what he was seeing.

"Jackrabbit," Shanley said, making his chair creak as he leaned back against the cabin's front wall with a weary groan.

Colter watched the rabbit bound off into a clump of brush and then he turned his gaze back to the portal standing sun-bleached out near the creek, its shadow angling down beneath it. Nothing beyond it but the creek, gnarled trees, and sage. Black flies stitched the air, and the late sun flashed golden off the wings of darting mud swallows.

There was no sound but the occasional gust of a breeze.

Later, when the night came down with that extra hush, they'd be able to hear the creek rushing softly in its bed, chuckling over stones. Several times, Colter had gone out there to fish, and he'd pulled up a couple of nice rainbow trout on grasshoppers. Tonight, he wouldn't be making that walk or that chill evening wade that had always set his mind at ease.

He didn't know what he'd be doing later tonight, if he'd be doing anything at all.

The tension raked his nerves, and he clenched his jaw, wishing they'd come.

Dawson felt the same way. He spat a wad of chew over the porch rail and growled, "Well, is he gonna come look for the damn saddlebags or ain't he?"

Cimarron sat on the front step of the porch, doffed his hat, and ran his brown fingers through his long, dark red hair. "Nah, he already knows it's not there. Likely, he has someone camped out in the brush on the ridge over yonder, glassing the ranch. He knows we ain't brought the gold out there. He's just waiting to make us wait."

And wait they did. Under a searing tension. All night long. Jerking their heads around at every owl hoot or sudden wind gust or horse stomp. They ate in turns, two always keeping watch outside. They slept in turns, too — if anyone did any sleeping.

Colter didn't.

He just lay staring at the bunkhouse ceiling, counting the poles that made up the roof and then the knots in the poles and then he scrutinized the initials that Cimarron's men had carved in the walls over the years, and a couple of lewd stick figures.

When dawn came, the tension increased, because it figured they'd attack at first light, trying to catch one of the Diamond Bar folks sleeping or owly from not having slept.

But the sun climbed, casting a lemon glow over the ranch stead. There was another clear sky. The horses stood in the corral, staring toward the cabin for breakfast.

The men had their own breakfast — sowbelly, beans, and eggs - on the front porch, their eyes tired-looking and red-veined and continually aimed toward the creek the way a compass needle was always jerking north.

Cimarron scrubbed his plate with a biscuit, stuffed it into his mouth, and glanced at Colter, sitting on the porch's far end, straddling the rail with his rifle leaning against his left thigh. "Son, let's you and me ride out, see if we can spot 'em. I'm starting to wonder if Stretch doesn't have it right, and they didn't light on out of here. It'd be just like La Brie to leave us wondering and getting a big chuckle out of it."

Colter nodded and continued eating though he wasn't all that hungry.

"That might be just what he wants," Shanley warned. "If he gets two of us out there, leaving two in here —"

"Three in here," Pearl corrected him sternly as she refilled his coffee cup from her big black pot.

"Three, I mean," Shanley said, contrite. "That might be a good hand of stud for ole La Brie."

"Maybe." Waving off Pearl's coffee, Cimarron rose and carried his plate into the cabin. "But we're gonna ride out anyway. If we see tracks near, we'll come back. If he ain't around, it's time we got some work done around the damn place."

Colter and Cimarron rode out under the ranch portal twenty minutes later.

They rode slowly, warily at first, craning their heads to peer in all directions at once as they held their rifles across their saddle-bows. When they were halfway to the other side of the valley, they started looking for sign that La Brie's gang might have moved up close to the ranch during the night and were possibly hunkered down behind a knoll. The valley might have looked flat from a distance, but it was anything but flat when you really scouted it out.

Directly across from the Diamond Bar headquarters was a steep, pine- and fir-covered ridge. The ridge was sort of an apron slope of the higher, rockier reaches of the Cheyennes. Northeast of the ranch, the valley widened and nudged slightly north-ward, and here were several low benches cut and shaped by the ancient river that had originally carved the valley.

These benches rose toward higher, for-ested ridges. It was the first of these benches that Cimarron told Colter he wanted to scout. If the gang was holed up out here, they'd likely taken cover on this bench from where they'd have a view of the ranch through a good set of field glasses.

Though you could see the bench from the ranch, Colter and Cimarron had been riding nearly an hour before they started up its blond-grassed slope, following an elk trail that rose at a forty-five-degree angle. The horses snorted and blew. The saddles creaked, and bridle chains jangled.

Gophers and field mice peeped and scuttled across the trail, sometimes frightening the horses. A hawk screeched somewhere in the bright blue sky.

They were nearly to the top of the bench when Cimarron glanced back at Colter, then tossed his head toward a fir standing straight and tall at the ridge crest, in a long line with many others. This tree stood where the trail flattened out at the top; from a dead branch about ten feet off the ground a rope swung in the morning breeze.

A rope in the form of a hangman's noose.

Cimarron snugged the butt of his Henry against his right thigh as he and Colter gained the crest of the ridge and sat staring up at the noose dancing and swaying in the breeze. Colter looked to each side along the bench that he could see now was merely a shelf in the apron slope rising toward toothy mountain peaks.

None of the La Brie riders seemed to be near, but the tracks of a half dozen shod hooves were plain in the thin soil and its scanty covering of coarse blond grass and wiry little wildflowers that grew close to the ground. There were several rocks beside the tree from which the noose dangled, and Colter was about to skid his gaze over them until he saw something peculiar about their arrangement.

He rode over and stared down at the flat

168

chunks of slide rock forming the Diamond Bar brand. On the "bar," five .45-caliber cartridges had been neatly arranged, lead heads pointing up.

Cimarron followed him over, and stared down. He said nothing as he scrutinized the rocks and the cartridges and then rode over them, scattering the .45 shells, and into the trees. Colter booted Northwest after his boss. Cimarron stopped his horse again, and Colter followed the rancher's gaze to a ring of fire-blackened stones in which gray ashes and part of a scorched log lay mounded.

Cimarron looked around, keeping his voice low. Colter could tell the noose and the rocks and the cartridges had gotten to him in much the same way they'd gotten to Colter. Made him feel owly as hell. Mocked. Trapped.

Targeted.

Cimarron's voice was low and tight, his dark eyes wary. "This is where they spent the night."

Colter rode back to the tree from which the noose dangled. Apprehension clung like bloodsuckers to his back. He held his rifle in one hand across his saddle horn as he stared out across the valley.

From the direction of the ranch, a rifle barked three times in quick succession, echoing flatly.

Cimarron bolted past Colter in a blur of man and horse, lunging down the bench.

Heart hammering, imagining all of La Brie's men storming the ranch and Pearl, Shanley, and Dawson, Colter put Northwest into an instant downslope lunge in his boss's dust.

CHAPTER 13

Spurr slid the Mexican whore, Carmelita, up and down on his lap as he sat on the edge of the bed in his dingy room in the Skinner House in Buffaloville. The naked, dusky-skinned, small-breasted pleasure girl straddled him. She had her arms wrapped around his neck, her heels pressing against his back.

She cooed, grunted, and groaned as he drove her up and down with his hands on her slender, bony hips.

"I please you — no?" the girl inquired anxiously as her hair bobbed across her shoulders.

"Shut up!" Spurr growled, bringing the little *puta* against him with even more fury.

"*Mierda!*" the girl cried. She rested her chin on Spurr's head, smoothed down his sleep-tangled hair with her hands. "You need relax, senor. Why don' you lay back, let Carmelita do the work, huh?"

"Goddamnit, girl," Spurr regaled the little whore bobbing up and down like a malfunctioning jack-in-the-box. "I done told you to shut up!" He squeezed his eyes closed and gritted his teeth, pressing his right cheek against the girl's breasts as he worked. "Can't . . . you see . . . I'm tryin' to *concentrate* . . . here?"

Beneath the squawking of the bedsprings, his own grunts, and the girl's groans, there was the scuttling of tiny toenails against the wood floor, and the *snick-snicks* of a leathery little tail. Spurr opened his eyes and peered through the girl's jostling black hair.

"Goddamnit, Lyle!" he wailed, bounding up off the bed and twisting around to grab his gun from the shell belts hanging off a front poster.

The girl screamed as she flew back off Spurr's naked lap and hit the floor with a loud thump. Spurr slid his horn-handled Starr .44 from its greased holster, thumbed back the hammer, and aimed at the rat just now poking its head down the fist-sized hole in the floor at the base of the wall.

Pow! Pow! Pow!

The three slugs only made the hole larger. The rat gave a mocking peep and slithered down it, pulling its twitching tail after it. The whore screamed again and, pushing herself up off the floor, dashed to the door. She gave Spurr a terrified look over her bare left shoulder as she fumbled the door open and then, sobbing, dashed out into the hall, leaving the door wide behind her.

Lyle Kingman's voice bellowed from the first story, "Spurr! What in the hell are you shooting at now, *you crazy son of a bitch?*"

Spurr heaved himself with effort from the bed. Naked, holding the smoking revolver up high in his hand as though certain he'd have another opportunity to use it, he walked through the open door and into the hall, and turned toward the stairs at the far end. "I'm shootin' your pet rat, you bald-headed bastard! You can subtract my fee for cleanin' up this rat trap from my bill!"

Drunken fury had lowered a red shade over the lawman's eyes. He aimed at the newell post at the top of the stairs, squinted one eye, and pulled the trigger.

The Starr leaped and roared like thunder in the close quarters. The .44 slug ripped the wooden ball atop the post completely off, bounced it off the wall behind it, and sailed it down the stairs.

"And send up another whore!" the drunken lawman shouted at the tops of his lungs, mindless of the hot hitch in his chest. "I done wore that one plumb out!"

Spurr turned to go back into his room, stopped. Two old gray-headed ladies — spinster sisters on their way to Chugwater for a funeral, he'd heard — peered out at him through their cracked room door. Spurr gave a growling chuckle and wagged his hips. "Sorry, ladies, but I don't think you'd want for your first time to be under a stallion like this'n here. I'd ruin you both for all the studs forever after!"

Both women shrieked and threw their shoulders against their door, slamming it.

Spurr guffawed and staggered back into his room, slamming his own door, then grabbed the nearly empty whiskey bottle off the dresser. He glanced at the rat hole, saw two dull yellow eyes staring up at him. Slamming the bottle back down on the dresser, Spurr leveled the Starr at the hole once more, and fired.

Bam!

The recoil was more than his inebriated, off-balance state could handle. He got his bare feet tangled, and suddenly the room was spinning and his feet were going one way, his shoulders another, and the floor came up to rap his back and the back of his head so hard that his vision turned fuzzy and his ears filled with songbirds.

The slowly revolving, pitching room went dark.

He had no idea how much time had elapsed before he found himself looking up into the lustrous brown eyes of Abilene. She was calling his name anxiously as she frowned down at him, rubbing his hair back from his forehead with one hand and dabbing a cool cloth at his temple with the other.

She was sitting with her back against his dresser. His head was propped on her soft thigh. She smelled like talcum and spring lilacs and very faintly of licorice and as he stared up into her worried eyes, he saw a single, large but faint freckle just right of her nose and up close to her eye. For some reason the freckle pinched his heart, made him poignantly sad and desperately eager to marry the woman and take her to Mexico with him.

"Spurr?" she said, her eyes probing his. "Spurr, are you still kicking, you besotted son of a bitch?"

Spurr heard himself chuckle and then he looked at her well-filled corset, could feel the soft edge of one full breast against the top of his head. Of course — why not take her to Mexico? He'd never find anything better than Abilene on the Sea of Cortez.

"Marry me, woman. Let's go to Mexico and diddle till the goats come home for milkin'!"

"Goddamnit, he's alive."

The gravelly voice belonged to a man. Spurr rolled his eyes back a little farther and saw the gnarled old visage of Sheriff Wilden staring down at him. The local lawman was bent low, vein-lined hands on his knees, to give Spurr the Indian eye. In one of his hands he clutched Spurr's revolver.

"Oh, no," Spurr groaned. "Tell me I didn't propose in front of this old bastard."

"You did," Wilden said. "Any woman would be a sorry-assed female to marry the likes of you. And she'd likely have to break you out of jail first, because that's where you'll end up if you keep shootin' up my town and scarin' the little *putas.* Good Lord, man — Carmelita's young enough to be your granddaughter!"

Spurr looked accusingly at Abilene. "I went lookin' for another'n, but she was busy with some mucky-muck from Cheyenne!"

"Oh, shut up, Spurr!" Abilene looked toward the door, where Lyle Kingman stood with his arms crossed reprovingly, staring down at the besotted lawman, who just now realized, looking up from his bare toes to the hotel proprietor, that he was buck-assed naked. "Lyle, fetch the doctor, will you?" Abilene said. "I don't like the way he looks."

"No!" Spurr tried heaving himself up and was surprised that he was able to do so without his chest filling with lead barbs. "I just stumbled and hit my head, 's all. Tryin' to kill the rats in that bastard's flea-infested pile of rotten boards is a risky damn business, don't ya know?"

He gained his feet, Wilden standing close in case the federal lawman should fall. Spurr sat on the edge of the bed, drew a sheet corner over his privates, ran a hand over his face, and smacked his lips. "How long was I down there?"

"Just a few minutes," Kingman growled, scowling at Spurr. "I heard ya fall, came up here, and when I started back downstairs to fetch the doc, the sheriff and Abilene were already heading up to your room. I hope you know you'll be paying to have my floor repaired."

"Diddle yourself, ya hog-wolloping lout." Spurr looked at Wilden and Abilene, who was sitting on the floor, the wet cloth wadded in her hand. "What was you two headin' my way for? How do you know I wasn't entertainin'?"

He laughed, then remembered Carmelita, and laughed again. "In fact, I was! Where in hell'd that girl go, anyways? We was just startin' to have a good time."

Kingman cast a bored, impatient look at Wilden. "If you don't want me to fetch the doc, I'll be downstairs. Some of us have work to do."

Wilden told the man to go ahead, and when Kingman was gone, Abilene gained her feet and crossed her arms in front of the dresser. Wilden held up the whiskey bottle to examine its contents, and whistled.

"Did you put all this away since yesterday? In your condition?" Wilden cast an exasperated look at the near-naked lawman sitting slouched on the bed. "Now, I know Mac-Gregor told you to go easy on the tanglefoot and mattress dances 'cause I talked to him last night over to the Beer Bucket, after he'd hazed you on out of his office and ordered you to bed for several days. A bed to *sleep in,* not to try to prove what a stud you still are with sportin' girls like Carmelita. My God, man, that girl has killed two gents in the past seven months through no fault of her own!"

"Heart attacks, both," Abilene added. "And they didn't even know they had bad tickers until they both collapsed in that child's crib!"

Spurr turned his mouth corners down as

he looked at Abilene. "You know, too?"

"Of course. Word spreads fast in Buffalo-ville. Half the town's drinking to your worn-out ticker while the other half's jumping for joy."

"Just don't let me catch the other half." Spurr extended his hand to Wilden. "Give me the bottle."

"Don't see how any more could hurt him worse," he told Abilene, who merely pursed her lips and shook her head.

Spurr took the bottle and tipped a long pull. His head had started aching, and the fresh whiskey doused the blaze. "Well, hell, Sheriff, if you come to take me in, let's get to it. I'm about ready for another nap and I reckon I can do it over to your hotbox as well as I can in here."

"Didn't come to take you in," Wilden said, doffing his hat and running a hand through his thin silver hair. "Me an' Abilene got to talkin' about you over lunch and decided to see if you was still kickin'. On the way over here, we heard the shootin' and the whore screamin', and we thought Red Cloud was on the rampage again."

Wilden shook his head. "Look at you. A man your age, with your experience. So you let a little heart fart take you down, try to prove yourself or die tryin' with Carmelita.

Shit, if I knew you wanted to prove you still had a few miles in your saddle, I'd've sent you off to the Diamond Bar for that stolen gold, which I'd been *intendin'* to do when you shot the horse thief Willard Coates over to the Wyoming House Saloon and seized up on me like a damn snake caught in the spokes of a wagon wheel."

Spurr took another, smaller pull from the bottle. "What stolen gold?"

"Cimarron Padilla over to Diamond Bar Creek ran across a pair of U.S. Army pouches filled with gold coins. He sent a rider to Crow Dance, and the constable of Crow Dance, George Nolan, rode over here to tell me, since I'm the county sheriff. Nolan didn't realize I been stove up and can't ride farther than the privy behind my house, so we thought you could go fetch the pouches, since it's a federal matter, it bein' stolen army loot an' all."

"Ah, hell."

"That's what I said. Anyway, Nolan's making the ride though he wasn't too happy about it. I told him I'd buy him a bottle and a good steak, so he went grumblin' off to fetch his no-account deputy Max Strong — somethin' tells me they might be nancy-boys, but let's not spread that around — and then they're headin' up to ole Cimarron's place. If they don't run off with the loot themselves, they'll likely be back here by the end of the week. It's a good two-day pull up to the Diamond Bar."

"I'm retired, anyways."

"That ain't official, you simple fool. Maybe, if you haven't killed yourself diddling fifteen-year-old whores, you could take it with you down to Denver and turn it in to the head law dog down there, same time you turn in your badge. By the by, it *might* just find its way back to its rightful owner."

Wilden set his funnel-brimmed Stetson on his head and started toward the door. "I believe I read in the *Rocky Mountain News* a few weeks back about an army payroll robbery over to Kansas. That's probably where the loot came from. Anyway, I'm gonna go over to the jailhouse and get a cell ready for you."

Wilden stopped at the door and turned to Abilene. "Unless Abilene can keep you out of trouble until we have the good fortune of watching you ride on out of here for good. Don't marry the man, Abilene. Good Lord, that'd be the end of such a sweet, long-suffering soul as yourself."

Abilene stared at Spurr, her eyes smokily admonishing. "Don't worry — he's not rich enough for me." She glanced at the splintery rat hole in the room's corner. "And I don't reckon I've known a man with worse aim. In Mexico, he'd let us get taken down by banditos in no time flat."

Wilden pinched his hat brim at her, gave a caustic chuff at Spurr, and went out.

Spurr looked up at Abilene with chagrin. She pushed away from the wall, her arms crossed on her breasts, and walked over to him. She extended a hand to him, as though he were an old cur she was allowing to sniff her, then brushed a lock of sweaty hair back from his forehead.

"Now, what's this all about? I know you don't like Carmelita more than me. She squeals a lot but the girl don't mean it."

Spurr dropped his eyes, cradling his bottle in one arm, pouting. "You was busy."

"Well, I'm not busy now."

Spurr arched a brow at her. She smiled coyly at him as she began unbuttoning her corset.

"Are you sure you can handle a real woman, Spurr?" she asked as her breasts sprang free.

Spurr swallowed the dry knot in his throat. "Damn it, Abilene," he rasped. "Are you sure you won't marry me?"

She dropped the corset and continued undressing. "Not a chance."

CHAPTER 14

As Colter and Cimarron bounded back across the valley, riding low in their saddles and whipping their mounts with their rein ends, the rifle barks continued. The shooting was sporadic at first. Then there was an angry but short-lived barrage.

By the time the two riders galloped under the ranch portal and into the yard, the shooting had ceased.

Colter and Cimarron checked their mounts down in front of the cabin, looking around wildly. The cabin door was open and there were a couple of rifle casings in the dust off the stoop, but there was no sign of Dawson, Shanley, and Pearl. The horses in the corral were all running in a broad circle led by a mud brown, white-chested stallion.

A shot sounded north of the cabin. A man shouted. Colter and Cimarron whipped around to see Shanley and Dawson moving toward the cabin from the brush of the branch creek that twisted toward the ranch yard from the base of the forested mountain. Dawson was injured, dragging one leg, while Shanley led him through the brush, Dawson's right arm thrown around Shanley's neck. Rifles dangled from the men's free hands.

Colter and Cimarron galloped toward them. When they were twenty feet away from the two men, Colter saw the blood on Dawson's upper left thigh, oozing through his batwing chap. Behind them, Pearl appeared from the willows and stunt cedars lining the creek, splashing through a freshet and holding her rifle in both hands, her hat flopping down her back by the rawhide thong around her neck.

"They came from the north creek!" Shanley shouted as he continued leading Dawson through the brush and over the grassy hummocks.

Dawson was pale. His lips were stretched back from his teeth, eyes bright with pain. He was putting very little weight on his left leg.

Cimarron and Colter reined the horses to skidding stops. Cimarron looked toward Pearl. "How many?"

"Only saw three!" Shanley said, breathless, as he led Dawson past Cimarron's horse. "Stretch here took one in the leg. I think they hightailed it. Don't ask me why — they had the jump on us."

Cimarron leaped out of his saddle, sliding his Henry into its scabbard. He grabbed Dawson's rifle, then threw the man's right arm over his shoulders and began helping Shanley lead him toward the cabin.

Colter looked at Pearl, who tripped a little as she turned to look behind her through the willows and cedars on the other side of the branch creek. He gigged Northwest toward her, stopped, reined the riled mount in a tight circle as he stared toward the north.

"How far away are they?"

"On horseback you might be able to catch 'em."

Colter put the steel to Northwest once more, and lunged off through the brush, splashing across the freshet, then through the thin willows and across the wide, shallow branch creek and up the other side. He galloped a hundred yards, paralleling the base of the mountain, and then he stopped and stared ahead.

Three riders were disappearing into a distant stand of willows along another branch creek. One had tufts of blond hair puffing out around the base of her bowler hat. The second rider was the black man whom La Brie had called Preston. The third was the rangy blond kid in the top hat and tan duster. They were well out of accurate rifle range, and following them through that scrub was a sure way to get bushwhacked.

Colter looked around. No sign of the others. Leading away from him were three swaths of bent weeds, marking the paths of only three riders.

Where were the other cutthroats?

Colter jerked Northwest around and galloped back in the direction of the cabin. A worm of dread was flopping around in his gut.

The noose swinging from the pine atop the bench, the ambush by only three riders . . .

It all added up to a cat-and-mouse game. Either La Brie was setting them up for a massive bushwhacking from the ranch's weak side, which was now its south side, or he was trying to scare the hell out of them, so they'd turn over the gold.

Fear was a dry knot in Colter's chest. Fury was a fully stoked furnace burning up from deep in his bowels. He didn't like being toyed with, and he didn't like seeing his friends shot. And in the month he'd been on the Diamond Bar, he come to count

Stretch Dawson as one of his rare friends.

The old cowboy didn't deserve that bullet in his leg.

Colter checked Northwest down in front of the cabin, leaped down from the saddle, and dropped the reins. Cimarron poked his head out the cabin door, his face taut, eyes grave.

"Turn the horses loose."

The young drover looked at the rancher, puzzled.

"They'll likely hit the horses next," Cimarron barked, then waved his arm. "Turn 'em out!"

Colter wheeled and ran over to the main corral where the horses were milling and nickering with their tails curled. He pried the wire loop up over the post, swung the gate wide, then worked his way in behind the remuda, and fired his Remington in the air twice.

Several of the horses screamed. A couple pitched and bucked, and in seconds they were all galloping in a large boiling dust cloud out the open gate, two colts following their mares. A few seconds after that, Colter stood in the middle of the yard, watching the entire remuda of a dozen mounts bounding off under the portal and splashing across the creek, spreading out as they hit the valley.

Their hoof thuds dwindled gradually, replaced by the din of anxious voices, the thud of heavy-heeled boots, and the *ching* of spurs emanating from inside the cabin.

Colter turned toward the cabin's open door. Northwest stood in front of the stoop, lifting his hooves anxiously but remaining where his reins tied him to the ground. Cimarron's horse remained where the rancher had dismounted fifty yards north. The paint was looking toward the cabin as though awaiting orders.

Colter leaped onto Northwest's back, rode over and grabbed the reins of Cimarron's paint, and led the horse into the pines behind the cabin. He left both horses in the fragrant shade of the tall pines angling down the steep mountain slope, then loosened the saddle cinches of both mounts and slipped their bridle bits.

He'd find out what Cimarron wanted to do, then see to both mounts later. He'd take his chances with Northwest in the yard where he could find the horse if he needed him.

"Colter!" Cimarron's shout echoed around the yard.

The young drover ran around the cabin and through the open door into the cabin's late-morning shadows still rife with the smells of coffee and the morning meal.

Cimarron and Shanley were holding Dawson's shoulders down on the kitchen table. The tall drover lay with his head back on the table, gritting his teeth, growling, panting, sweating, his bullet-pierced left leg shaking. Pearl stood near Dawson's bloody thigh, holding a glowing fireplace poker. They'd removed the drover's chaps and cut open his pants leg to reveal the bloody wound about the size of a silver dollar midway between his knee and hip. Dark red blood braided from it thickly.

Cimarron turned to Colter. "Hold his legs down while Pearl cauterizes the wound!"

Colter hunched down over the opposite end of the table, draping his arms over Dawson's ankles, pinning his calves to the table's scarred, scorched, ten-inch-wide pine planks.

"I got him!"

"Hold him steady," Pearl ordered the men as she lowered the smoking poker toward Dawson's leg.

"Shit fire!" Dawson groused.

"Don't look at it, ye damn fool," Shanley advised through gritted teeth as he pinned his partner's right shoulder to the table.

Colter didn't want to watch, but something kept his attention pinned on the glowing poker that shed feathers of white smoke and tiny red sparks. The coal oil smell of the hot iron seemed to fill the cabin. Pearl glanced at Colter, then winced and bit her lower lip as she jammed the poker into the wound.

Dawson screamed, tried to thrash.

Colter held the man's legs fast to the table, the stench of burning flesh and scorched blood nearly overpowering him so that he had to fight to keep a hold on Dawson's jerking feet. He stared at the end of the poker, which Pearl had nearly buried in Dawson's bloody thigh, but in Colter's own mind it was Bill Rondo's glowing S iron he watched drop toward his face.

The grinning visage of Sheriff Rondo hovered behind and above the pulsating S until Rondo gritted his teeth and jerked the brand down sharply.

Colter pulled his head back away from the smell of his own burning blood and flesh and from the agony of the molten iron searing into his face as if a gallon of flaming oil.

"Colter, hold him!"

Cimarron's shout dispersed the living nightmare, and Colter looked down to see that the screaming Dawson had nearly pulled his ankles free of Colter's grasp.

Colter renewed his hold on the man's ankles, pushing Dawson's shins down with his chest.

The wounded puncher wailed, his mouth foaming, his eyes ringed white as he pulled every muscle in his long body taut.

"Okay, Pearl," Cimarron yelled above Dawson's mewls and shouted curses.

Pearl pulled the poker back out of the wound, blood on it sizzling liking burning grease. Suddenly, she ripped her gaze from the poker's sputtering end toward the door, and her jaw dropped. What happened next Colter was never sure about, because time began to race suddenly and his vision was obscured by the smoke from Dawson's cauterized wound and by the smoke of a half dozen popping guns.

There was one clear image, of a man standing in the doorway as the door blew back against the wall — a tall, long-haired man with fire in his eyes, both flaps of his duster pulled back and thonged behind the two cross-draw holsters on his hips. As the door bounced back toward the frame, the man stepped into the cabin, catching the door with his left boot while he raised two long-barreled Army Colts in his gloved fists.

The pistols roared, stabbing smoke and flames.

Pearl screamed.

Cimarron shouted.

Colter bolted back away from Dawson's ankles as the cold sting of a bullet brushed his right cheek. He reached for his Remington, but he hadn't gotten the piece half out of its holster before he felt the burn of two more slugs across his chest and belly and was flung against the kitchen's back wall.

Cimarron and Shanley were shouting, standing facing the door and lifting their six-shooters from their holsters.

As Colter jerked a quick look left of the table, he saw a half dozen shadowy images obscured by smoke and the bright morning light from the doorway behind them. All six had flashing, roaring guns in their fists, and they were waving the smoking weapons this way and that as Cimarron and Shanley went spinning off toward the cabin's opposite end and Dawson flew sideways from the table and piled up against the kitchen range.

Colter looked for Pearl but saw no sign of her before the back of his head smashed glass and then he was automatically throwing himself through the window's broken frame, clawing at the wall and pushing off the floor with his boots. Bullets thudded into the wall around him. They screeched through the opening, plucking his hat from his head and parting his hair.

Vaguely, he felt blood oozing down his cheeks and down his chin from his cut lip, and then he was on the ground outside the cabin, pushing himself up with his raw, burning hands.

Voices rose from the window behind him, amid the gunfire and the screams of dying men. Colter gained his feet and, running on raw energy and the primitive need to stay alive, he staggered back into the pines and the mossy boulders that had been left by a long-ago glacier. He passed Pearl's chicken coop from which the din of squawking chickens sounded.

Behind him, guns popped. A girl shouted. Not Pearl's voice but the mannish, nasal voice of Mercy.

Boots thumped behind Colter. Ahead, Northwest appeared, standing beside Cimarron's paint, both horses looking toward Colter and twitching their ears nervously.

Pistols popped from the direction of the cabin. A slug passed over Colter's head. The paint shied, jerked its reins loose from the branch Colter had tied it to, and galloped off. Northwest was about to do the same, but Colter grabbed the reins. He cast a look through the trees toward the cabin, saw three men and Mercy running toward him. The black man stopped and fired a pistol. Bark flew from one of the trees between him and Colter.

Colter toed a stirrup, and, groaning against the pain searing both sides and his belly as well as his face and hands — he didn't know how many times he'd been shot or how serious any of the wounds were, but he felt plenty of oozing blood — he grabbed the horn and pried himself up against the fender.

"Go, boy!" he raked out.

Northwest lunged into a gallop away from the cabin.

More pistols popped, bullets spanging off rocks or plunking into trees. Colter's boot slipped out of the stirrup and he nearly went tumbling but managed to summon all his strength to his hands and arms and heaved himself up into the saddle.

Casting a fearful look over his right shoulder, he saw the big-bellied man with the bear-tooth earrings and Mercy dwindling behind him, smoke puffing from their guns as they zigzagged through the pines. Colter turned forward in the saddle, lowered his head, and gave Northwest free rein, squeezing his eyes closed against the nausea flooding his belly, the weakness in his over-stressed arms and legs.

Northwest's hooves crunched gravel and snapped branches, splashed across one stream and then another. Colter heard none of these sounds. All he heard were Pearl's initial scream and the gunfire and the agonized, exasperated, terrified wails of Cimarron, Griff Shanley, and Stretch Dawson.

The shock of what had just occurred held him in its taut, numbing grip. But the horror of it slithered through the numbness to the tender nerves of his awareness.

As Northwest galloped through the willows and traced a lazy arc out into the valley — the horse wanting only to be far, far away from the din and the smell of blood and gun smoke — Colter convulsed with a sob.

Chapter 15

Sitting on the veranda of the Skinner House Hotel in Buffaloville, on a quiet midweek afternoon under a clear Wyoming sky, Deputy U.S. Marshal Spurr raised his beer schooner to his bearded lips and drained it.

The malty brew crackled down his throat and warmed his belly. It made his head feel light and cast a dreamy glow upon the dusty, sun-bleached little ranch town that always looked its ugliest about now. At three p.m., Buffaloville was all sharp edges and garish hues. It was all dust and tumbleweeds and squawky ranch wagons and the flat barks of some riled-up old hound. The toneless snicks of a shopkeeper sweeping the horse dung from his porch, or the hammering hooves of drovers heading back to their ranch after visiting the mercantile for coffee and tobacco or windmill parts.

This time of the day, the world lacked dimension, laughter, and the soft prattle of a piano or a guitar emanating from a dark, smoky cantina. It lacked the sublimity of females no matter how fallen, painted, or toothless.

This time of the day, the town lacked a soul.

The beer gave the town back its soul, re-acquainted the place with a higher power, turned the occasional breeze shepherding tumbleweeds down a trash-strewn alley into a poem.

Spurr studied the empty glass, watched with a sour expression, the last beer bubbles and lines of froth clinging to the inside of the schooner. Cunning crept into the lawman's mind on little cat feet. He looked toward Abilene's tidy blue frame house set slightly back from the main street, surrounded with a picket fence in need of fresh paint and boasting a small but healthy-looking ponderosa pine just off her front porch.

Abilene herself was nowhere to be seen. Her curtains were drawn over her windows.

Spurr's heart picked up its beat. He turned his attention to the Cheyenne Saloon across the street on his left — a simple, log structure with a shake roof and elk antlers over its pine-plank door that was propped open with a stone. His heart quickened even more.

He cleared his throat and turned his head a little to call behind him, "Lyle? Hey, Lyle, you in there?"

Behind him, silence. A fly buzzed and ticked against the hotel's screen door.

A rocking chair squawked and a man grunted.

"Lyle? Wake up, damn it. The pestilence committee needs you out here at once. Pronto."

In the lobby behind Spurr, the hotel proprietor sighed. "Goddamnit, Spurr, I was dead asleep. What the hell do you want now?"

"Go over to the Cheyenne and fetch me another beer."

"You know I can't fetch you more than one beer, Spurr. Abilene's orders."

"Abilene's gettin' her beauty sleep. Besides, Lyle, when did you start takin' orders from women?"

"Well, let's see — I'm fifty-six years old . . ."

"Lyle, if you fetch me another beer, I'll give you a dollar. The beer's a nickel. You, bein' a businessman, should appreciate such a wide profit margin."

Lyle chuffed. The chair in the lobby

squawked and there was the thud of Kingman slapping the arms of his rocking chair in frustration. Footsteps sounded, and then Kingman's voice said directly behind Spurr through the screen door: "Spurr, I'm gonna fetch you that beer but not for the profit margin. Maybe that extra beer will kill you or at the very least shut you up."

The screen door squawked. Kingman stepped onto the veranda, running a hand over his bald head and yawning. He held his shabby bowler in his other hand. "If Abilene finds out, I reckon I can tell her you threatened me at pistol point. I know I won't be the first man who ever lied to her."

"You won't be the last, neither," Spurr chuckled as the hotel proprietor grabbed the schooner from his hand and, setting his hat on his head, moseyed down the veranda steps and out into the deserted street, angling toward the Cheyenne.

Spurr hiked up his boots on the railing, gently crossed his ankles, wincing against the slight strain he could feel in his logy ticker, and sat back in his chair. He laced his hands behind his head and sighed.

The life of an invalid maybe wasn't too bad as long as he had a lackey to shag suds for him. Once he was down in Mexico, he'd have to find a senorita who'd do the same but stay with him and squirm around on his lap until he needed her to fetch another.

Spurr chuckled at the thought, then slid his gaze across the toes of his worn, high-topped moccasins toward the Cheyenne Saloon. Movement directly over his toes caught his eye, and, frowning, he slid his gaze back until he could pick out the brown speck of a rider moving toward Buffaloville from the north, trailing a miniature mare's tail of dust.

"Gonna kill that hoss," Spurr chided the rider crossing the sage flat at a hell-for-leather run, hunkered low in his saddle, hat flopping across his shoulders.

He was following no trail but heading cross-country, having traversed the Wagon Mound bluffs and now having a clear shot at the town.

"Sumbitch must be needin' a drink mighty bad."

The thought reminded Spurr of his own beer, and he looked at the Cheyenne. He couldn't see movement through the door's dark opening, but he could hear the low rumble of conversation from within, thought he recognized the voice of Lyle Kingman.

The bastard must have decided to have a drink himself before bringing Spurr his beer. He was probably standing at the bar, gassing with the apron or one of the two Indian whores who tended the place. "I'll give the bastard a fifty-cent piece," Spurr muttered. "That's enough of a profit margin for the lazy son of a buck who lets rats runs rampant in his flea-bit digs and diddles Mescin whores in his lobby for all the world to see."

He swiveled his head slightly to see that the rider had slowed his horse, a long-legged pinto, to a trot as he approached the corrals and tumbledown log shacks on Buffaloville's shaggy fringe. The horse was blowing hard and it moved shamble-footed, the sun reflecting off the lather on its neck and across its withers.

Blown.

The rider was young and long-haired, a white boy, but that's about all that Spurr could tell from this distance. The kid put the horse across a dry gulley and then turned him slightly west until he was threading the gap between the Cheyenne Saloon and a Chinese laundry shack in which three Chinese women bustled around steaming copper washtubs. As the horse and rider emerged from the gap, the kid gigged the ragged pinto up past the front of the saloon to the hitch rack fronting the log building housing the sheriff's office just beyond it, and slid wearily down from the saddle, wincing as though he were stiff and sore from the long, hard ride.

"Nope, it ain't a drink he wants," Spurr muttered, frowning over the porch rail. "It's Wilden."

Batwing chaps flapped against the kid's legs as he quickly, expertly uncinched the pinto's saddle, tossed the gear with its bedroll and rifle scabbard onto the ground with a puff of clay-colored dust, then reached up with one hand and removed the horse's bridle. Tossing the bridle onto the saddle, the kid slapped dust from his chaps with his hat and mounted the sheriff's narrow veranda.

He was heavy-footed, and his spurs rang raucously.

Behind the rider, the pinto gave a relieved nicker, dropped, and rolled in the street, sending up a churning dust cloud. The rider pounded on the sheriff's door, called for Wilden, then opened the door, went in, and closed the door behind him.

"Probably rustlers," Spurr said to himself.

He watched the sheriff's closed door with an uneasy feeling. An entire minute hadn't passed before it opened again and Bill Wilden hobbled out, hooking his cane over the hitch rack fronting the office, then wrapping his gun and shell belt around his waist. He had his funnel-brimmed hat on his head, a pair of saddlebags draped over a shoulder.

The young rider followed the sheriff out, and they were speaking, but Spurr couldn't hear what they were saying. He recognized the anxious tones, however. Wilden seemed deeply troubled, his craggy, hollow-cheeked face flushed.

When Wilden had donned his gun, he took up his cane and glanced at the kid, jaws moving. The kid turned and went back into the jailhouse, reemerging a few seconds later with Wilden's rifle scabbard and bedroll.

Wilden said something else to the young rider and then the sheriff started hobbling eastward along the street, the kid walking beside him carrying the sheriff's scabbard and bedroll, the kid continuing to chatter at Wilden but Wilden now saying nothing but staring straight ahead and leaning hard on his cane.

Spurr arched a curious brow. When the sheriff and the kid were passing the Skinner House on the other side of the street, Spurr yelled, "What's up, Wilden? Rustlers?"

The sheriff stopped and turned his anxious gaze to Spurr, and shook his head darkly. He kept his voice just loud enough for Spurr to hear from a hundred feet away.

"That constable I sent to the Diamond Bar — him and his deputy's hosses turned up back in Crow Dance this morning minus Nolan and Strong. Blood on their saddles. I'm ridin' out. Keep an eye on the town for me."

Wilden continued limping up the street.

"Hell, Bill — you can't ride," Spurr shouted. "That's why you sent Nolan in the first consarned place!"

Wilden didn't so much as glance behind him. He just kept walking, thc kid tramping along beside him with the sheriff's rifle and bedroll on his shoulder. The pinto flanked the men from thirty feet or so, the dust and manure of the street clinging to its sweaty back.

"Ah, hell," Spurr growled, watching Wilden and the kid approach the livery barn.

Spurr turncd away. It wasn't any of his business. Hell, he had a bad ticker. As soon as he was strong enough, he was turning in his badge and heading to Mexico. If Wilden wanted to make that trek when he couldn't ride as far as his own privy, let him try. He'd end up back here in a half hour, forty-five minutes, deputizing some out-of-work saddle tramp in one of the saloons.

Spurr sat there on the porch of the Skinner House, getting more and more owly as he waited for his beer and thought about the constables and that damn federal gold and Wilden's gimped-up leg. The owlishness turned plain rancid when he watched Wilden trot past the hotel on his ewe-necked sorrel, yelling at Spurr to keep an eye on things, and whether he needed any help to deputize Kingman.

"You deputize Kingman," he growled at the sheriff's back. "You'll be back here inside of an hour and confined to bed for the rest of the week with hot water bottles around your crooked old leg."

Fool.

Spurr stared at Wilden's gradually diminishing form until the sheriff was a brown speck bobbing amongst the silver-green sage, the purple-green slopes and red-rock bluffs of the Cheyennes rising beyond him. Guilt raked Spurr like the harsh notes of an out-of-tune piano, and the more he tried to deny the guilt and the shame of his sitting here like a lump on a log, awaiting a forbidden beer, while a stove-up old sheriff rode out to do his work for him, the worse the guilt got.

It was like a fist-sized tumor burning behind his failing heart.

Kingman finally showed up with the beer

from the Cheyenne Saloon, truckling as he said, "Sorry for the holdup there, Spurr. Me and Spook Lawson got into a cribbage game, and you know how I am about cribbage."

Spurr had only vaguely noticed Kingman's appearance beside him. Now he looked at the frothy beer that the hotel proprietor was extending in his fist, the man's eyes owning a sheepish cast behind his silver-framed spectacles.

"Why, Lyle," Spurr said. "Didn't you hear Abilene? She gave me strict orders to indulge in one beer a day, and one beer only. Now put down that demon brew and fetch my hoss!"

Kingman sputtered and stammered, aghast, for nearly a minute. When he'd finally wheeled and stomped down the hotel veranda and up the street, taking long pulls from Spurr's beer glass, the deputy U.S. marshal heaved himself up out of his chair. He strode into the hotel, crossing the dingy lobby and mounting the stairs, walking hard and fast, testing his heart out, wondering if he'd die before he reached the top.

When he reached the top and he was still breathing, felt only a very slight tightness in his chest, only the usual shortness of breath, he ran his hand across his nose. His washed-out eyes acquired a pensive expression.

Hell, maybe he wasn't as sick as he thought he was.

Maybe he wasn't as sick as the doc told him he was.

Maybe all he really needed to do was to stop sitting around waiting to die, and straddle a horse, and head on out of here, the devil take the hindmost.

Feeling somehow lighter if not necessarily better, Spurr stomped around his room, packing and gathering his gear. When he descended the stairs and threw the door open to the veranda, Kingman was leading his big, saddled roan up to the hotel. Cochise bobbed his head when he saw Spurr and gave a whinny, happy to see its old master up and around and only semi-drunk.

"Where the hell you going, you old fool?" Kingman said, tossing Spurr the horse's reins.

"You got that right," Spurr said, tying his rifle scabbard to his saddle. "I'm likely goin' straight to hell. But I might as well ride there as walk or enter the pearly gates in that rickety hide-bottom chair of yours."

Spurr tied his bedroll behind his cantle, then toed a stirrup and pulled himself into the saddle, settling his weight, liking the familiar way the ancient saddle creaked beneath him. "Do me a favor while I'm gone, Lyle?"

From the hotel veranda, Kingman glowered at him.

"Get rid o' them damn rats and save me on forty-four shells!"

Spurr reined the snorting Cochise around, touched spurs to the horse's quivering flanks, and lunged into a ground-eating lope, heading west toward the Diamond Bar.

Dust sifted behind him.

Kingman coughed and waved it out of his face.

CHAPTER 16

Colter opened his eyes, lifted his head.

It was almost as though Northwest had known where he'd wanted to go, for the horse had stopped about thirty yards from the cabin of Charlie Benbow. It was a squat, part-log, part–mud brick hovel with a connecting corral and a privy behind it. Little Sandy Creek traced a horseshoe in front of the place. It was from the creek that Northwest was thirstily drawing water, rattling his bit chains, and shifting his weight from one hoof to the other.

Colter had met Benbow when the prospector had hired on with Cimarron's crew during the fall gather, and he'd instantly liked the soft-spoken, kind-eyed man. Benbow was a prospector most of the year, with several cabins spread throughout the Cheyennes.

Colter winced at the pain from his multiple wounds, and licked his cracked, windburned lips. "Mr. Benbow?"

No answer.

He didn't bother calling again. The cabin was closed up tight, windows shuttered, even a log stuffed down the chimney pipe to keeps birds out of the flue. Benbow was obviously working one of the other creeks near one of his other cabins. It was just as well. If La Brie's gang managed to track him here, it would go as badly for Benbow as for him.

Colter had directed his horse here because, aside from one remote and likely abandoned line shack, Benbow's was the closest cabin to the Diamond Bar, and he needed somewhere relatively safe to tend his wounds. He'd wanted to stay and fight the La Brie bunch and to save Pearl if she hadn't been killed when they'd first burst into the cabin, but he'd been too shot-up to do much more but get himself killed. And he'd be no good to anyone dead.

Like Cimarron, Shanley, and Dawson. All three, dead.

Pearl had likely been killed, too, in that massive fusillade La Brie had stormed into the cabin with. Colter wasn't sure what had saved him. The luck of a fool, he reckoned. But he hadn't been saved yet. He snarled a curse as he examined his right side where blood oozed out around the bandanna, which he'd used to compress his most severe wound, just above his left hip.

He'd thought he'd gotten the blood stopped. But that had been several miles back. The hard ride into these red rock canyons and sage-sheathed dry washes in the southeastern foothills of the Cheyennes had nearly done him in.

Damn, he wished Benbow were here. He knew that despite the danger the old prospector wouldn't begrudge helping him, a friend of Cimarron's, and Benbow likely could tend his wounds, get the blood stopped and the holes sewn shut. He might even have helped him get Pearl back.

Out here, folks took care of their own, and "their own" included their friends and neighbors.

But Benbow was gone and there was no telling when he'd be back. There was no point crying about it. Colter knew the man wouldn't mind his breaking into his cabin and helping himself to whatever he needed to sustain himself.

Backing Northwest away from the creek, as the horse was too hot to hold much water, Colter eased himself out of the saddle, dropped to his hands and knees beside the creek, and buried his face in the cold, rushing stream. Fed by a deep spring, the water was cold even this late in the summer. Tooth-splintering cold, and refreshing.

When he'd had so much that his jaws and head ached, he wrung the blood out of his neckerchief, soaked it in the water, and cleaned the wound as well as he could, then stuffed a corner of the cold cloth into the hole and pushed himself to his feet.

He looked back the way he'd come. The trail threaded a narrow, sage-spotted valley between sandstone ridges. Nothing back there but the adobe-colored land, the red rocks, and the blue, arching sky.

Colter led Northwest across the creek via Benbow's log bridge. Unsaddling the horse was a grueling process, and he could feel blood oozing from his several wounds, making his head spin and his knees shake. But it was a job he had to do, and one he was damn glad he had finished once he'd turned the horse into the corral sporting a crib with a few bites of hay remaining inside.

Apparently, Benbow hadn't left more than a day or so ago, which meant he probably wouldn't be back soon, either.

Colter wrestled his saddle over the top of the closed gate, then, carrying his rifle, bedroll, and saddlebags, tramped heavy-heeled to the cabin. As was the custom of the country, Benbow's door wasn't locked. The prospector likely left provisions for weary travelers, too. Colter let the door hang wide on its rusty hinges and went inside, looking around.

The table, plank shelves, sheet-iron stove, and single, quilt-covered bed were all neat and clean, the earthen floor freshly swept. A pyramid of canned vegetables stood on a shelf behind the table, as well as several hide sacks; one was probably filled with jerky. What interested Colter most, though, was the stove. Beside it were two splintery peach crates, one filled with kindling in the form of feather sticks and yellowed newspapers, the other heaped with split stove wood.

Quickly, feeling the wound in his left side oozing more blood, Colter opened the stove's single iron door and laid in some kindling. He lit the kindling with a stove match from a jelly jar on the table, and babied the fledgling flames until adding more feather sticks and, eventually, a few of the small logs from the second crate. When the blaze was crackling and snapping and the stove was ticking as it warmed, Colter added one of the large logs and then a few minutes later, another.

When the fire was going good, and the stove was hot, he plucked the iron poker from the second wood box and laid the business end inside the stove. He found a couple of clothes, then shucked out of his shirt, pants, and long-handles, sat naked save his hat on the floor in front of the stove, legs bent in front of him, and dabbed at his several other bullet burns — one on each thigh, one across his chest, another on his right forearm — with damp cloths before finally dragging the poker out of the stove.

He sat back against a leg of the table and looked down at the blood oozing from the hole in his left side. His taut, pale belly rose and fell as he panted against the pain and the even severer agony he knew was coming.

Looking at the poker once more, he remembered La Brie standing in Cimarron's cabin doorway, both guns blazing, and he hardened his jaw against his fury and what he knew he was going to do — or die trying to do — about it.

Keeping his jaw hard and his anger up, inviting the screams of Cimarron, Shanley, and Dawson back into his head for sustenance, he rammed the glowing end of the poker against his side and held it there, snarling like a trapped bobcat, until black smoke rose in front of him and he could smell the nauseating fetor of his own burning flesh.

Then he tossed it away and heard it clank against the earthen floor a second before his head hit the floor, and he was out.

He wasn't sure what woke him, but when he lifted his head from the floor, it took him nearly a full minute to remember where he was and what he was doing there. The raw, gnawing ache in his side reminded him. He sat up against the table leg and inspected the cauterization.

The bleeding was stopped. The flesh over the wound had the texture of jelly, it was oozing pus, and it felt as if a rat were inside and trying to eat its way out of him. But he'd stopped the bleeding. And since the bullet had gone all the way through without hitting anything vital, not even a rib, he considered himself on the mend.

His upper right arm needed rewrapping, but it could wait. The other grazes were little more than bloody burns, and they were already scabbing up.

Again, he heard the sound that had awakened him. His reflexes were as slow as his mind, so it took him a moment to find the Remington on the floor beneath the table. Once he had it, he cocked it and, mindless of his nakedness, walked barefoot over to the open door.

In the waning afternoon light, a mule deer doe and a fawn were nibbling the spindly brown brush growing along the creek. The doe spied Colter out the corner of its eye, and jerked its head up. The skittish fawn, its spots just fading, leaped back partly behind its mother's twitching black tail, staring wide-eyed at the cabin.

Nothing as serene as two grazing deer, but Colter knew enough about survival to consider downing one of the two animals. Likely, he would have plugged the fawn, as it would have been easier for him to dress and haul to the cabin for roasting.

But he didn't have the energy to clean a rabbit, much less a fawn.

"You're dang lucky," Colter rasped at the two deer staring at him with their wide brown eyes, the creek twinkling green and silver in front of them.

He depressed the revolver's hammer and tossed it onto the table. Clutching his burning side, he looked around the cabin, spied a stone jug on a shelf near a stretched bobcat hide, and carried it over to the bed in the back corner opposite the kitchen. He sat gingerly down on the bed and plucked the cork from the jug's chipped mouth. He was so weak that it took both hands to lift the heavy vessel to his lips. When he got it there, he couldn't lower it fast enough, and the peppery firewater plunged down his throat and exploded in his chest, detonating cannons in his head.

Quickly, he set the bottle on the floor.

Gasping, he lay back on the bed, drew the single quilt over his body, and felt the pleasant numbing of his brain as the fire in his belly burned itself out slowly. He drifted into darkness populated with screams and gunfire and hammering nightmares from which he awoke occasionally, burning up with fever. At one point, he realized it was cold and dark in the room, so he closed the cabin door, then sat back down on the bed and took another pull from the bottle.

He'd taken enough swigs that he'd somewhat gotten used to the burn, and the painkilling properties of the tarantula juice were a blessing he'd thank Charlie Benbow for if he ever saw him again.

He woke near dawn feeling as if he'd been dragged kicking and screaming through a hungry bobcat's den, each of several cats having taken a bite. He lay awake for a time, his mind acquiring a haunting clarity.

He was alone once more. He'd had a home and friends, folks he'd trusted and felt comfortable around, and now they'd been taken from him just as Trace Cassidy had been taken.

And Marianna Claymore and Jennifer Spurlock.

Cimarron, Shanley, Dawson, and Pearl — all murdered.

A venal, gnawing depression took hold of him and pulled him down into a deep, stygian pit. Beneath the quilt, he curled into a tight ball and felt the tears gush out from behind his squeezed-shut lids as his body convulsed with sorrow and misery.

His sobs echoed in the silent darkness.

He slept.

When he opened his eyes again, buttery light poured through the cabin's dusty windows. Automatically, he tried to stretch, and an angry beaver buried its toothy head in his left side, just up from his hip. He snarled and cursed and flung the quilt away, dropped his bare feet to the floor.

As the cold morning air wrapped against his naked body, he realized his fever had broken. He felt weak, and his head throbbed a little from the whiskey, but he wasn't as sick as he'd felt last night. He thought he might even be able to swallow a few bites of food. Pulling out a fresh pair of long-handles, he dressed, then built a fire in the woodstove. When he had the cabin warm, he went out and checked on Northwest, then filled his canteen at the creek, looking around warily for La Brie.

There'd been little reason for the outlaws to follow him. It was the gold they were after, and there was no reason for them to think he had it. Likely they were tearing the ranch apart, looking for it, unless they'd already found it and were on the trail again, leaving death and destruction behind them.

He draped a feed sack of oats over Northwest's ears, then went back inside the warm cabin, pulled a can and a hide sack off the shelf, and had a breakfast of stewed tomatoes and jerky washed down with water. Coffee would have been nice, but he needed food in his stomach first. Then maybe he'd have the energy to make a good strong pot of mud; he'd almost depleted himself with dressing, walking to the creek, and tending the horse.

After breakfast, he indeed felt better.

He found a coffee pouch tucked behind the other vegetable tins, and a mill and a coffeepot in an apple crate stuffed with various possibles. Filling the pot with water from the creek, he set the coffee to boil on the stove and then hauled more wood into the cabin from the split pine logs neatly stacked against its rear wall.

Soon, he had the cabin as warm as a Chinese laundry and filled with the aroma of fresh coffee. While drinking the belly wash from a cracked stone mug, he tended his wounds with water and whiskey from the crock jug; then, satisfied he really was on the mend, he laid his rifle and pistol on a dry rag on the table.

Slowly and carefully, he cleaned each weapon, taking it apart, taking his time, then loading them both so they were ready for his ride back to the Diamond Bar. His gut recoiled at what he'd find there, but he had to go back and see about Pearl.

If he found her dead, which seemed likely, he'd bury her along with the men. Probably, La Brie had found the money and had lit out by now. If so, Colter would track him.

It would be a tough ride. Colter had no delusions. La Brie and his gang were seasoned outlaws. His chances of bringing them all down, giving them their reckoning, were slim. But he had to do it. He owed it to Pearl, Cimarron, and the other two ranch hands. He'd likely die, and while he felt himself automatically quaking at the prospect, he wasn't sure the dread was deep or genuine.

Nothing in life had turned out right for him so far. Being dead couldn't really be all that bad.

When he'd finished the pot of coffee, he rewrapped the wound in his upper right arm, glad to see it was healing, then closed the damper on the stove and wrapped his shell belt and Remy around his waist. He donned his hat, picked up his rifle and saddle gear. Giving the cabin a quick straightening, and swabbing the table with a torn rag, he headed outside and closed the door behind him.

He stood looking around the canyon bathed in harsh noon light. He took a deep breath. He felt good. Strong. Determined. Only a little frightened.

He went over and saddled Northwest, tied his rifle scabbard to the saddle, and adjusted his bedroll and saddlebags.

Yes, he felt strong. He was ready to wreak some vengeance today.

He led the horse out of the corral. The light around him dimmed, and he looked at the sky. A storm must be moving in. He shaded his eyes with his hand, and frowned.

No clouds in sight.

Suddenly, his stomach heaved. His knees knocked together. He took another step, but the ground seemed a long ways away. Then suddenly it pitched toward him and smacked him in the face.

The last thing he heard before his senses went out was Northwest nickering curiously.

CHAPTER 17

"Benbow?"

Spurr sat his big roan on the other side of the creek from the cabin, waiting. The cabin's shutters were open, smoke issued from the chimney pipe, and there was a horse in the corral. The prospector had to be around here somewhere.

"Benbow? It's Spurr. Come out, come out, wherever you are! Less'n you gotta a gal in there. Don't come out here nekkid, whatever you do!"

Spurr chuckled, stared at the cabin's closed door. Except for the gurgle of the creek in front of him, silence. He looked around the barren yard shaded by both the cabin and the rimrock rising behind the log-and-mud hovel. He hipped himself around in the saddle, looking behind him. Seeing nothing, he turned to the cabin once more, glanced at the corral.

There was a horse there, all right. Not

necessarily Charlie Benbow's, though. The last time Spurr was through this country and overnighted with the prospector, Benbow had had only two mules. There were no mules around now, and the old Conestoga wagon that Benbow had been using the last time Spurr had been through here, chasing whiskey runners, was nowhere to be seen.

The hairs under Spurr's collar pricked. He spat a wad of chaw to one side, then eased his Winchester '66 from the scabbard under his right thigh. He cocked it one-handed, hearing the metallic rasp echo around the cabin yard. Holding the rifle across his saddlebows, he gigged the roan across the creek, the shod hooves clattering on the wet, mossy stones, and up the opposite bank. He stopped the horse about fifty feet from the cabin's door, looked cautiously around once more, then stepped down from the saddle.

"Benbow?" he called, louder this time, in case the prospector was out behind the place at his woodpile. Or maybe his hearing had gotten worse. "It's Spurr!" Then, in case someone else was around — someone he didn't know — he added, "Deputy United States marshal."

Slowly he moved forward, taking one slow

step at a time, pressing the butt of the old Winchester against the cartridge belts looped over his right hip, and swinging his head from left to right. Just in front of the cabin, he turned fully around to eye the creek, wary of an ambush, then turned to the cabin again and rapped on the door with his Winchester's butt.

"Ben —"

The bark of a shell being levered into a rifle breech cut him off. The sound had come from above. He lifted his eyes to the roof of the cabin to see a rifle maw yawning at him — cold and dark as the grave he'd been dreaming about for the past several nights.

From up beyond the maw, a kid narrowed an eye down the barrel at him. The kid's pale, scarred cheek was pressed against the stalk of the old Henry repeater. The kid's long red hair blew around his head and freckled face, marred by an S brand, in the wind. His pink lips were set in a straight, hard line.

Spurr felt his face warm with disdain. Nothing burned him more than having a gun aimed at him. Especially one aimed at him by a younker. "If you're gonna pull that trigger, pull it, and stop wasting my time, you little privy snipe!"

The kid opened both eyes and lifted his chin slightly away from the Henry's brass receiver. "Who the hell are you?"

"Deputy United States marshal. Name's Spurr. Who the hell are you?"

"Colter Farrow."

He studied Spurr skeptically, giving him the slow up and down. This man didn't look like any federal marshal he'd ever seen before. Not that he'd seen that many. In his buckskins, hickory shirt, and moccasins, craggy face behind a patchy, gray-brown beard, this man looked like an old trapper or Indian trader. Maybe a waddie who'd been kicked out of the bunkhouse for drunkenness.

"I don't see no badge."

Spurr reached up and slid his beaded deerskin vest slightly back from the vest pocket of his shirt, revealing the moon-and-star U.S. marshal's badge.

"No shit?" Colter said, mostly to himself though he'd voiced it loud enough for Spurr to hear.

Spurr's loins burned once more with annoyance. "No shit. Now get that rifle out of my face, Colter Farrow, and tell me what in the holy hell you're doin' here on the roof of Charlie Benbow's cabin." He glanced around. "Where the hell is old Benbow, anyway?"

"Hold on."

Spurr watched as Colter pushed himself up off the roof and then crabbed back away from the peak. Spurr walked around the side of the cabin to the back, saw the kid drop his legs down over the edge while clinging to the roof with one hand, keeping the rifle in the other.

Colter grunted as he slowly lowered his boots toward the woodpile, the wound in his left side stretching painfully.

"Young man, why don't you hand me that rifle?" Spurr said, reaching toward Colter with his left hand. "Make it some easier for you to crawl down from —"

Just then Colter let go of the edge of the roof. His feet dropped to the woodpile. He groaned, losing his balance, his side burning up, and threw out his arms for balance but didn't manage to attain it before he was tumbling through the air and piling up on the ground several feet away from the woodpile. Dust wafted around him.

He lifted his head, set his jaw, and groaned once more, dropping the rifle and clamping his left hand to his side.

Spurr walked over to him. "See there? That's just what I was afraid would happen. If young men listened to their elders, they'd be spared a whole pile of unnecessary grief."

Colter glared up at the craggy, hazel-eyed countenance staring down at him in mild reproof. "As soon as I can find a pencil, Mr. Spurr, I'll write that one down and try to abide by it and turn my rifle over to a stranger, next time I'm crawling off a roof."

Spurr's gaze drifted to the side that Colter was holding with his hand, saw the blood staining the kid's underwear shirt. " 'Pears you been shot."

As the pain abated a bit, Colter turned onto his hands and knees and began pushing himself to his feet. "The slug went all the way through, but it made a nice little hole in my side. I closed it with Benbow's fireplace poker."

Colter saw the lawman staring at his cheek.

"That ain't what I used on my face," he added, feeling the brand heat up with embarrassment.

"Didn't think it was," Spurr said, silently chastising himself for staring as he grabbed Colter's arm and helped the young drover to his feet. "What happened? Who shot ya?"

"You come for the money?"

"If you mean the stolen army loot — yep. Now, suppose you answer my questions? Who shot ya and where's Benbow?"

"You're too late for the loot. Them who lost it probably have it back by now. They killed Cimarron and two other good men over to the Diamond Bar. Probably Cimarron's daughter, too." Colter stood slightly crouched, holding a hand over the wound spotting his shirt. "I made it out of the cabin with this burn here and a few others, came here to get tended. I don't know where Mr. Benbow is. Probably off at one of his other claims."

"Cimarron's dead?"

Colter felt a tightness in his throat, and he nodded. "You knew him?"

"Shared a few pulls of a jug with the man, time or two. Come on, boy. Let's get you inside the cabin before you open that hole up all the way."

Colter pulled his arm away from Spurr. "I can make it."

"All right," Spurr said, standing back and lowering his Winchester to his side, watching the young, scar-faced firebrand stride stiffly around the cabin.

The kid had sand — Spurr would give him that. That brand on his cheek had to be a heavy burden. The lawman wondered where he'd gotten it. A devilish thing to do to anyone — especially to one so young. Spurr had seen rustlers and cardsharps branded in the arms or legs. Once even on the back of the neck.

Never the face. The thought repelled him, filled him with sympathy for the stalwart lad.

Halfway to the cabin's front, Colter stopped, glanced over his shoulder. "You stayin' here tonight?"

Spurr narrowed an eye at the sky. The sun was almost down. "I figured to. Light out for the Diamond Bar first thing in the mornin'."

"I'll be lightin' out with you, Marshal Spurr."

"The name's Spurr. Just Spurr. And . . . like hell you will, boy."

The lawman strode on past Colter to where the big roan stood waiting for him, ground-tied. Colter curled his lip and hardened his jaw at the lawman's slightly stooped back.

Spurr stripped the tack from Cochise, and rubbed the horse down good before leading him back over to the creek to draw his fill of water. When the lawman had corralled the mount with the boy's blaze-faced coyote dun that hustled over to cautiously greet its new corral mate, Spurr hauled his rifle, saddlebags, bedroll, and two dead jackrabbits over to the cabin.

Inside, he found Colter on the bed, semi-reclined with his head and shoulders against the wall behind him, one knee raised, his left hand on his side. The wound on his upper right arm was wrapped with burlap. With all his scrapes and sundry other bruises, he looked like a prime candidate for a hospital tent. He also looked frustrated, impatient. Spurr had a feeling he was going to have his hands full come morning, when the kid was going to insist on shadowing him over to the Diamond Bar. The kid had sand, but Spurr wasn't going to let him get himself killed. Besides, this was law business.

Spurr moved into the cabin, slung his gear and both field-dressed rabbits onto the table, and, winded, he sucked a deep breath. Damn, he wished that knot in his chest would loosen up.

"You want me to take a look at that bloody side of yours, kid, I'll be happy to do so. That arm could use a look, too."

"No, thanks. I just strained it a bit. It's healin' just fine. By morning I'll be ready to ride." Colter pitched his voice with challenge.

"You think so, do you?" Spurr growled. Holding up the rabbits, he looked at the kid. "Hungry? I shot both o' these big jacks on the way out from Buffaloville. Figured to feed old Benbow in exchange for a roof and a few pulls from his jug." He glanced at the jug sitting on the floor beneath the bed. "I see you already been into it."

"Just had me enough to get to sleep last night."

"I don't begrudge ya. I'd likely have killed that jug there and gone probin' the yard for more. From all the dirt on them jugs, I assume he buys a big cache in Crow Dance, then buries 'em out here for when he's away."

Spurr dragged a chair out from the table and plopped into it. The long ride from Buffaloville had blown him out good. He probably shouldn't have come out here, but he had a job to do and his pride wouldn't let him sit on the stoop of the Skinner House, drinking beer, while someone else did it.

He'd overtaken Bill Wilden a few miles from town, and sent the sheriff and his mangled leg back home.

He tossed his hat onto the table, slid his saddlebags to one side so he could see Colter on the bed. Leaning back in his chair, he let a few seconds pass, catching his breath, feeling the fatigue loosen a little, before he said, "Tell me about it, boy."

Colter turned his head to him. "It was a man named La Brie that done it. He and his gang — four other men and La Brie's sister, Mercy, stormed into the cabin while we was tending a wound Stretch took in the thigh. They busted in, firing. There was so much smoke I couldn't see much except men flying around, yelling, before I skinned out a window. Figured on riding away and coming back when I had a chance against those bastards."

"La Brie?"

Colter nodded.

"Big man, early forties, long gray-brown hair? Ridin' with a butt-ugly woman and a black man named Preston?"

"That's him."

Spurr nodded grimly, dropping his eyes. "Skylar La Brie, then. He's back in the country."

"You know 'im?"

"I do. Him and his bunch . . . pack o' scalawags down from Canada. That woman — Mercy, she calls herself now — is La Brie's half sister, Bethel Nordquist. Her husband ran with the gang till he was shot by marshals out of Bismark in the Dakota Territory. They'd robbed several banks in Dakota, killing all sorts of innocent folks including a couple sheriffs and a town

234

marshal that rode after 'em, then disappeared up into Canada. Holed up in the
Sweet Grass Hills, I heard. The paper on
them's been circulatin' the past two years.
The law's been wantin' 'em bad."

Spurr scrubbed his jaw. "Shit." Now, the
gang was down here, in Wyoming. And
Spurr had no posse to help him run them
down. Only a vengeance-hungry kid and a
bad ticker. Any one of that bunch was wool-
lier than an old bull griz with a sow and
cubs to protect.

"Don't worry," Colter said. "You won't be
tangling with them alone."

"Kid," Spurr said, leaning forward and
resting an elbow on the table while pointing
a dirty finger at Colter. "I'm gonna tell you
this just one more . . ."

He let his voice trail off. He could tell by
the look the young drover was sending him,
he might as well be counseling a stone boat
loaded with field rocks on the benefits of
the Christian religion.

"Ah, hell."

The old marshal kicked his chair back,
used the edge of the table to push himself
to his feet. He felt as though a colt kicked
his breastbone from the other side, and he
gave a grunt, standing still, slightly wobbly,
for a second, feeling the blood rush out of

his face. Grimacing, he stared at the black stove flue on the other side of the room, waiting for the pain to pass, debating whether he needed one of the precious tablets that the sawbones in Buffaloville had given him. His heart seemed to labor and flutter as though under a heavy strain.

Spurr felt Colter's eyes on him, and his ears warmed with shame.

"You okay, Marshal Spurr?" Colter asked him.

He could see the man was having a bad moment. His craggy face was pale, and his eyes appeared pain-racked as they stared across the table. Colter had just dropped a foot to the floor, ready to go to the man, when Spurr turned to him, lilac eyes sharp with unwarranted fury.

"I'm just fine, young man. Don't you worry about this old stallion. And what'd I tell you about that Marshal Spurr business? Don't you heed nothin' your elders tell ya?"

With that, he stumbled forward and began knocking around the kitchen, making coffee. Colter's side hurt so bad that he let the man go about his business without offering to help, merely rested his head back against the log wall and closed his eyes. He'd need all the rest he could get.

Despite what the marshal had told him,

he was going after La Brie. The old lawman was so stove-up and sickly, there wasn't anything he could do about it. There wasn't much Spurr could do about La Brie, either. Hell, La Brie would fill that old hide sack — he must be seventy years old at least — with hot lead at the first sight of him, and toss him in the nearest ravine.

From the look of him, it would be a merciful end. Sorta like shootin' a blind old hound.

When Spurr had poured himself a cup of coffee and offered one to Colter, who declined it, Spurr set his cup on the table, then rolled up his shirtsleeves and started skinning the rabbits. He seemed an old hand at cooking for himself — Colter would give the old goat that. Probably spent a lot of time on the trail alone. He had the look of a man of many hard miles on countless lonely trails. He'd likely emptied a few bottles in his day, chased a few less than respectable women.

Spurr kept cutting curious glances at Colter while he worked, until Colter said, "I fell on a branding iron. That answer the question?"

Spurr had set a board on the table, and now he began chopping the rabbits with a meat cleaver. "It sure got you good, that iron did. It's right where a man would place it, if'n he was good and mean enough." Spurr shook his head and continued hacking away at the big liver-colored jack streaked with fat and sinew. "Don't mind me, younker. It's in my nature to be curious, that's all."

He shuttled a cunning glance back over at Colter. "Just so happens I heard a few weeks ago about some county sheriff in southern Colorado puttin' a bounty on some kid, about the same age as you — sixteen, seventeen — with an S brand on his left cheek." Spurr wagged his head but kept his face expressionless as he gave the rabbit one last chop, then started shoveling the pieces into a cast-iron stew pot. "Coincidences abound, I reckon."

Colter studied the old lawman skeptically. Tentatively, he said, "You ain't in the market for illegal bounties — are ya, Spurr? And since the bounty was put out by a son-of-a-bitch sheriff who by rights should be dead instead of just crippled for what he done to my foster pa, that'd be a county matter, wouldn't it? You're federal."

"That's right," Spurr said as he started chopping the second rabbit. "You been learning, haven't ya?"

Colter rested his head back against the

wall. He didn't know why, but something told him he could trust this man. He might be old and stove-up and not much good at his job anymore, but at least he wouldn't try to gun Colter down and cut his head off, sack it up, and send it back to Bill Rondo in Sapinero. "Yeah, I learned a lot in the past few months."

"I bet you have." Spurr stopped chopping to sip his coffee. "How'd Cimarron come to get his hands on the gold?"

Colter considered his answer. He didn't know whether he should tell Spurr he was responsible for securing the stolen army loot, or not. Why tip his hand to a stranger about how fast he was with his old Remington? Trusting the man but still feeling wary from all the long miles he'd covered from Colorado, and from his recent dustup with the bounty killers, Colter scuttled down in the bed and turned onto his right side, facing the wall. He slid his right hand against the cold, firm butt of the Remy he'd placed beneath the pillow.

"I'm feelin' some peaked, Spurr. Reckon I'll shut my eyes for a bit."

"All right, kid," Spurr growled, chopping away at the rabbit. "You do that."

CHAPTER 18

Spurr shuffled the whiskey-stained deck of cards in his big gnarled hands, causing the candle on the table before him to sputter. He was about to begin laying down the pasteboards for a one-handed game of war when Colter groaned in his sleep.

Spurr looked over the table at the boy asleep on the floor against the front wall, left of the door, head resting on his saddle. Since there was only one bed in the cabin, the boy had insisted he'd take the floor despite the ugly-looking knot in his side, which Spurr had gotten a look at when Colter had dressed the wound as well as the one in his arm before turning in.

Now the kid, wrapped in blankets as he lay with his head back against his saddle, hat pulled down over his eyes, said, "No . . ."

Colter shook his head, jostling the hat around enough that it revealed his eyes, which were fluttering.

"No." He clucked and snorted, frustrated. "Dang it all, Marianna!" Then he sort of whimpered and swallowed hard.

Gradually, his muscles relaxed. His breathing became slow and even. His eyes and lips stopped moving. The candle spread a wan glow of saffron light across the right side of his face, casting the scarred left side in shadow. The S stuck out darkly, like a small coiled snake laid out there under the kid's eye.

Colter's breathing became heavy, and his jaw hardened, the left hinge dimpling in the candlelight.

The old lawman started laying down cards, swiping the pairs off to one side or the other. Poor kid. You couldn't really blame him for having vengeance on his mind, after being marked in such a grisly fashion by Bill Rondo. Also, he was young. Spurr had been the same way. Even now, he'd probably go after such men as La Brie if they'd killed friends of his. But there was no such thing as getting even for a killing. The proof lay in the fact that folks didn't just waltz up out of their graves to rejoin the living as soon as they were avenged.

The law corrected no wrongs, either. But Spurr figured that following it had in some way saved his soul. At least, on this side of the sod, anyway.

He intended to ride out of here alone in the morning. No vengeance-hungry younker was going to weigh him down, distract him, make his job more difficult than it already was. Besides, there were enough vengeance-seeking young men pushing up sage on the boot hills across the frontier. Spurr had found himself liking this one, and he didn't want to see young Colter Farrow shot out of his saddle, a bullet between his eyes.

Something deep inside the logy-hearted old lawman told him he wouldn't be able to handle the La Brie bunch alone. This secret thought lay very deep in a very small pocket in his brain that did not communicate with the rest of itself. But in this pocket Spurr was also thinking that facing the La Brie bunch, the worst gang of killers currently running roughshod across the frontier, would be one hell of a way to go out. . . .

He'd probably never make it to Mexico, anyway. If his luck held and he did make it, the whores down there would kill him within a week. He'd have laid heavy odds on it, if he'd really thought about, which he didn't.

But he knew . . .

He set a seven of heart downs on a jack of spades.

In the far distance, a horse whinnied.

Spurr lifted his eyes across the guttering candle at the door. His heart sputtered. He leaned forward, blew out the candle, and sat there for a moment in the darkness that still smelled like the rabbit stew he'd made for supper. The silence was dense and ominous.

In the corral just outside the cabin, one of the horses snorted. There was the thud of a stomping hoof.

Spurr jerked himself to his feet . . . too fast. His weak heart revolted. He felt as though tough hands were pushing him back down while a third one squeezed his ticker. Ignoring the pain, he grabbed one of his cartridge belts hanging over the chair beside him, and wrapped it with his holster and pistol around his waist. As he reached for his rifle, he glanced at the kid.

Colter was snoring very softly, occasionally moving his lips, the scar on his cheek twitching every so often. A troubled sleeper. But he continued sleeping. Spurr would let him sleep. Chances were, the horses had only been riled by a coyote or some other night critter padding around along the creek.

Spurr left his hat on the table. He crossed the room, his heart thudding slowly, painfully, and slowly lifted the steel and leather latch until the door slackened. He pulled it open quickly, wincing at the hinges' squawk, and stepped out. Drawing the door closed behind him, he moved to the left and, wincing at the continued heavy ache in his chest, hunkered down on his haunches.

His chest felt tighter, heavier. With a shaking hand, he reached into the left breast pocket of his shirt and withdrew the small hide pouch in which he'd poured the pills the sawbones had given him. He popped one in his mouth — it tasted like tin as it dissolved beneath his tongue.

Almost instantly, he felt the affects. His chest lightened. With each breath he seemed to draw more air. His strength returned, his senses growing keener.

He looked around the cabin's dark yard, pricking his ears.

A half-moon hovered over a southwestern butte, giving enough light that he could make out the furry line of the creek. He waited for his eyes to adjust. After a time, staring out beyond the creek, he picked out two silhouetted horses standing with their heads down. They were tied in a copse of piñons, and he wouldn't have seen them if the moon hadn't been angling just right.

He chuffed softly to himself. His ticker

was weak, but his distance vision was as keen as ever. His hearing, too. He picked out the slight stumble of someone walking across the creek, and a muttered curse.

It wasn't a coyote out there, after all. At least, not the animal kind.

Spurr stood slowly, then eased off to the cabin's left side, where the shadow of a low, steep-sided bluff cast a pie-wedged shadow across the yard and corral. As his and Colter's horses continued to nicker and fidget around in the paddock behind him, Spurr stole through the shadow out to the creek. At the edge of the brush lining the stream, he stopped, looked upstream, in the direction from which he'd heard the splash.

Spying nothing, he continued on into the brush, forded the creek via half-submerged stones, getting the soles of his moccasins wet enough to be irksome though not dangerous, and began tramping upstream, keeping close to the dark shadows of the brush. No telling who was out here. It was remote country, so it could be anyone from rustlers to Cheyenne Indians looking for a larder to raid.

Spurr was holding out the hope it was Charlie Benbow, having seen the two horses in his corral, scouting the layout here before entering. But Charlie had always preferred mules to horses, and Spurr had been able to tell that the two animals tied to the brush yonder were horses.

Spurr stopped suddenly, straining his eyes to see into the darkness ahead of him. A man knelt on one knee about thirty feet away, holding a rifle and facing the cabin. All Spurr could tell about the man was that he was lanky and wore a shabby cream hat and long denim jacket. The eyelets of his tall, lace-up boots — miners' boots — shone in the moonlight.

He was studying the cabin, likely backing up the man who'd crossed the creek.

Anxiety nipped at Spurr. The kid was in the cabin, asleep on the floor, helpless.

As Spurr approached the kneeling interloper, he could see the man's jaws nervously working a wad of chew. Just as the man lowered his head to spit a long wet stream into the brush, Spurr stopped ten feet away from him.

"Hold it."

The man froze. Suddenly, he whipped around, bringing a Spencer carbine to bear on Spurr, who cursed as he fired his Winchester twice — *bam! bam!* — both spent cartridges dropping in the short, wiry grass behind him.

The man triggered his Spencer over

Spurr's head as he gave a shrill cry and went flying off into the creek. He hit the water with a splash, his rifle landing on the rocks and water a half second later.

"Damn fool." Spurr bolted forward, saw the man bobbing slightly in the eight-inch-deep water, limbs akimbo. His hat had fallen just beyond him. It was being carried slowly downstream, weaving among the rocks and branches.

Spurr hurried across the creek, his heart pounding. He'd left the kid alone. The other would-be ambusher was likely headed for him. . . .

As he started across the yard as fast as his old legs would carry him, he saw a shadow move against the darker shadow of the cabin door. There was the heavy rap of a rifle butt against wood and the cracking of the latch, the ping of the steel bolt hitting the cabin floor.

"I'm here, you bastard!" Spurr shouted, hoping to distract the man from the cabin.

Too late.

A gun flashed three times inside the cabin. The bark of the rifle sounded strange and hollow as it echoed off the cabin's stout walls. A thick shadow flew back from the door. It arced high in the air and came down and hit the ground hard with a yelp.

There was another, slender shadow. It arced higher and came down farther away from the cabin than the man had.

The attacker's rifle clattered when it struck the ground.

Another figure stepped out of the cabin. The moonlight washed over the kid's long-handles and hat and the Tyler Henry he aimed straight out from his left shoulder.

"Colter!" the old marshal said, stopping about twenty feet from the front door. He leaned forward, a hand on a knee. "Hold on — it's Spurr."

Colter moved toward him. Above the kid, yet another shadow moved atop the cabin. Instantly, Spurr straightened, bringing up his rifle.

"Drop, junior!"

Colter threw himself flat.

Spurr's old Winchester leaped and roared in his hands. The man atop the cabin groaned and triggered one shot that sent a slug burning across Spurr's left cheek. Then he spun and hit the cabin's brush roof with a curse. A second later he was on his hands and knees and crawling quickly toward the cabin's rear, groaning and panting.

"I'll be damned if I don't know that son of a bitch!"

Spurr racked a fresh cartridge, leaped over

Colter's sprawled figure, and dashed around the cabin toward the rear. As he rounded the corner, the wounded bushwhacker leaped from the roof to the woodpile. He careened off the woodpile, scattering logs, and hit the ground with another groan and a sob.

"Ah . . . goddamn your eyes, Spurr!" He rolled around on his back, grabbing his knee. The ankle of the same leg hung limp and crooked. "You shot me, ya sumbitch. Ya busted my fuckin' ankle!"

"Toad Johnson, you bushwhackin' fool." Spurr stood over the man, aiming his Winchester one-handed at the man's head that shone pale in the moonlight angling over the cabin. Johnson had lost his hat in the fall. He had close-cropped dark hair, a blunt-nosed face, jug ears, and a week's growth of black beard. "Would you mind tellin' me just what in the *hell* you think you're doin'?"

"Ah, shit." Johnson lowered his leg, sort of resting the broken ankle atop the other one. "I'm gonna die, ain't I?"

"Looks like I buried one in your belly. Best sweep out the chimney before you're judged by ole St. Pete." Spurr dropped to a knee beside the dying man. "What're you doin' out here, ya damn bushwhackin' id-jit?"

"What the hell ya think? The gold!"

Spurr chuckled without mirth. "I don't even have it yet, Toad."

Johnson's pain-racked face gained a befuddled expression. He shifted his gaze to Colter, who stood beside Spurr. He looked at the rifle hanging limp in Colter's hand. "We . . . we thought . . ."

"The kid was one of the gang? Pshaw! You shoulda stuck to sellin' whiskey and gold pans, Toad." Spurr shook his head. "You're a day early and about twenty-six thousand short. Who're you friends?"

Toad just stared up at Spurr, that befuddled look pasted on his face. His eyes were glassy. His chest fell still.

Colter glanced at Spurr. "He followed you out from Buffaloville?"

The old lawman looked indignantly back at the young drover. "I don't let no one, and I mean no one, fog my back trail, younker. Toad here's from Crow Dance. His dry goods store went belly-up last winter. It never was much more than a tent over an old Murphy freight wagon. When he heard about the gold that Cimarron had, he must have gathered up some of his down-at-heel friends to come gunnin' for it. They likely spied me and you here at the cabin, figured you was my prisoner, and I'd somehow gotten the gold already."

Spurr straightened, his old knees popping, breath sounding raspy. He stared down at the dead dry goods man. "The heart is deceitful above all things, and desperately wicked."

Colter looked at him.

"I never could get through the Good Book, but my dear old aunt that raised me quoted to me from it all the time. I reckon some of it stuck." Spurr shouldered his rifle. "That was some fancy shootin', kid."

Colter shouldered his own rifle and gave the old lawman a direct, determined look. "Deputize me, Spurr. You've seen here how I can back your play. We'll go after the La Brie gang and bring 'em down hard. Together, we can do it."

He didn't want to go against the old law dog. Why not throw in with him? Despite his weakened state, he looked as though he could take care of himself. Besides, two had a better chance than one against the La Brie gang.

Spurr chuckled and started back around the cabin. "I ride alone, junior."

CHAPTER 19

Pearl gritted her teeth and snarled like an enraged bobcat as she pulled at the four stakes pinning her, naked and spread-eagle, in the middle of the Diamond Bar yard.

The two La Brie gang members — the big man with the calico bandanna and bear-tooth earrings, whom the other gang members called Big Norm, and the kid in the top hat whom everyone called Yukon — had tied her wrists and ankles to the stakes with rawhide that had no give in it at all.

Pearl gave the stakes and tethers one more try, lifting her head and drawing the cords in her neck taut as she snarled and cursed as quietly as she could, for the gang members were all sacked out nearby. Pearl didn't want to give them the satisfaction of knowing how miserable her night had been.

And how discouraged she'd become.

Defeated.

Not only was Cimarron dead — he and

Dawson and Shanley were still lying in bloody, twisted heaps in the cabin — but her own spirit was all but broken. Several times over the course of the long night, when the temperature must have gotten down to around forty degrees and her muscles had burned from the position she'd been held in since they'd dragged her out of the cabin and she'd refused to tell them where the stolen army gold was hidden, she'd half wished that death would swoop down like a big black bird and claim her.

Only half wished. Dead, she wouldn't be able to exact revenge on the killers of Cimarron.

Only luck had saved her from being killed with the others — the luck of Stretch Dawson flying into her when bullets had plunked through him, and her hitting her head on the range so hard she'd been knocked out until La Brie had dragged her out from under Dawson's bloody body, and out of the cabin.

Letting her body fall slack against the cold, hard ground once more, she felt herself convulse for the half-dozenth time that night in a sob of wretched, all-consuming sorrow. Tears oozed out from her closed eyelids and washed down her cheeks, and she swallowed the sobs that threatened to well up from her chest.

Cimarron . . .

The man who'd taken her in and given her a home when she was half as old as she was now, and who'd adopted and loved her like one of his own, was dead and cold as he lay with open, sightless eyes in a large pool of his own blood in the cabin he'd raised her in.

But it did no good to cry. Crying wouldn't bring Cimarron back. Nothing would do that. But over the long night she'd found a modicum of comfort in the thought of slitting La Brie's throat from ear to ear, and killing one by one the rest of his gang, including his fat, mean, stupid, curly-headed sister whom everyone inexplicably called Mercy.

Whatever her real name, she would die screaming. Pearl would see to that.

But the only way she could accomplish the task was to keep herself alive. It was clear to her now, after lying here staked out on the ground all night, watching the stars revolve and feeling the chill of the high-mountain air like blunt spikes hammering into her, that the only chance she had at staying alive was to tell La Brie where Cimarron had hidden the money. They might very well kill her once they'd gotten it, but something in the way La Brie had looked at her told her there was a chance they wouldn't.

Her numb lips quivering from the brutal chill, she turned to where the gang was bedded down about forty yards away from her and directly in front of the cabin. Mercy and most of the men had wanted to sleep in the bunkhouse, but when they'd found out that La Brie had intended to sleep in the yard with Pearl, they'd all decided to throw down out there, too. Either they didn't trust him with the gold, or they didn't want to be left out if La Brie tried to take Pearl by force. Mercy hadn't wanted any "funny business," but Pearl doubted that would stop La Brie once he'd made his mind up.

All the men were snoring. Pearl could tell where Mercy lay by the curly blond head turned to one side, by the large hump of the woman's ass pushing her wool blankets up, as though a barrel were under there, and by one fat, white calf of a stubby leg sticking out to one side.

As it was false dawn, there was a milky cast to the brown air, and birds were chirping.

Pearl was shivering, but she tried to keep her voice from shaking. "La Brie?"

The black man called Ten grunted and

snorted under his tan hat, then continued snoring. The others didn't move.

Pearl cleared her throat. "La Brie?"

La Brie jerked his head up suddenly, his hat tumbling into his lap. Instantly, he had a cocked pistol in each hand and he was swinging his head around anxiously.

"Over here," Pearl said.

La Brie turned his head toward her. The others, all nearly as cagey as La Brie, were jerking awake, as well, reaching for guns holstered beside them or hidden beneath the saddles that they'd been sleeping on. The black man had grabbed a rifle, and he was loudly racking a round into the chamber. The top of his head was as bald as an egg, but he wore a neatly trimmed beard and mustache. A scar from what appeared barbed wire angled pinkly across his forehead.

"Pull your horns in, Ten," La Brie ordered, his voice thick with sleep.

"What the hell is it?" Mercy wanted to know.

She had a Colt revolver in each hand and was looking beyond the corral as if expecting a posse to be approaching from the creek.

"Put up them hoglegs, sis," La Brie said raspily. "It's our purty little Injun gal." He swept his blankets aside and, keeping his guns in his hands but depressing the hammers, rose with a weary groan.

In his stocking feet, he walked over to where Pearl lay, and looked down at her.

La Brie was a big man. He had a slight paunch, but his shoulders, while always slightly stooped, were thick and broad. His face would have been handsome except for his eyes, which were flat and a strange blue-gray color. He had a pouncing hawk tattooed on his neck. While some women might have seen him as rakish and flirtatious, maybe even charming in a devilish way, Pearl saw the casual killer in the man.

Those weirdly colored eyes raked her body as she lay supine and naked before him. They flickered a little, snakelike, appreciating her. That was what she had to bank her fate on — his appreciation of her. His obvious desire for her as well as his outlaw's brand of nobility that had so far kept him from taking her against her will or allowing the others to rape her.

"Good mornin', my purty Injun gal." He knelt down beside her and slid a lock of her black hair away from her right eye. "Did you have a good night's sleep? Damn, but your lips are about as blue as overripe plums." He pressed two fingers across her quivering lips, and smiled. "You didn't get cold, did you?"

He had the same northern accent they all did except for the black man, who was from Texas. La Brie and the others all spoke with clipped vowels and strangely accented consonants, so that "about" sounded like "boot," "short" came out as "shirt," and cold was "colt." Canadians, most likely. Several Canadian cowboys had worked for Cimarron over the years.

"I got a couple hours in," Pearl said defiantly, continuing to try to keep her voice from shaking.

"Well, what'd you call me over here for?" La Brie smiled again as his eyes raked her. "Lonely?"

The others were following him over, some draping blankets over their shoulders against the chill. Mercy gave a loud shiver, rubbing her hands together.

Pearl swallowed, licked her lips. "I'll tell you where the money's hid."

"So it is still around here." Pulling a boot on while hopping around on one stockinged foot, Mercy looked at La Brie with victory in her sleep-bleary eyes. "I knew they hadn't taken it to town!"

"Where is it?" La Brie asked Pearl calmly, giving her that rakish little half grin of his

258

as he ran a hand through his longish, gray-streaked dark brown hair, which was the same color as his beard. He yawned. "And you better not be wastin' my time."

"Will you let me go?"

"I'll untie you and give your clothes back. I ain't promisin' I'll let you go. Why, don't you know?" With mock gentleness in both his hands and in his eyes, he smoothed her hair back from her forehead. "I've grown kind of fond of you."

Wearing only one boot, Mercy aimed both her pistols down at Pearl, clicking the hammers back and glaring down their barrels. "Quit horsin' around, brother. Where's the goddamn money, squaw? No deals. Where is it or stay tied out here through another sunny day and another long, cold night!"

La Brie scowled up at his sister. "Mercy, that is no way to talk to this poor girl."

"Hell, she's a damn Injun."

"A good-lookin' one, though," said Big Norm, his bushy gray handlebar mustache fluttering slightly in the chill morning breeze. "Me, I never had me a squaw. Feared I'd catch somethin'. But this one here — shit, I might just risk it."

Pearl kept her eyes on La Brie. "If you let me go, I'll tell you where the gold's hid. If not, I'll stay here until the sun burns straight through me or I freeze to death."

Mercy gritted her teeth and sucked a sharp, infuriated breath. She opened her mouth to speak, but La Brie held up his hand, cutting her off, keeping his attention on Pearl.

"How 'bout we do it this way? You tell us where the gold is, and once we've hauled it out here, then we untie you." La Brie held up his hands. "I make no promises to turn you loose on the world. Maybe in a few days, but not now so's you can go squeal to the authorities so we have more like them constables interruptin' our lunch break."

He chuckled at his joke, squinting his weird eyes.

"I won't squeal."

La Brie said firmly, "No, you won't. At least, not so's it can cause us trouble."

Pearl stared at him, sort of caressed him with her eyes. She knew he liked her, wanted her but only if she was willing and made it pleasant for him. "You promise to untie me, let me dress?"

"After we've hauled the gold out here."

Pearl glanced at the cabin. The door was open and she could see the arm of one of the dead men — Shanley, she thought — lying in front of the doorjamb. Sorrow and fury blew through her like a hot summer wind, but she suppressed the emotion, tossing her head to indicate the back of the cabin, saying, "There's a root cellar a hundred feet behind the cabin. There's a stone boat on top of it. The door's beneath the boat."

La Brie glanced at the other men and Mercy. Their eyes snapped wide and they jerked around and started stomping excitedly into their boots. When they'd all trotted off around the cabin, Big Norm threatening, "She better not be playin' some kinda squaw games, La Brie, or she's mine!"

La Brie remained on one knee beside Pearl, staring down at her with a weird mix of mockery and tenderness. "Nah. She ain't lyin'. I put my faith in her."

He grabbed Pearl's hair in his right hand and pulled it steadily so that it just started to hurt. Pearl did not wince. As cold and stiff as she was, she kept her face stony. That was the Sioux in her, she figured. From somewhere she got that primitive, iron resolve. She would not want to tangle with anyone like herself when she was mad.

La Brie would find that out in Pearl's own good time.

She stretched her lips slightly in a smile. "Don't worry. When I give my word, it's good. Is yours?"

"I reckon you might be about to find that out." Raking his eyes down the length of her cherry red body, parts of which quivered involuntarily from the night's endless chill, he shook his head in amazement. "Damn, but you're a good-lookin' girl. It'd be a shame to have to cut your throat for mocking me, makin' me look foolish in front of my amigos. You know what I think, Pearl?"

"What's that?"

"I think you and me are a lot alike. We're iron tough. Survivors. You and me would work well together, given half a chance."

"Maybe."

"The problem is, trustin' a tough-assed little squaw like you is just a might on the dangerous side."

"The rewards might even things out."

La Brie nodded pensively, ran the first two fingers of his left hand through the deep valley between her breasts. "Maybe." He continued running his fingers down her belly, and lower.

Pearl tightened her voice. "Don't."

He turned the corners of his mouth down. The hawk tattoo on the left side of his neck got darker. He removed his hand. "You'd have to get over this touchiness."

"You lie out here naked all night, and we'll see how touchy you get."

A smile blossomed on La Brie's face. His strange eyes flashed. "Damn, Pearl, I like you. I really do like you. You're as sassy and tough as you are purty." He pressed his fingers to her lips once more, and his smile tightened with menace. "You'd better not be messin' with me. . . ."

In the distance, spurs rattled and boots thumped. "Brother!"

La Brie turned. Pearl craned her head as far as she could to see Mercy striding quickly on her short legs around the corner of the cabin and into the front yard. The men flanked her, Ten holding the saddlebags over his shoulder and the others sticking close to him, lifting the flaps on the pouches to admire the loot.

"It's here!" Mercy said, approaching La Brie and Pearl.

La Brie stood. The men were oohing and aahing over the loot, chuckling and elbowing one another. La Brie stuck his hand inside one of the pouches and pulled up a handful of coins, letting them dribble back into the bag as he turned his approving gaze on Pearl.

"Well, I'll be damned. My purty little Pearl squaw girl came through."

"Yep," Mercy said, drawing one of her pistols from a holster hanging low on her soiled wool skirt. "Now it's time to say good-bye to the little bitch!"

CHAPTER 20

Colter rose in the murky light of false dawn and dressed slowly, with painstaking quiet, in the still-dark cabin while Spurr snored atop the cabin's single bed. The shooting last night, on top of his long ride out here to Benbow's hovel, had taken a lot out of the old lawman. He might sleep till eight or nine o'clock this morning. Hell, he might sleep all day.

That was fine with Colter. Since Spurr didn't want Colter teaming up with him, the young drover would have to ride the vengeance trail his own way.

Without Spurr. . . .

Colter plucked his hat off the table. He jerked with a start when Spurr fired an extra loud and grating snore at the rafters. The young drover looked over his shoulder. The lawman lay on his back, head resting on a stuffed toe sack pillow, lower jaw hanging, his open mouth making a large dark hole in the lower half of his thin-bearded, well-seasoned face.

Twice last night Colter had had to get up from his pallet on the floor and nudge the old man over onto his belly, to quell the snoring that had echoed off the cabin's stout walls like light cannonades. Otherwise, he wouldn't have gotten any sleep at all, and he'd needed a good night's rest to heal the bullet hole in his side well enough that he could ride the long, hard trail if that was what he was in for.

Colter snugged his hat down tight on his head, picked up his rifle and spurs, and ever so gently opened the door, wincing at the low creaking sounds emanating from the rusty hinges. When he had the door open two feet, he cast one more backward glance at Spurr, then sidestepped through the opening and used the same painstaking caution in drawing the door closed behind him.

When the latch clicked softly, he sighed with relief and sat down on the top porch step to put his spurs on. He chuckled softly to himself as he continued to hear the old law dog sawing logs in the cabin. When he had both spurs buckled, he strode across the yard toward the corral where Northwest and the lawman's big roan stared at him with their heads over the gate, both expecting their morning grub.

It was cold enough, getting on late in the summer, that breath jetted from the horses' nostrils.

Northwest nickered and shook his head. Colter winced and stopped, holding a finger to his lips, shushing the beast.

The horse stared at him curiously, twitching one ear. Colter continued forward and went on into the corral, pushed past both horses that jostled him for their morning feed, and continued into the lean-to shed where he'd stashed his tack. Looking at the crude wooden bench, he froze. He set his lips in a straight line and hardened his jaw, feeling warm blood rush to his head.

Swinging around, he leaned his rifle across a hay trough. He tramped back out of the corral and across the hard-packed yard to the cabin, letting his spurs ching raucously, and threw the cabin door open so hard that it banged off the wall. Standing just back of the opening, fully dressed with even his hat on his head and his saddle on his shoulder, his rifle in his other hand, Spurr grinned.

"Lookin' for your tack?"

Colter was furious, indignant. He'd let the old bastard hornswoggle him. "Where is it?"

"Behind the shed."

Colter swung around and stomped off

behind the cabin. Sure enough, his saddle was on the woodpile along with blanket, bridle, saddlebags, and bedroll. The young puncher sighed. Despite his fury, he chuckled as he slung the saddle over one shoulder, his bedroll and bags over the other, and continued around the cabin to the corral, where Spurr was grunting as he heaved his saddle onto his roan's back.

Both the roan and Northwest had feed sacks draped over their snoots, and were hungrily munching parched corn.

Colter strode through the open gate and walked up to Northwest. He narrowed an eye at the old lawman, who he could tell was thoroughly enjoying his ruse. Colter dropped his gear at his feet, then tossed his blanket up onto Northwest's back.

"All right, maybe I didn't get the jump on you. But there's nothing you can do to prevent me from riding over to the Diamond Bar."

Spurr was tightening his saddle's latigo, scowling at the big roan's head. "Let your air out, you stubborn bastard!" Then, fastening the strap's buckle and facing his horse, he said to Colter, "I figured that out on my own, younker. I reckon we're partnered up."

He picked up his rifle from where it lay

beside Colter's, then went around to the other side of the horse and slid the old Winchester into its scabbard. He entwined his hands atop the saddle and looked over them at Colter, his eyes hard and no longer owning any humor at all.

"But if you get in my way, try to take matters into your own hands, I'll cuff you and shackle you, tie you belly down over your horse, and haul your skinny ass back to Denver, where you'll stand trial for interfering with a federal lawman. In case you're too fired up to understand what that means, I'll tell ya — it means at least a year in the federal pen. I hear they got them boys diggin' out a tunnel for some narrow-gauge railroad up high in the Rockies."

He spat a wad of chew to one side, then, chewing his cud and grinning with satisfaction, added, "Cold up there of a winter."

Colter snorted his derision, grabbed his Henry, and slid it into his saddle scabbard. He glanced over his shoulder at Spurr now tying his bedroll over his saddlebags behind the cantle of his saddle. "Those men were good to me. Gave me a job for the winter, and Cimarron would have kept me on through next summer. He told me so, and his word was good."

"Probably the only family you have 'bout now."

"That's right. And La Brie killed 'em. Stormed into the cabin and shot 'em in cold blood. Likely killed Pearl, or worse. All for that damn money I shot off them cousins of La Brie's!"

Colter's voice broke on this last. Tears oozed out of his eyes, dribbled down his cheeks. Quickly, he swiped at them with a sleeve of his denim jacket, but he could not keep his lips from quivering.

Removing the feed sack from his roan's head, Spurr looked at him. "So it was you that got the gold."

Colter sniffed, swallowed, turned to look in the direction of the Diamond Bar.

"Sorta makes you feel responsible for what happened, don't it?"

"That's right, it does."

"Comes with the territory, kid."

Colter turned to Spurr, who was removing the feed sack from Northwest's ears. The young drover frowned at him.

"That old six-shooter of yours. Goes with the territory of knowin' how to use it." Spurr glanced at him as he went over and opened one of his saddlebag flaps. "Knowin' how to use it keeps you alive, but it sorta starts a habit. The more you use it, the more you have to use it."

He stuffed the feed sacks into the saddle-bag pouch.

"You sayin' I shoulda just let La Brie's cousins blow me and Shanley and ole Stretch out of our saddles?"

"Nope." Spurr shook his head. When he'd buckled the flap down tight over the pouch, he turned a direct look on Colter. "I'm sayin' you reap what you sow whether you deserve it or not. And there's no point in gettin' on your high horse about it."

He toed his left stirrup, grabbed his saddle horn with both hands, and his face colored up as he winced and heaved himself into his saddle, the leather creaking along with his joints. When he got himself settled in the leather, he turned that direct look on Colter once more. "This ain't no pistolero fandango, understand? This here's a ride after owl hoots ramrodded by a deputy United States marshal."

He tapped the badge pinned to his elk-skin vest. "We're out to secure stolen army gold and bring the thieves to justice as allowed for by the code of the U.S. Marshal's Service and the Constitution. Nothing more, nothing less. You try any Black Bart or Billy the Kid imitations, you'll spend this winter and next summer breakin' rock for the railroad."

Spurr ground his heels against the roan's flanks. "Hee-yaa!"

And galloped out through the open corral gate.

From a hundred yards away, Colter thought the object hanging from the lone, dead aspen tree along a sharp bend in Diamond Creek was a hunter's cache of elk or venison. As he and the old lawman closed on it, however, his gut tightened.

There wasn't just one object, but two.

Gradually, Colter made out the hair-capped heads of two separate men hanging naked, necks stretched by the nooses that hung down from a stout branch, the ends of both ropes tied off on a low knob on the opposite side of the tree from the bodies. They were pale, gaunt, and red from the blood that had leaked from the several bullet holes in their chests and heads.

Colter and Spurr checked their mounts down ten feet from the dead men, who swung two and fro in the gusting afternoon breeze. The ropes squawked. The branch above their heads groaned from the strain of their shifting weight. Their blood-splattered clothes including boots and hats were strewn about the willows lining the creek.

Colter felt sick to his stomach as he stared up at them, their eyelids heavy in death.

Spurr clucked his disgust. "Nolan and Strong. Shot 'em and stripped 'em, hung up as a warning for others."

Colter looked at the men again. He wouldn't have recognized the two bodies if Spurr hadn't named them. Death had leeched out their distinguishing characteristics, so that now they were just two dead human bodies looking grisly and terrible as the breeze nudged them this way and that, their stark, pale feet brushing the tops of the blond needlegrass. Strong's right big toe was purple — likely a horse had stepped on it some time ago.

The body of Constable Nolan twisted around to face Colter with its slitted eyes reflecting the afternoon light and the man's thick brown hair curling down over his ears. Colter turned away to stare southwest along the valley.

Again, his gut tightened as he made out the black smoke billowing up from behind a fir-covered southern ridge jutting into the canyon, between him and the ranch. He threw out an arm. "Look!"

He and Spurr both put the steel to their

mounts, lunging into lurching, hard-thudding gallops. Colter's heart raced. He knew the men were dead, but he'd still been terrified of seeing it all again. He'd dreaded learning of Pearl's fate. Something had told him he'd find her slumped in the cabin with Cimarron, Shanley, and Dawson, but he knew now he'd imagined it all wrong.

As he and Spurr rode hard around the ridge and then plunged across the creek, they slipped their rifles from their scabbards. As they rode under the Diamond Bar portal and past the corral on their right, they could feel the heat of the burning cabin. The pops of the burning resin sounded like the reports of small-caliber pistols.

Nothing. He'd find nothing here now. They'd burned it all up.

Colter checked Northwest down and held the reins up taut against his chest. The horse pitched and whinnied at the snapping, crackling flames and the *whoosh* of the fire wind. As the cabin's right wall suddenly shuddered and tumbled inward into the swirling orange conflagaration, the horse reared sharply, and Colter gigged him farther back toward where the bunkhouse hunched in grim silence.

The gold . . .

Colter neck-reined Northwest around sharply, then gigged him into a trot, tracing a broad circle around the burning cabin and into the pines behind it. He reined up again when he saw the stone boat sitting several feet from the cellar, the cellar door lying back away from the gaping, black hole.

Clucking to the horse once more, Colter galloped back around to the front of the cabin. Spurr was riding back and forth across the yard on his nervous roan, keeping the horse's head up with a tight rein while he himself leaned out from his saddle, scouring the ground with his eyes.

"They got the loot!" Colter yelled above the fire, the smoke making his eyes water.

Spurr reined his horse around suddenly and rode off toward the creek, continuing to scour the ground with his eyes before he rode back into the yard and put the roan up beside Northwest. Colter was staring at the fire, his heart both sick and burning with fury. Could he smell the bodies burning in there or was it just his imagination? Likely, they were all burned up by now.

Was Pearl in there, too? Nothing but melting flesh and charred bones . . .

Spurr set his carbine across his saddle-bows and leaned forward against the horn. "How many were with La Brie?"

Colter couldn't help venting his impatience at the lawman's question. "I done already told you they were six!"

Spurr returned his calm gaze to the cabin. "Seven rode out of here a little over an hour ago."

Colter jerked a surprised look at him. "You think Pearl's alive?"

"All I'm sayin' is seven riders rode back out under that portal a little over an hour ago. And they had someone staked out on the ground last night."

"What?"

"Look down."

Colter looked at the ground. Not far off his right stirrup fender, four stakes poked several inches out of the pocked and scuffed dust of the yard, two broken off at ground level.

Colter looked at the cabin. "Pearl," he muttered. His heartbeat increased, and urgency raked him. "Pearl's gotta be with 'em."

"Maybe."

"Maybe, hell! Who else could it be?" Colter reined Northwest around to face the portal. "Let's get after the sons o' bitches!"

Before he could put steel to the dun, Spurr reached out and grabbed Northwest's bridle, hauling horse and rider up short.

Colter cast an exasperated look at the old lout, but something in Spurr's hard, level gaze rendered his objection stillborn on his tongue.

"We rest the horses one half hour," Spurr said evenly. "Otherwise, we'll never catch 'em. You understand me now, Colter Farrow, or do I need to get my ankle chains out?"

Gradually, the taut muscles in Colter's face slackened. He gave his mind enough rein to remember his promise to toe Spurr's line, and to realize the wily old lawman was right.

Northwest was nearly blown from the ride out there, as was the roan, and they wouldn't catch the gang afoot. He hated the idea of the gang, with Pearl in tow, moving farther and farther away from him, but maybe Spurr wasn't quite as beat-up and burnt-out as he looked.

Colter blew a hard sigh and reluctantly swung down from his saddle.

CHAPTER 21

Three days from the Diamond Bar, La Brie's bunch with the gold and Pearl in tow drifted up into the higher reaches of the Cheyennes, where the nights were so cold the water in their canteens remained frozen until several hours after sunup. The pines were mixed with turning aspens, and the rivers ran hard and fast through their rocky chasms.

Pearl wasn't sure where the gang was headed. She'd thought she'd heard one of the men mention Laramie, but that couldn't be their final destination.

Likely, they intended to hop the train there and head as far from this country as they could, probably make their way to the West Coast or Mexico, where they could spend the stolen loot in relative peace. She often found herself wondering what they would do with her once they reached Laramie, but she tried to keep such thoughts from her mind.

Cimarron had had a saying in the fall when they were busy with the roundup and again in the spring when they were calving: "One job o' work at a time."

For now, her main job was figuring out how to get away from the gang despite their keeping her wrists tied to her horse's saddle horn and watching her closely every minute of every day, even making her sleep with her wrists tied together, her ankles tied to a tree. It was Cimarron's horse that La Brie had ridden down for Pearl to ride. So not only was she stuck in the company of the killers who'd killed Cimarron, but she'd been condemned to ride Cimarron's horse, Hair Trigger, who constantly reminded her of Cimarron himself until she often found herself with an apple-sized knot in her throat and tears dribbling down her dusty cheeks.

Farther and farther the killers hauled her away from the Diamond Bar, with no one to help her but herself. Nevertheless, she often found herself glancing back along their back trail, as though half expecting to find Colter behind her. Likely, the young Colorado drover was dead. He'd probably ridden away from the cabin that horrible morning, wounded, and died in a ravine somewhere.

If he'd managed to survive, Pearl was sure he'd try to rescue her. But rescuing her from killers such as these would be impossible for anything but a small army of gun-savvy men.

She was alone out here. She doubted the gang would take her beyond Laramie. The only reason they'd kept her alive this long was for the amusement of La Brie. She had to find a way, alone, to free herself. It wouldn't be easy, and she'd probably die doing it, because she did not intend to leave without first killing La Brie.

Without first cutting the killer's throat from ear to ear and allowing him the horror of watching her smile down at him as he bled himself dry.

She had to be patient and careful, wait for just the right moment to spring her trap. That moment came sooner than she'd expected — or what she thought was that moment. . . .

"We'll stop here and build a coffee fire, rest the horses," La Brie shouted back over his shoulder at the others as they approached a broad horseshoe in the river they'd been following.

" 'Bout time, brother," Mercy said, riding directly behind Pearl, who was straddling

Hair Trigger directly behind La Brie. The outlaw boss was leading the horse by a rope clipped to its halter. "My ass has about grown into this saddle."

A couple of the men snickered. Mercy turned to them, fire in her eyes. "Shut up, you mangy coyotes! My ass ain't no bigger than a girl's ass oughta be. That squaw's hindquarters wouldn't please no man where I come from. Why, up in Moose Jaw, real men like their women big, round, and warm!"

Mercy laughed her grating, raspy laugh, causing Pearl to grind her jaws. The only one of the bunch she wanted to kill worse than La Brie was La Brie's sister. Not only because she was the most grating, ugly bitch that Pearl had ever known, but because the fat, mannish woman always tied Pearl's wrists so tight it was hard for her to sleep at night.

She had to hand it to the woman, however. She made it known she didn't want to see Pearl taken by force. Though this sentiment mostly stemmed from jealousy — it was obvious that Mercy would have shared her blankets with any of them, possibly even her brother, but none of them would have her — she kept the men away from Pearl. Once, when La Brie had disappeared for a couple of hours, scouting their back trail, Mercy had kept Yukon from following Pearl during a nature call by the point of both her guns.

"Forget it, Yukon," Mercy had warned, clicking both gun hammers back. "If you're gonna take that rock-worshippin' heathen squaw, you gotta take me first!"

Yukon had drifted on back to the coffee fire.

Now, as Mercy and the men except for La Brie dismounted at the edge of the thick brush bordering an aspen copse, then led their mounts into the woods, La Brie stepped down from his bay and tied Hair Trigger's lead rope to his saddle horn. He glanced at Pearl out the corner of his eye.

"How you doin' up there, Miss Pearl?"

Pearl let the vaguely taunting question go. She had other things on her mind as she watched the others lead their horses off into the woods. "You have a first name, La Brie?"

"Yep."

"What is it?"

La Brie walked back to Hair Trigger and squinted one eye up at Pearl from the shading brim of his Stetson. "Why should I tell you?"

"I don't know." Pearl innocently hiked her shoulder. She pitched her voice with a coquettish sauciness as she looked off with a bored, tired air. "Just curious. Never mind."

La Brie cut her wrists free of the horn. "Skylar. I go by Sky to them's I'm on a first-name basis with."

He kept squinting an eye at her with interest. "You thinkin' you're ready to start callin' me by my first name?" He let the un-squinted eye drift down to Pearl's well-filled wool shirt under which she wore only a thin cotton camisole. She also wore an unbuttoned old wolf coat, tassled buckskin breeches, and moccasins — all of which she'd pulled out of the cabin before the killers had set fire to it.

Pearl pulled her wrists away from the apple, rubbing them. "I reckon it depends on what a girl has to do to start callin' you by your first name." She let that hang there, obliquely, and enjoyed the slight flush it lifted in the killer's face. She jerked her head toward the stream. "I think I'll just wander over there and have a scrub."

La Brie backed away from her horse as Pearl swung down from Cimarron's saddle, her right thigh nudging the empty scabbard. What she wouldn't give to get her hands on a gun . . . La Brie stepped toward her, planting both hands on her saddle, on either side of her, pinning her against the horse.

He smiled his snaky smile, the pupils of his gray-green eyes expanding and contracting, catlike. "You think I'm just gonna let you wander off alone? Without no chaperone?" He smiled at his rhyme.

"Where'm I gonna run? Hell, I'm safer with your bunch than bein' on foot alone out here."

"You know — I like the way you curse."

"I bet you say that to all the girls."

He placed the palm of his left hand on her right breast, lifting it slightly. "Only the ones that fill their blouses nice."

She flicked his hand away with her forearm and turned to dig into her saddlebags for a bar of soap and a gunnysack.

"Come on, Miss Pearl. I never been with a squaw. Well, there was a fat one up in Devil's Lake, but she weren't like you."

"We squaws are right picky about who we throw in with." Pearl tossed her hair as she swung around and started striding off down toward the river, aware of how her hips swung, drawing the seat of her buckskins taut across each buttock in turn.

"You might need help!" La Brie called behind her.

Swinging around and walking backward a few steps, Pearl said, "It'd take more man than you" — she let her eyes flicker across his crotch — "to help a girl like me."

Tossing her hair again, she swung back around and continued strolling toward the stream, chewing her bottom lip, hoping he didn't suspect what she had planned for him.

Behind her, he gave a lusty chuckle. Then he whistled. Moving through the rustling trees, Pearl kept her head forward and allowed herself a smile. With a man like La Brie, you couldn't overplay it. Such a man was so full of himself that he'd never get into a woman's mind long enough to know what she needed from him, what she desired, dreamed about, what she really thought about him, or how she planned to kill him.

A man like La Brie deserved exactly the bloody, howling death she had planned for him. It wouldn't be until after he was shaking hands with the devil himself that he'd start to realize he'd been hornswoggled.

Pearl did not look back as she continued through the trees and onto the rocks along the shallow, tea-colored stream that ruffled over stones and around branch snags. She could hear the other men talking and laughing and Mercy occasionally joining in the conversation in her raucous voice that was always raised either in anger or sarcasm.

Pearl couldn't see La Brie's eyes on her. But she could feel them.

She felt her mouth corners rise in a devilish smile as she began unbuttoning the wool shirt. Facing the stream, she slid the shirt off her shoulders but did not yet shed the light cotton camisole that hung down low on her chest, exposing nearly all of her ample breasts. She kicked out of her moccasins, one after another, then sat down on a rock near the edge of the stream and slowly, deliberately removed her gray wool socks.

When her feet were bare, she sat up slightly from the rock and pulled her buckskin pants down beneath her rump. Settling herself back on top of the rock, she curled both legs out in front of her and squirmed around a little, sliding the skintight breeches down her thighs. When she had them down around her calves, she gave them a kick, and they fell in the rocks near the water's edge.

Pearl wore only a pair of thin cotton underwear under the breeches. They hiked up high on her thighs as she extended her long, golden brown legs out in front of her again, stretching the muscles and waggling her feet, enjoying the warmth of the sun on her bare skin, which shone like polished cherry wood. Shaking her hair back, she stood and finally pulled the camisole up over her head. She tossed the garment on top of her breeches and felt her long, straight black hair tumble down her shoulders and back, enjoying the light rake of it on her bare skin.

She stared at the water, pricking her ears to listen around her. Hearing nothing but the laughter and conversational voices coming from over where the gang was unsaddling their horses and building a coffee fire, but sure that La Brie was around here somewhere, Pearl cupped the tips of her breasts in her palms and shoved them up against her chest.

She looked down to see them bulging out around her palms. They were good, heavy, well-formed breasts. Even tressed up behind coarse wool or red calico working shirts, they'd drawn the admiring stares of many men.

She just hoped she was drawing the stare and raising the body temperture of the man she wished to kill.

Pearl stepped into the water and bit her tongue at the stinging chill. She took another step, feeling the cold water rise up her shins. After a minute, she started getting used to it. The nights were cold up here, but the water was shallow and the sun shone on it most of the day, warming it. She could stand it. After all, she'd often enjoyed bathing in Diamond Creek when it was swollen with fast-rushing snowmelt in the spring — a pleasure she'd acquired from Cimarron, who'd rarely bathed in the winter and felt the icy spring water was a good way to get his winter-strangled circulation popping and sputtering through his aging veins again.

She walked out a good twenty yards into the stream, her feet sliding off the polished stones, then turned to face the shore she'd just left, and sank down into a sandy patch of stream bottom between two large pale rocks. The cold water covered her thighs and crotch, making her light-headed and pinching her lungs. The sandy bottom coupled with the icy water soothed her saddle-sore rump, raking it delightfully, working the blood back into it.

She took only passing notice of these sensations. Her mind was on La Brie.

Her eyes raked the rocky shore and the knee-high grass, but there were only the breeze-brushed aspens. He wasn't there. Frowning, wondering whether she had gone through this charade for nothing, she slid her gaze left along the shoreline to where she could see pale smoke rising from low flames about thirty yards in from the river and another forty or fifty yards upstream. The men and Mercy were moving around the fire, tossing down their gear.

Pearl probed the figures, looking for La Brie's long, silver-brown hair hanging straight down from beneath his cream Stetson banded with silver conchos.

"Lookin' for someone?"

La Brie's voice swiveled her head back right, where the outlaw leader was just now stepping out from behind a wagon-sized boulder clad in only his long-handles, hat, and socks. He had his cartridge belt looped over his right shoulder. He leaned his rifle against the boulder and walked out across the rocks to the edge of the water, where he set his holstered .45s and shell belt down. Smiling lasciviously at Pearl sitting in the water and cupping her breasts in her hands, he tossed his hat down on the guns and began unbuttoning his long-handles.

Pearl looked at the pistols, quickly looked away from them to La Brie, her heartbeat quickening. She fashioned a sidelong, flirtatious smile. "Don't get any ideas. I told you — there's only a certain kinda man who can satisfy a girl like me."

"That right?"

"That's right."

"And just what kinda man is that if it ain't me?" La Brie stepped out of the long-handles and kicked them away, glanced down past his belly to his jutting dong. "Huh? You just tell me. I don't see no Hunkpoppy braves around here anywheres. And I know how you Injun girls are. Less'n you're gettin' it regular, you get fidgety as a damn bobcat in the springtime."

Pearl looked at him. She manufactured an impressed look and, keeping her eyes on the man's crotch, slowly lowered her hands from her breasts, giving him a good, full view.

"I don't know." Pearl kicked at the water, now looking coy. "Maybe . . . but. . . ."

"Maybe but hell!" La Brie walked into the water, taking long strides and swinging his arms back for balance, hardening his jaw at the cold inching up his flour white legs. "I'm gettin' a little tired of your foolishness, girl. When I get my hands on you . . ."

Pearl feigned shock and fear, snapping her eyes wide, and heaving herself to her feet. "Wait, now, I never said —"

She started toward the far side of the stream. La Brie grabbed her arm and jerked her back around. "You might not have said it out loud, but I seen it in your eyes when I

290

first laid eyes on you. You're Injun all over." He placed a brash hand on her, clamping the other hand against the back of her neck and holding her head so that she was looking straight into his eyes. "I killed the man who raised you. Still . . ." He let a fascinated, beguiled grin play across his thin lips. ". . . you were thinkin' about your wild squaw needs."

Rage stoked a fire behind Pearl's heart. She suppressed it and grabbed him down below, gently squeezing, letting her anger harden her jaw so it looked like untrammeled lust. "You gonna stand here all day chinning, or we gonna get down to it?"

La Brie laughed, his eyes narrowing at her expert manipulation of his manhood.

She released him, stepped back. "I like it in the water." She jerked her head toward the gurgling stream.

La Brie laughed again and dropped to his hands and knees. Pearl, taking charge, pushed him back down on his ass, then straddled him, casting a hard, devilish grin at him. His eyes were wide with want as they raked across her golden brown body with the hard, upthrust breasts.

"All right," he rasped. "This how you like it? Okay, girl. That's just fine with me."

Pearl sank down on top of him, then

291

leaned forward on her knees, reaching between her legs to find him. At the same time, she dipped her right hand into the river, felt around for a rock.

La Brie was grinning dreamily and dropping his chin toward his chest to watch her other hand. Suddenly, just before she slipped him into her, she raised her right hand. The fist-sized rock in her palm dripped water.

She gritted her teeth. Her black eyes flashed savagely.

La Brie's eyes found the rock, and widened. He opened his mouth to scream, but before he could get a sound out, Pearl grunted and swung her arm down.

Smack!

She'd struck his temple so hard that the rock slipped out of her hand and plopped into the water. The blow had jerked La Brie's head to one side, his face instantly turning pale. His eyes fluttered and he tried raising his hands to his head, but they appeared too heavy for him. They dropped into the water. Pearl looked around for another rock. She'd smash his head to a bloody pulp before she . . .

A yell from the direction of the camp broke off her thoughts, distracted her. She hadn't been able to make out what the yeller had yelled, as the river was too loud, but she turned with a gasp to look back through the brush and trees. All she could see was pale smoke unraveling against the branches, and a few hatted heads jostling around the coffee fire.

Pearl's heart was turning somersaults. She was cold and frightened and hadn't planned what she'd do after she'd killed La Brie. Maybe she really hadn't figured she'd get this far.

She rose from the man's belly, staring down at him. He lolled sideways in the water, groaning and blinking his eyes, scissoring his white legs slowly as though in a futile effort to stand. His left temple was turning purple, but there was only a small trickle of blood dribbling down over that eye.

Pearl gave up looking for another rock to strike him with. She'd get dressed and grab his gun and finish him with the gun, then hide out in the brush on the other side of the creek and pick off the rest of his gang one by one as they came for her. Crouching so she wouldn't be seen from the camp, Pearl hurried back to shore, casting anxious glances at La Brie.

She'd let him lie there in agony for a while. He was too addled to call out.

She hoped the image of that rock smashing down against his forehead was being played out over and over again behind his eyes.

When her feet hit dry land, she turned her head forward.

She stopped suddenly, her jaw dropping in shock.

The black man, Tenbow Preston, stood only a few feet away, arms crossed on his chest. He was grinning so broadly that she could see nearly all of his bone white teeth.

CHAPTER 22

"Mercy sent me out here to see what you and her brother was up to." Preston's voice was deep and resonant, threatening.

Grinning, he stared over Pearl's bare right shoulder to where La Brie was still lolling, half conscious, in the river.

"You kill him?" Preston wanted to know.

Pearl just stared at him as she stood, naked and wet, at the edge of the shore. In the corner of her eyes, she saw La Brie's pistols and shell belt.

"Don't worry," the black man said. "I don't mind. If he's dead, that's just one less man I gotta worry about splittin' the gold with. Never cared for La Brie, anyway. Too damn bossy." His black eyes scuttled down and up Pearl's dripping body. "But he sure had some fine taste in female flesh."

As Preston moved toward Pearl, Pearl lunged away and dove for one of La Brie's pistols. She'd just gotten her hands on it when Preston wrapped a strong hand around her arm and jerked her around so violently that her hand slipped off the .45's ivory grips.

On her back, Pearl stared up at Preston, who scowled down at her. He hadn't filled his hands with any of the three pistols bristling on his stocky frame that was clad in brown leggings, white pin-striped shirt, and billowy red neckerchief. His eyes bored into hers, and then suddenly he doffed his brown hat and began unknotting the neckerchief.

"Think I'll give ya a try my own sel—"

The man's word was clipped by a soft plunking sound. The top of his head exploded, blood geysering across Pearl's legs and onto the rocks beside her. Preston nodded his head as though he couldn't agree more with something Pearl had said, and then his knees buckled.

The whip-crack of the rifle that had killed him echoed across the chuckling stream, and Pearl scrambled sideways as Preston tumbled straight forward and piled up on the rocks and sand where she'd been sprawled a second before.

His body quivered, legs kicking, arms flopping wildly.

Someone from the direction of the camp

yelled. It sounded like Mercy's screeching voice.

Pearl looked across the stream, confused and disoriented from all that had happened coupled with the chill of the early-autumn breeze raking her wet flesh, and saw a man in buckskin pants and elk-skin vest hunkered on one knee and pumping a fresh shell into his rifle. He had a gray-brown beard, and it was hard to tell from this distance, but his face under the funneled brim of his tobacco-colored hat looked craggy and gaunt.

Pearl had no idea who he was, and she didn't have time to think about it, because a second man — this one on a blaze-faced coyote dun — was galloping across the stream, heading toward her. Not a man. A kid in suspenders, brush-scarred chaps, and blanket coat, a floppy-brimmed brown hat on his head. His left cheek was badly marked.

Pearl stared and worked her lips silently. "Colter Farrow . . ."

Now several men in addition to Mercy were shouting from the direction of the camp. The man on the other side of the screen — Marshal Spurr, she suddenly realized, not having seen him in a year or two — was levering and firing the Winchester that leaped and roared in his hands as he laid down covering fire for Colter.

The coyote dun approached Pearl, splashing water up high around its rider's head, and Colter yelled, "Pearl, come on!"

"Wait!"

As the horse leaped onto the shore and Colter extended a hand to her, Pearl quickly dropped her camisole over her head, covering her breasts, then quickly gathered up the rest of her clothes.

"Forget 'em!" Colter was casting nervous glances back toward the fire from which direction pistols and rifles were beginning to pop.

Pearl grabbed her wolf coat, then threw her hand toward Colter's hand as the horse pranced and snorted as it curveted at the edge of the water. Remembering La Brie's shell belt and guns, Pearl snapped her hand back down. It was a compulsive move, but she desperately wanted a gun, and what better gun than the killer's own prized shooting irons?

From the other side of the stream, Spurr shouted in his gravelly voice, "What the hell are you *doin'* over there?" He was punching fresh cartridges into his Winchester from his shell belt while several bullets punked into the water before him and off the rocks around him.

Colter's eyes flashed with exasperation as he shook his outstretched hand at her. *"Pearl!"*

Slinging the shell belt and both holstered pistols over her shoulder and clutching her bundle of clothes under the same arm, Pearl ran over to Colter and flung her hand into his. At the same time, she thrust her knee against the dun's belly. Colter put the steel to Northwest's flanks and jerked the horse back into the stream, and Pearl swung up onto the horse's rump and Colter's bedroll.

As the horse plunged back into the river where Spurr was now firing from behind a large boulder a ways farther upstream, Colter felt a hot slug curl the air just inches in front of his face. Northwest felt it, too, and shook his head.

"Keep your head down!" Colter shouted at Pearl, whose arms he could feel tightly around him with the soft lump of her clothes wedged between them.

As Northwest lunged up the opposite bank about twenty yards downstream from Spurr, more bullets hammered the ground around him. One bullet broke a twig off the aspen branch over Spurr's head.

"Come on!" Colter urged.

"Keep goin'!" Spurr triggered two more

quick shots toward the killers lunging and dodging in the weeds and trees on the stream's other side. He looked over his shoulder at Colter, who'd slowed down, and jerked his thumb to indicate the high, rocky hill beyond the river. "Head straight up that ridge and keep goin'! I'll be right behind ya!"

Colter put the spurs to Northwest once more, and the horse lunged off its rear hooves, first heading straight up the ridge, then angling for easier going. The terrain was rocky with tufts of yucca and sage, but the mustang had been bred in the Lunatic Mountains, and it was broad-barreled, stout-legged, and surefooted. Colter let it pick its own way, hearing the occasional screech of lead just behind him, and the spangs of errant rounds ricocheting off rocks.

The horse lunged, digging its front hooves into the chalky soil, blowing, the tack squawking, stones rattling down the hill behind them. Pearl's body felt good behind Colter — warm and reassuring. He'd thought he'd find her dead. He could hear her grunting and sighing with each of the horse's hard lunges and sudden swerves around a cactus patch or a large rock. The breeze blew her wet hair against the back of his neck, cooling him.

When they were nearly to the top of the ridge, Colter looked down their back trail. Spurr was riding up the slope behind him, reins in his teeth, letting the big roan pick its own way. Spurr himself was hipped around in his saddle, shooting at the killers, who were now running out into the stream, firing and yelling and cursing at the tops of their lungs. Clutching his saddle hard with both knees, Spurr rammed a fresh shell into his old Winchester, raised the rifle to his shoulder, and snapped off another shot.

One of the men running into the stream yelped and grabbed his knee.

Colter turned forward to peer over Northwest's bobbing head as the horse climbed up onto the lip of the ridge. The young drover snorted and shook his head at the old lawman's grit. Pearl must have felt the same way.

"I never knew he could ride and shoot like that," she said a little breathlessly in Colter's right ear.

"You know Spurr?"

"Who doesn't know Spurr? I heard the whores and bartenders knew him better than anyone."

Colter shook his head again as Northwest lunged off in a lope onto the tableland that stretched off across the top of the ridge, away from the canyon and the stream behind him. As much to himself as to Pearl, he said with pensive amazement, "Don't sell that old mossy-horn short."

The tableland was treeless, with short, wiry, brown grass and occasional tufts of mountain sage and wildflowers. That was everything up here — grass, sage, and a vault of silver-blue sky. The mesa or plateau they were on seemed to stretch away to the far end of the earth.

"How'd you catch up to us?" Pearl asked above Northwest's thudding hooves.

"Spurr ain't a bad tracker, neither."

She was silent a moment. He could feel her weight shift as she turned to peer behind them. Then she leaned toward him once more to say into his ear, her voice pitched with concern: "Hey, did you see La Brie in the water?"

"The only two people I saw was you and the black man Spurr perforated with his Winchester."

Pearl looked behind her once more, a chill running up her spine. In her confusion and panic, she'd forgotten to look around for La Brie after Colter had pulled her onto Northwest's back. Surely he was still in the stream. Dead. Maybe as the life left him, the river had washed him downstream.

Damn, she wished now she'd have given him one more good smack with that stone.

Shouts behind her swung her gaze to her dust-sifting back trail.

Spurr was galloping toward them, hunkered low in his saddle, the brim of his weather-stained hat pasted against his leathery forehead. He had his rifle in his right hand and he was thrusting it up and forward, jerking the long gun at Pearl and Colter and shouting something Pearl couldn't hear above the wind and the loud raps of Northwest's ground-churning hooves.

Pearl said into Colter's right ear, "I think Spurr's trying to get your attention."

Colter looked back over his right shoulder. The old lawman was about seventy yards behind and gaining on Colter and Pearl, the big roan chewing up the ground and sending large doggets of sod into the air behind it. Colter frowned. Beneath the wind and hoof thuds, he could hear Spurr shouting as the lawman thrust his rifle forward.

Colter looked ahead. The flat plateau stretched on to the distant pearl horizon.

He looked behind once more, muttering, "What the hell's he want?"

"Looks like he wants us to keep going."

"Hell," Colter said, "I wasn't thinkin' about stopping for lunch."

He turned his head forward. His heart sprang up into his throat. His eyes grew wide as saucers.

He'd been wrong about the plateau going on forever. It was opening up in front of him now as though a massive earthquake were splitting the earth in two.

Just as Colter realized that he was galloping right up onto the lip of another, deeper canyon, seeing the dark green furs carpeting the canyon's opposite ridge just down from its lip, he hauled back on Northwest's reins, bellowing, *"Whoooo-awwwww!"*

The horse dug its rear hooves in, giving a shrill, enraged whinny.

Colter said, "Hold on!"

Pearl screamed.

As the horse skidded to a rocking stop, its momentum was like a giant hand thrusting both Colter and Pearl straight up and over the coyote dun's arched neck and lowered head. Colter hit the ground on his bad side, feeling as though someone had smacked his bullet wound with a shovel, and felt the ground churning beneath him as his momentum continued tossing him head over heels toward the canyon.

In the periphery of his vision, he saw

Northwest lose his footing as he tried to turn away from the canyon, and roll.

The horse was suddenly as large as a locomotive barreling toward Colter in a churning cloud of tan-colored dust and gravel and flying sage branches and flapping stirrups. Northwest grunted and snorted beneath the thunder of his heavy, slamming roll, and Colter, who'd stopped his own plunge toward the canyon about six feet from the chasm's lip, saw an iron-shod hoof slash toward him.

He threw himself straight back and sideways, pressing his scarred left cheek to the prickly ground. A hard, hot wind rife with the smell of horse washed over him, blowing his hair.

When he looked up, gasping for a breath and feeling blood oozing from his wounded left side, he looked over to see Northwest climbing heavily to his feet, less than ten feet from Colter. The dun was wide-eyed, indignantly snorting. Colter's saddle hung down beneath its broad belly.

Sucking air through his teeth, Colter sat up, his legs extended before him. Northwest shook, nearly shedding the saddle entirely. Hoof thuds hammered, and Colter looked straight out along his back trail to see Spurr approaching at a hammering gallop before, thirty feet away, pulling back on his own reins and bringing the roan to a hard but far more graceful halt than the one Colter had brought Northwest to.

His red face creased with exasperation, the lawman swung down from his saddle and, holding his rifle low in his right hand, strode bandy-legged and heavy-footed toward Colter. His eyes blazed with fury. *"You hard o' hearin', you loco pup? Didn't you hear me yellin' at you?"*

Colter nodded weakly. "Yeah. Thought . . . you wanted us to go faster. . . ."

Spurr looked around. "Where the hell's Pearl?"

Colter looked around, too. There were only he and Spurr and the two dusty, sweat-lathered horses.

Pearl's strained voice rose, just loudly enough to be heard above the wind rushing up out of the canyon. "Here."

Spurr strode quickly toward the lip of the canyon. Colter pushed himself to his feet, amazed that his legs weren't broken, and followed the lawman. Standing at the canyon's lip, he looked down. His loins tingled, and his stomach flipped over.

The canyon yawned, broad and deep, sucking at him.

Pearl looked up at him, face taut with the

strain of clinging with both hands to the thin knob of rock jutting out from the canyon's sheer, steep wall about fifteen feet down from the toes of Spurr's moccasins.

Her black hair blew around her head in the wind.

"Could you give me a hand up?"

CHAPTER 23

"Hang on, girl!" Spurr ran back to his roan and plucked his lariat from his saddle horn. He was huffing and puffing by the time he'd hustled back to the edge of the cliff and tossed a small loop down to Pearl.

"Don't grab it yet! Wait till I say so."

Colter knelt at the edge of the cliff, his strength waning as blood leaked from his wounded side. He hadn't looked under his shirt, but he must have opened the bullet hole again in that tumble with Pearl and Northwest. What an idiot he was. You'd think he'd been raised on the flatlands, not able to see that canyon moving toward him.

He gazed down at Pearl, silently willing the girl to hold on to the rock ledge on which he could see her fingers turning white from the strain. The small noose dangled beside her left shoulder. She lowered her head, and her dusty camisole blew around in the wind shooting up out of the canyon yawning below and all around her. The garment sort of twisted around her neck, revealing nearly all of her golden brown body hanging there by about four inches of none-too-solid-looking rock.

"Hold on, Pearl," Colter said, watching her fingernails turning as white as her fingers.

Pearl said nothing but continued to hold on in spite of the fact that her fingers seemed to be slipping closer to the edge of the thin stone knob.

Spurr, who was mounting his horse clumsily, twice missed the stirrup before finally poking his boot toe into it.

"Hurry up, damn it!" Colter urged the old lawman.

Spurr's face looked ashen as he swung up into the leather. "Ain't movin' as fast as I once did." Quickly, bunching his lips, he looped the riata around the horn. He looked at Colter and bobbed his head.

Colter jerked another look over the edge. "Grab the rope."

Pearl lifted her chin. Her dark eyes, pinched with strain, found Colter. Maybe gaining some strength from the glance, she closed her upper front teeth over her bottom lip, removed one hand from the stone knob, and swiped it at the noose. She missed, nudged the noose sideways, causing it to swing like a metronome, then flutter in the wind.

"Pearl!"

She tried to grab the rope again with her free hand, and missed. She gasped and groaned and looked down as her free arm dropped to her side, only one hand with not much of a hold saving her from oblivion.

Sucking air through his teeth, Colter grabbed the rope and tried to steady it. "Try again."

Pearl looked up at him once more, then, gritting her teeth, threw her free hand up at the rope again. Colter's chest lightened slightly as he watched her hand close around the rope, just above the loop.

He jerked his head toward Spurr, who was staring back at him anxiously, waiting. "She got it!"

Spurr pulled up and back on Cochise's reins, and the horse began stepping straight backward. Looking back down the canyon wall, Colter saw Pearl wrap her other hand around the rope and clench her jaw as she began moving slowly up the side of the rocky chasm. The camisole fluttered up to reveal her breasts and slightly rounded belly. As her head gained the top of the ridge, her eyes found Colter once more, and she said,

"A gentleman would avert his eyes."

He grabbed one of her arms and then wrapped his own arm around her waist and hauled her up and over the lip of the ridge, calling for Spurr to stop the roan. When the rope slackened and Pearl lay facedown in the wiry grass and gravel a few feet from the edge of the canyon, Colter sat back on his heels, breathing hard.

"Christ, Pearl — I sure am sorry about that."

Pearl was trembling, not caring that she was mostly naked. Her hair had dried and it blew like a large black tumbleweed in the wind that had seemed to have picked up and acquired a chill. She looked up at Colter, and he was surprised to see a wry cast to her eyes. "Don't take this wrong, but next time I need rescuing from savage killers, I think I'll wait for someone else to come along."

She rose onto her knees. He thought for a moment she was going to punch him. But then her eyes softened with the first emotion he'd ever seen in them. Lunging toward the young drover, she threw her arms around Colter's neck, and pressed her lips against the S brand on his cheek.

"But for now," she said with relief, "I reckon you'll do."

Spurr tramped over, looping his lariat over his arm. "You all right, girl?"

"I'll live."

"I hope so," Spurr said. "Two things could get in all our ways." He stared at the western sky that was suddenly as purple as a bushel of ripe plums, arrow-shaped and sliding straight toward them. It was shepherded by a stiff, cold wind that flattened Spurr's hat brim against his forehead and blew his longish hair back from his collar.

"What's the second thing?" Pearl said as she and Colter gained their feet, both wincing with the agony of the pummeling they'd endured.

Spurr swung around to peer back across the plateau. "That there."

Colter and Pearl both turned to stare along their back trail. A billowing dust cloud pushed almost half a dozen horseback riders straight toward them, silhouetted against the dust and sky behind them. As the storm clouds rumbled in the western sky, the thunder of the approaching riders slowly grew within Colter's hearing.

Colter ran over to Northwest and, deeming the horse uninjured except for a few minor scrapes and bruises, began quickly reseating his saddle. He cast an anxious glance at the La Brie bunch bobbing and pitching atop their galloping horses. "They sure got those mounts saddled fast."

"Nah," Spurr grumbled, limping over to his roan and dropping the riata over the saddle horn. "We just got waylaid."

Pearl was gathering the clothes she'd dropped in the fall, as well as La Brie's guns and shell belt. "Who'm I riding with?"

"You best try the kid again, but say your prayers."

Colter rammed a fist against Northwest's side, forcing the horse to let out its breath as he tightened the latigo strap. He looked over his reset saddle at Spurr, who was heaving his withered and bowed frame onto the roan's back. "We gonna stay and fight?"

Spurr turned his horse to face La Brie's bunch. They were within two hundred yards and closing fast.

The lawman's calm voice belied the nerves sparking inside him. "Oh, nah. Five seasoned shooters against a man and two children aren't usually the kinda odds I look for when I'm considerin' a lead swap. Especially with someone of La Brie's killin' caliber."

Colter figured he had that coming, so he kept his mouth shut. Pearl hurried over to him, casting anxious looks at the approaching killers and wondering whether La Brie was one of them.

He couldn't be. She'd let him have it hard with that rock. Maybe not hard enough to kill him but hard enough to put him out of commission for a while.

Colter swung her up behind him, and winced regretfully when he saw the skinning both her legs and one shoulder had taken. Like him, she was dusty from head to toe.

Spurr rode past them, following the uneven line of the canyon lip southward toward the building storm, yelling above the whipping wind that was beginning to blow rain, "Come on, children. We're gonna get us into that canyon by a slightly different route than the one you two just about took!"

As Colter ground his spurs against Northwest's flanks, and they lunged off after the lawman on the big roan, Pearl put her lips up close to Colter's right ear. "He's feelin' good."

"Yeah, downright scrappy. But if he really does know a way into this canyon" — Colter tossed another glance at the gang now thundering to within seventy yards and turning as a group to follow their now-galloping quarry — "I'll likely forgive him for it."

They rode down a slight slope, continuing

to hug the canyon lip from about twenty yards away from it, and then Spurr reined up suddenly nearer the edge, leaning out away from his saddle to peer apprehensively into the chasm. Colter hauled Northwest to a stop beside the lawman.

"There's a trail here." Spurr looked at Colter, then on past him toward the gang, whose hoof thuds now mixed with the building thunder. The sun was still shining on the other side of the canyon, but the clouds were almost over Colter's, Spurr's, and Pearl's side, whipping their hat brims, neckerchiefs, and Pearl's hair. "It ain't a good one. An elk path to the river down there. I took it once, so I know you can make it if you're careful. Of course . . ."

He let his voice trail off as he slipped his rifle from its scabbard and cocked it one-handed.

"Of course what?" Colter inquired.

"Of course I didn't have a passel of blood-hungry lobos nippin' at my heels. Haul ass, junior!"

Spurr stepped down from the saddle, facing the oncoming gang that was unclumping and spreading out slightly, slowing their pace and riding abreast as they drew within fifty yards. Colter eased Northwest over to the canyon edge, saw the trail snaking down

315

the side of the ridge. The slope was far less steep than where Pearl had nearly fallen, but the journey down it would still be a tricky one on a narrow path twisting around boulders and stunt cedars and over large patches of slide rock.

The way the slope laid out, Colter couldn't see much of the trail at all, so there was no telling how the entire ride would be. Dangerous, for sure. Especially riding double. One fall and Colter, Pearl, and Northwest would likely roll all the way to the bottom.

There wasn't much choice.

Colter gigged Northwest ahead. The horse balked a little, then started down, Colter bracing his arms against the apple, feeling Pearl lean back toward the horse's rump, knowing they needed to distribute their weight as best they could. Above them, thunder clapped. Lightning flashed all around in the purple sky, and the rain was starting to slash.

That's all they needed — rain to make a perilous trail even more dangerous.

As his and Pearl's heads dropped beneath the plateau, Colter glanced back and up toward Spurr but couldn't see him atop the ridge wall. There was a rifle crack and then another. They were followed by the cracks of several more distant guns. Beneath the intermittent thunder clamps, Colter could hear the rumble of oncoming hooves.

Colter's gut tightened as he swung his head to look over the bobbing head of his horse. Northwest was handling the steep trail in expert, surefooted fashion. Only when they made a talus slide that had become extra slippery from the rain that was beginning to hammer, did the horse slip. Northwest shook his head but continued, and when they were past the slide, Colter heaved a relieved sigh.

Behind him, he felt Pearl do the same.

As they turned down another switchback in the game trail and were about to pass through a nest of large boulders humping on the upslope, Colter cast a look back up toward the ridge crest, squinting his eyes against the rain that was pelting his face and funneling off his hat brim. The gunfire beneath the thunder and the roaring rain sounded like distant knuckles popping. He couldn't see the ridge crest because of a low cloud, and anxiety pinched his belly.

"Spurr!" Colter yelled.

Just then, as if answering the young man's summons, the old lawman and the big roan galloped down out of the cloud, Spurr hunkered low in his saddle, holding his rifle across the cantle and giving his horse its head. Rain dribbled down over the man's craggy red face from his hat's funneled brim.

Spurr and the roan barreled down the ridge and across the talus patch at such a fast clip that Colter gritted his teeth, certain that the horse would lose his footing and he and Spurr would tumble straight down into the canyon.

Colter had stopped Northwest behind a boulder, and he could hear the roan's hooves clacking on the wet rocks as the roan and Spurr wheeled down the last switch-back and came hammering toward him and Pearl. Colter's face slackened, amazed at the lawman's wicked riding.

Spurr galloped past them, giving a whoop as he leveled out on the canyon bottom. He shouted above the thunder and hammering rain, "What the hell you two waitin' for — *Halloween?* Bad men on our trail. Let's go, children!"

CHAPTER 24

Colter put the spurs to Northwest, and the dun whinnied anxiously as it raced down the last stretch of trail and leaped onto the canyon bottom between two large cedar trees. Colter could see the river ahead of him sheathed in pines, aspens, and firs that thrashed and creaked in the wind and the screening rain.

Spurr raced upstream along a trail on the outside of the trees. Colter put the dun after him.

"The son of a bitch's crazy . . . treatin' a horse like that in this weather," he grumbled as the canyon walls tightened around him, blocking out what little light the storm was letting into the canyon.

As they thundered into a heavy stand of pines, he cast a look behind him to see several jostling horseback figures hammering toward him. Pinpricks of red light flashed. As the rifle reports flatted off the canyon walls, a slug thumped into a tree bole to his left. Behind him, Pearl clenched her half-naked body and tightened her arms around his waist.

Colter turned forward again and ducked his head low. Spurr was galloping a dozen yards ahead of him. As they followed the twisting canyon trail through pines, lightning bolts hammered the sides of the walls a hundred feet up and lower. The smell of brimstone filled the damp air.

The rain plopped into puddles. The wind thrashed the trees — a chill wind that must have penetrated deep into Pearl's bones. Colter felt her shivering and pressing her body hard against his. They had to stop soon and let her get dressed or she'd freeze to death. But if they stopped now, with La Brie's bunch dogging them like the devil's hounds, they'd have one hell of a battle on their hands.

Pearl wasn't dressed for a fight and Colter felt weak and sick from the open hole in his side.

Suddenly, the trail forked. Spurr took the fork's left tine into an intersecting canyon.

The trail widened, and Colter saw another stream push up on his right. Shortly, they angled away from the stream and rose up a pass that was steep enough to slow Northwest down and cause the horse to lunge harder, blowing, his muscles straining.

Behind Colter, guns popped. Men shouted. Shod hooves clacked on the canyon's stone floor.

Spurr, Colter, and Pearl dropped down the other side of the pass. Spurr checked the big roan and slid quickly down from his saddle. Northwest's momentum pushed Colter and Pearl a little past the roan. When Colter got the horse stopped, he turned to see Spurr jog back to a slight bend in the trail, drop to a knee, and raise his Winchester to his shoulder.

Behind Spurr, shadows jostled as the gang galloped around the bend. Spurr whooped and hollered. The Winchester leaped and roared in his hands, the maw stabbing smoke and flames into the storm's dusky grimness.

When the old lawman had fired off eight or nine rounds, likely emptying his chamber, he snapped a look over his shoulder. "Get dressed, girl!"

As Pearl clambered down from Northwest's back, her bundle of clothes in her arms, Spurr turned forward again, staring in the direction of the gang that he seemed to have held at bay for the time being, and quickly plucked fresh shells from his double cartridge belts. He slid them into the Winchester's chamber.

As Pearl dressed in the driving rain, Colter ran back to where Spurr was hunkered down under a knob of shrub-studded rock jutting into the canyon over the lawman's head. Colter racked a shell into his Henry's breech and was about to fire when he saw a rider wheel his horse around and, hunkering low in his saddle, ride back around a bend and out of sight.

Spurr glanced back at Pearl, who'd pulled her shirt on but was struggling with her buckskin breeches, hopping around on one foot and trying to balance between the roan and Northwest.

"Help her," Spurr told Colter. Then he smiled. "I would but my ticker wouldn't take it. When she's ready, we're gonna ride like bats out of hell down this canyon and up a trail I know."

Colter began to rise but jerked back down when a lightning bolt blasted into the ridge just ahead and above them fifty or sixty feet. Rocks rained down, peppering the narrow trace in front of them.

He turned to Spurr, who was staring down the canyon. "Maybe we'd best hole up, wait out the storm."

"That's likely what La Brie'll do . . . now that I put the idea in his head." Spurr chuckled. He looked gaunt and pale, but his eyes were wild.

Colter went back to where Pearl had finally gotten her pants on. "That crazy bastard has La Brie pinned down back there. He sent me back to help you get dressed."

Pearl's blue lips were quivering. Her hair was plastered straight down against her head and shoulders. She looked miserable but she shot him a grim smile as she slapped one of her moccasins against his chest, then stepped into the other one. "You've seen enough of me to hold you for a while."

Colter smiled in spite of his own misery. "Maybe a little while."

When Pearl had gotten both moccasins on as well as her wolf coat, Spurr strode quickly toward them. He opened his mouth to yell something when he stopped suddenly, dropped his rifle, and grabbed his left arm. He made a pained expression, spreading his lips back from his teeth, and staggered backward.

Colter and Pearl ran over to him, each taking an arm. Colter raised his voice above the storm: "Your heart again?"

"It ain't gas." Spurr glanced at the jutting

ledge, which offered relative shelter from the driving rain. "Get me over there — sit me down. Don't forget my rifle."

Colter picked up the lawman's rifle. Then he and Pearl guided him under the dripping ledge. Spurr sat down on a rock, bunching his lips and looking even paler than before. He chewed off a glove and reached into a shirt pocket for a small canvas pouch. He knocked a pill out of the pouch and into his other, gloved hand, and popped the tablet into his mouth.

"Should wash this down with a shot of whiskey," he grunted, wincing as another chest pain bit him deep. "No time for hooch. If I kick off, you two head straight up and out of this canyon. Leads into a valley. Light a shuck out of here. You try tanglin' with this bunch on your own, you'll only be feedin' the bobcats."

Colter had been staring out from beneath the ledge. He saw a hatted head lean out away from the side of the canyon, just beyond the bedge, and, dropping to one knee, he fired three quick rounds. The bullets slammed off the rock wall, echoing loudly.

The man's head jerked back against the canyon wall.

Kneeling beside the lawman, Pearl said, "I

don't think any of us plan to go anywhere until this bunch is feedin' the bobcats, Spurr."

Spurr nodded as he sucked the pill. "I figured as much. Just trying to impart some wisdom on a coupla foolish hearts." He sighed. "I'm feelin' better now."

"What's in those pills?" Colter asked him.

"Strychnine, likely. Seems to work." The old lawman grabbed his rifle, and Pearl and Colter helped him to his feet. "Let's haul ass. This ain't no place to wage a war. We'll get 'im out in the valley and make him wish his ma never shitted him out in the first place."

Colter tried to help Spurr into his saddle, but the lawman waved him away. As Spurr fired another couple of rounds down-canyon, keeping La Brie's bunch pinned back behind the bend in the wall, he urged the roan forward. Colter swung Pearl up behind him, then kneed Northwest into a trot, seeing in the corner of his eye the girl cast an anxious glance behind them.

Mercy held a wadded-up neckerchief into the stream of rainwater dribbling down over the ledge under which her gang crouched from the storm. She rang some water out of the cloth, then pressed it against her brother's swollen temple, wincing.

"I don't know, brother — that squaw sure tattooed you good. Teach you to go waggin' your pecker around like you was a water witch."

La Brie sat back against the rock wall, panting against the pain in his head. He lifted a bottle to his mouth, took a long pull, then lowered the bottle as several streams of the potent brew dribbled down his chin.

His face was pale and gaunt, dark rings around both eyes. His body felt hot despite being soaked under his riding slicker. "I . . . I can't seem to see nothin' outta my left eye."

Mercy looked into that eye, and a look of deep concern washed across her face. She stared hard, probing the eye with her own.

"What the hell is it?" La Brie asked her. "Still there, ain't it?"

"Yeah . . ." Mercy nodded slowly, then elbowed the young rangy outlaw who was crouched next to her, staring down-canyon, water dribbling off his top hat's narrow brim. "Yukon, take a look at this."

"At what?"

"My brother's eye."

Yukon continued to peer down-canyon, fingering the repeater in his hands. He and Tenbow Preston had been riding the owl-hoot trail together for nearly six years, and Yukon was itching to kill the man who'd drilled a slug through the back of Ten's head. "What about his eye?"

Mercy rammed her elbow against his ribs. "Turn around here and look at it, damn you!"

Yukon snarled and turned, crouching beneath the low ledge but adjusting his head to see into La Brie's pain-racked face. Yukon's lightly beard stubbled face acquired its own anguished look as he studied the outlaw leader's eye. "Damn."

"What the hell is it?" La Brie demanded.

Yukon turned to Beaver Charlie, who was hunkered on his haunches and smoking a quirley while looking toward where the lawman was holed up with the squaw bitch and the scar-faced boy. "Charlie, take a look at this."

Beaver Charlie took a drag from his quirley, then rose to a crouch and angled his head over La Brie's. He shook his own head slowly, the nostrils of his long, slender nose expanding and contracting like that of an animal on a fresh scent. "Jumpin' Jesus. That's just queer."

"What's just queer?" La Brie said, sounding shrill. "Will one of you stupid sons o' bitches please tell me what in the hell is wrong with my eye?"

"Looks like someone's shutterin' a damn window," Yukon opined.

"What?" La Brie squawked, his good eye sparking fiercely.

Mercy dabbed at her brother's forehead again with the wet neckerchief. "It's . . . well, it's . . . turning pale," she said, staring into the eye again. "Sort of milky. You can't see anything out of it at all, brother?"

La Brie looked up with his good eye. It was hard to tell where the other eye was looking exactly because, as Mercy had said, the iris and pupil looked bizarrely bleached out. The outlaw leader held the bottom of the bottle over his good eye and continued to stare at the ceiling of the rock ledge that hovered only about four feet above his head.

"Blinded me." It was part whisper, part rasp. "Bitch blinded my eye."

"Maybe it'll come back," Mercy said with concern, not quite believing it herself. "Maybe it just needs to heal, Skylar. You know what? I think we oughta forget the lawman and the girl and take the gold and head for Mexico. They'll all get theirs, soon enough. Folks like that always do."

"No, they don't." Big Norm walked out of the rain to crouch beneath the ledge, and looked down into La Brie's face. He shook his head, and sighed. "They'll just go back and send a posse after us. I say we hunt 'em down and kill 'em, and *then* hightail it the hell south and west."

La Brie took another hard pull from the bottle. He shuttled his good eye from Big Norm to Yukon and Beaver Charlie. The latter two cutthroaats were looking at him apprehensively, Charlie puffing his quirley. The smoke from the quirley webbed in the darkness beneath the ledge.

"Charlie, Yukon — you boys go see if they're still holed up yondcr."

The two men looked at each other apprehensively.

"Go on, boys," La Brie said, pitching his voice with authority. "Scout 'em out for me."

Yukon nodded, pooching his lips out, his eyes hardening as he remembered seeing his pal Tenbow Preston lying there along the stream, his blood and brains oozing out onto the rocks. "You got it."

He slapped Beaver Charlie's chest as he turned and, hefting his rifle high, edged out from beneath the ledge and began making his way slowly down the canyon. Beaver Charlie glanced once more at La Brie and then at the gold-stuffed saddlebags they'd draped over Preston's saddled horse standing with the others back up the canyon a dozen yards. He sighed, stepped his quirley out in the wet sand, and began moving down-canyon behind Yukon.

La Brie continued to drink from the bottle and stare up with his good eye at the roof of the ledge as his sister swabbed his forehead. Big Norm stood guard with his Sharps carbine and staring up-canyon, squeezing the gun as though to wring water from it. His wet braid flopped down his back from his soggy blue bandanna, like a drowned snake.

It wasn't long before the two scouts returned, both running, breathing hard.

"They've moved," Yukon said, heading for the horses. "Bastards are gettin' away!"

La Brie corked his bottle and pushed himself up from his rock, jaw set with barely contained fury. "Oh, no, they are not."

CHAPTER 25

The rain had lightened to a fine mist, so Spurr did not have to raise his voice overly loud as he hipped himself around in his saddle toward Colter and Pearl. "That's the trail right there. Up through them rocks." He swung down from his saddle, breathing hard, soaked clothes hanging against his stooped frame. "We best lead our mounts. We lose one, our goose is cooked."

Colter reined down Northwest and looked up the side of the canyon wall. It was a sheer sandstone wall except along the very bottom, where he could see a trail snaking among the boulders that had likely dropped long ago from the ridge. The trail appeared to twist upward along a ledge, rising gradually up ahead of them and out of sight.

"How do you know it'll take us out of here?" Colter asked as he began leading Northwest behind Spurr, who'd begun climbing the slight rise, leading the big roan.

" 'Cause I got myself trapped down here by Utes about six years ago. Had a right fine time, pinned down here. Spent three or four days tryin' to get shed of them loco coyotes slatherin' after my topknot till I found this trail. Don't think even them Injuns knew about it."

As they made the bottom of the sheer sandstone wall, they followed the trail along the base of it and around a bend, climbing gradually higher. Several waterfalls slithered down over the ridge above and to their right, splashing onto the rocks below, then snaking down toward the rock- and brush-strewn canyon floor.

The horses slipped on the wet shale. When the trail rose steeply, they slipped even more, and even Colter, Spurr, and Pearl were having trouble keeping their footing. The last fifty feet was the worst stretch. Spurr led the roan up the path with a lot of coaxing and cursing. Northwest dropped to his haunches, then gave a furious whinny and dug his rear hooves into the slick clay as hard as he could, and Colter dropped the reins and stepped aside as the horse bounded up past him and onto the ridge crest.

Colter climbed to the crest then, too, and reached down to give Pearl a hand. As

Northwest shook himself, both horses snorting as they regained their wind, Colter looked around. They were in a valley over which clouds of different shades of gray hung like smoke and gauze. The ridges to either side were low and pine-studded. Straight out away from the canyon, a creek snaked across the valley floor, emptying into the canyon from which they'd just escaped, a hundred yards to Colter's left.

Spurr dropped the roan's reins, walked over to the edge of the canyon, and looked down at the steep trail they'd climbed. The canyon was a narrow, dripping, nasty gash before them, a hundred to a hundred and fifty feet deep, the red clay and sandstone looking darkly wet. The chasm took the shape of a boot as it curved away toward the main canyon.

Pearl, with La Brie's cartridge belt and guns draped over her right shoulder, came up to stand beside Colter, who stood near Spurr, appraising the canyon.

"Might be a good place to take the gang," he suggested. "We could pick 'em off as they tried to climb up out of there."

Spurr shook his head. "They'd just slip back into the canyon as soon as we started tossing lead at 'em. Then they might just decide to call it quits with us and sneak away with the gold. Besides, I'm runnin' low on ammunition." He shook his head again, scratched his gray-streaked chin whiskers. "I know a better way."

The old lawman limped over to his roan. Colter looked down at his own shell belt, counted thirteen cartridges in the small leather loops. That was all the ammo he had on him. He was glad Spurr had thought about that before they'd gotten themselves into a lead swap they couldn't finish.

Glad but not surprised. The old lawman seemed to think of quite a few things. And it was damn sure he had more gravel than Colter had given him credit for.

Pearl must have been thinking the same thing, for she was studying the old lawman with faint admiration in her dark eyes as Spurr grunted and groaned and pulled himself up onto the roan's back.

"I reckon we're moseyin'," Colter said.

La Brie, Mercy, and Big Norm sat their horses at the bottom of the trail the old lawman and the squaw and the scar-faced kid had recently taken up and out of the canyon. On the canyon ridge now, Beaver Charlie and Yukon both looked down at La Brie's group, beckoning.

"All clear!" Yukon's voice echoed eerily in

the sopping canyon.

La Brie was sitting slouched in his saddle, a pain spasm shooting through his battered temple nearly paralyzing him and causing him to ball his pale cheeks and grind his back teeth.

"Brother," Mercy said, sitting her gray-speckled gelding beside him. "You sure you wanna go through with this? Hell, we got the gold. We could head on down to Mexico and get you healed."

"Sure, just run and let them three send for a posse!" Big Norm said, standing beside his beefy buckskin beside La Brie and his sister.

Mercy whipped around. "Shut up, Norm! If I want any shit out o' you, I'll squeeze your big ugly head!"

La Brie turned to his sister. His pale eye had turned even paler, almost eggshell white. That and his gaunt cheeks and pain-racked other eye gave him a horrific, cadaverous look. "For the last time, Mercy," he rasped just loudly enough for her to hear him in spite of the post-storm silence, "I am going to run that squaw bitch down and after I've burned both her eyes out, I'm gonna skin her and bury her up to her neck in a whiskey-soaked anthill."

"Yeah, you mentioned that, brother."

Mercy laughed uneasily. It sounded like the squawk of a hen with a fox in the yard. "At least you still got your spirit. Glad to hear it. Well, then . . ." She nodded at the trail climbing up the canyon wall. "Shall we?"

"After you, sis."

"You better ride first, brother." Judging by how miserable the man looked, Mercy figured he could roll out of his saddle at any time. She'd better ride drag so she could maybe catch him.

La Brie cursed and toed his dun up the trail. When the trace got steep and perilous with mud and eroded gravel, he dismounted and led the beast. Behind him, Mercy and Big Norm did likewise. Cursing and wheezing, his head pounding as if there were a little man inside it wielding a ball-peen hammer, he crawled up out of the canyon a good fifteen minutes later.

Beaver Charlie reached down to give him a hand.

"Get your hands off me," La Brie scolded the man. "Help my sister."

When Beaver Charlie and Yukon had helped the pear-shaped, short-legged Mercy and her gelding up to the crest of the ridge, and Big Norm had climbed up huffing and puffing after them, they all stood staring off across the clouded-over valley. Beaver Charlie had rolled another cigarette, and he was puffing like a steam engine on a long uphill climb.

"Well, their tracks are plain enough." Yukon looked at La Brie. "Sure you're well enough to go on, boss?"

La Brie spat and stepped into his saddle. "I sure wish everybody'd quit worryin' about my health." His good eye bored into both Yukon and Beaver Charlie. "Unless it ain't really my health you're worried about, but maybe how I might slow you down. I know you, Yukon. You and Preston both thought you could lead this outfit just as well as me. Been thinkin' that ever since we left Kansas with the gold. I could tell it in your eyes. Only got worse after that mixup with my brother and cousins not findin' the right roadhouse we was to meet at."

Yukon scowled back at the outlaw leader, a wing of wet blond hair falling down from beneath his top hat and hovering above his left eye. His cheeks colored slightly, guiltily. He had the uncomfortable feeling that La Brie had been crawling around inside his head.

His voice was shrill with indignance. "Now, boss, you ain't got no call to accuse me of a double cross like that. You know how Ten was. Nobody could do nothin' better than he could. That stage station business graveled him, it did. But not me. No, sir. We been ridin' together three years now, and I got no argument about how you do things."

La Brie was partly right, the sneaky bastard. But it wasn't the job of ramrodding this group that Yukon and Tenbow Preston had coveted. They'd been wanting all the gold for themselves since about two days out of Kansas, when they'd suspected La Brie of planning a double cross with his cousins.

"I might have a sore noggin and only one good eye," La Brie rasped, staring hard at Yukon, whom he seemed to be able to see right through even with that eye that was turning white as a flour sack even as Yukon stared at it. "But don't think I'm some old bull buff ripe for the cull. Me, I got three good eyes in the back of my head, and with two I'm gonna be watchin' you." He turned to Beaver Charlie. "And with the third one, I'm gonna be watchin' you, Charlie."

"Them three rear eyes run in the family, boys," Mercy added, dipping her chin and pitching her croaky voice with bald menace, both hands on her holstered six-shooters, which she'd hooked both sides of her long, hide coat behind.

"You two got no call to talk that way to either one of us," Beaver Charlie said, sounding hurt. "We all been tight. Tighter than most gangs." He couldn't help his eyes flicking guiltily toward the bulging gold sacks draped over Tenbow Preston's black horse. As if to compensate for the indiscretion, he shook his head sadly. "Maybe we best get to ridin' before my feelin's get any more hurt than they already is."

He flipped his quirley into the wet grass and stalked haughtily over to his horse.

The La Brie bunch pushed as hard as their horses, tired from the long climb out of the canyon, would allow. With Big Norm doing the tracking from the back of his buckskin, they followed the tracks of two riders, both sets of shod prints intermittently deeper than the other, indicating that the double rider — the squaw bitch who'd led La Brie into her witch's trap — was switching horses.

By turns trotting and then loping and briefly resting their mounts, they made their way up the broad valley until the sun dropped behind the western ridges, and dark shadows slid down the high, pine-clad slope on their right. The air turned brisk, with even colder pockets along the creeks.

Stars kindled bright as near fires in a sky that had turned a faultless blue after the storm.

The tracks led to a small ranch cabin flanking an empty corral and lean-to shelter. Here, under cover of good dark, only the tiniest strip of salmon and green showing between the western mountains, the gang reined up along an aspen-lined creek.

La Brie waved Mercy away from him, and climbed down from his saddle without help. He'd drunk an entire bottle of forty-rod since leaving the canyon, but instead of seeming drunk, he appeared more determined than ever. To everyone else, including his sister, he seemed, despite his white, sightless eye, to be regaining his strength and maybe even his health.

He grabbed his army field glasses from his saddlebags. The rest of the gang flanking him as though in order of superiority — Mercy second, Big Norm, Yukon, and Beaver Charlie second, third, and fourth respectively — La Brie waded the shallow stream to the aspens on the other side, where he hunkered belly down in some chokecherry shrubs, shielded from the cabin a hundred yards away.

The cabin's front windows were lit, and the cold air was tinged with the smell of pine smoke.

"I sure would like to get inside by that fire," Yukon said, giving a shiver. "I still ain't dried out from that storm, and I swear this cold mountain air's freezin' my pecker to my left thigh."

"Shut up," Mercy scolded the outlaw. "That ain't no way to talk in the presence of a lady, ya damn buffoon."

Big Norm chuckled.

"All of ya shut up," La Brie growled, staring through the field glasses. "Let me hear myself think for a change."

"Sorry, brother." Hunkered down beside the one-eyed outlaw leader, Mercy reached out and kneaded the back of his neck. "I don't blame ya for feelin' cross, after what you been through."

"They're in there." La Brie paused, continuing to study the front of the brush-roofed, mud-brick shack and the dilapidated corral fronting the place. "There's two horses in the corral. Weeds grown up around it, several poles missin'. This place ain't been lived in regular in at least a year." He paused again. "It's them, all right."

"Kinda strange," Mercy said. "Them not coverin' their tracks, I mean, brother. They lead right across the creek here. A blind man could —" Mercy cut herself off quickly, then added somberly, "Sorry."

"You mean maybe they've lured us into an ambush?" asked Beaver Charlie. He still hadn't gotten over his indignance at La Brie's earlier accusation, and his voice and countenance owned a sullen air.

Big Norm said, "Could be they figured they lost us in that rocky draw."

La Brie lowered the field glasses. "Mercy's right. That mossy-horned old law dog wouldn't give up the gold that easy. He's either layin' for us or plannin' on trackin' us again, once he's got them two younkers put up safe somewhere. We'd best play this like it's a trap."

He ordered Mercy and Beaver Charlie to steal around to the back of the cabin, giving them fifteeen minutes to get into position. La Brie himself, Big Norm, and Yukon would approach the cabin from the front, spread wide and moving slowly. If any of them saw anyone lying in wait for them, they were to shoot first and ask questions later.

"But leave that squaw bitch for me," he ordered under his breath as Mercy and Beaver Charlie moved out, each stealing around opposite sides of the cabin, Beaver Charlie swinging far wide of the corral and the two horses.

La Brie ordered Yukon to make sure their own horses were secure — especially Tenbow Preston's black, which was carrying the gold. "And if you got any ideas about lighting out with the loot, my good friend Yukon," La Brie said, his pale eye showing eerily in the darkness, "just know I'm so hopped up on pain and hooch I'd shoot you out of the saddle at three hundred yards, then run you down and kick your mangy, double-crossing ass up around your ears and turn you inside out by your belly button."

He smiled.

Big Norm covered his mouth with a meaty hand to muffle his laughter.

CHAPTER 26

Yukon stared at La Brie, mouth agape.

The blond outlaw backed away slowly, shaking his head in awe at the outlaw leader's wrath, then turned and tramped off in the darkness. When he returned a few minutes later, crawling up beside La Brie but watching the obviously touched man cautiously, he said, "They're all good. The gold's good, too. And it's right there on Ten's black. All twenty-six thousand in coins . . . though of course I didn't take the time to count 'em."

"Let's go."

La Brie backed out of the shrubs, then stood, waved Yukon out to his right, Big Norm out to his left, and started slowly toward the cabin from which no sounds had issued since he and the gang had taken up positions near the creek. He could still smell the wood smoke, though it might have grown a little more faint. The lights still burned in the curtained windows.

In the corral, the two horses stood head to tail, heads and tails drooping, tired.

La Brie took one slow step toward the cabin at a time. Glancing thirty yards to his right, he saw Yukon doing the same, holding his Winchester up high across his chest. The outlaw from northern Canada was a rangy silhouette in his top hat and duster that hung a little stiffly, still damp from the storm. La Brie smiled with satisfaction. If Yukon had been thinking about taking advantage of La Brie's condition, the outlaw leader was fairly certain he'd purged the notion from the man's head.

Yukon was simple. And like most simple men, he was easy to cow. And now that Preston was dead, which was no skin off La Brie's teeth, he had no one to back his play. It might even be that after they'd gotten the loot to Mexico and split it up, he'd continue to let Yukon ride with him. No one was better at holdups, and Yukon had nerves of steel when it came to killing. It never seemed to give him pause or bother him afterward — two characteristics that were getting damn hard to find these days.

He didn't know about Big Norm. The big outlaw from Manitoba was a wild card in La Brie's eyes, which meant he'd probably have to kill him at some point. Now he merely glanced toward Big Norm, who held pace with him twenty yards to his left, and waved.

Norm waved back.

When La Brie was twenty yards from the cabin's left front corner, he waved for Yukon and Big Norm to hold their positions. Then La Brie continued to the cabin's front wall and, brushing his left elbow along the wall of uneven mud bricks, eased up to a window. He tried to glance inside, but the flour sack curtains were drawn, and he couldn't see either around them or through them.

He pricked his ears but he couldn't hear anything above the hammering of the little demon inside his head, who was hard at work making La Brie suffer for letting himself walk buck-naked into the squaw bitch's trap.

His heart thudded anxiously, and he caressed his Winchester's trigger with his gloved right index finger. Remaining by the window, he looked at Yukon standing between the corral and the cabin, then jerked his head toward the cabin's front door. Since Yukon had the use of both eyes, he'd have the northern Canadian brigand kick the door in and then La Brie would ram his rifle through the glass and trigger several shots through the window. That way, he wouldn't need to see anything. Just stand back and listen to the screams. Mercy and Beaver Charlie were under orders to shoot through the side windows as soon as they heard La Brie and Yukon open up. Big Norm would back everyone's play with his Sharps.

Hopefully, the squaw would survive the first onslaught, and La Brie would be able to haul her out into the yard and spend the whole night making her scream.

La Brie stepped back from the window, giving himself enough room to work. He glanced over at Yukon, who was within ten yards of the front door and closing fast. La Brie had just turned his head back toward the window when he heard a crunching noise following by a spine-splintering scream.

"*Ahhhhhh!*" someone cried as though from deep inside a cave. There was a splintering sound, like a dead tree branch breaking over a knee.

The cry became even more agonized, desperate. La Brie jerked his head toward the front door.

"*Ohhhhhhhh, mother of God! Ohhhh, Lordy — help me, help me, help me!*"

Yukon was nowhere to be seen. It was as

though the earth had swallowed him up.

"La Brie!" Yukon cried, his voice so pinched with misery as to be almost unrecognizeable.

La Brie gritted his teeth and jumped back farther away from the cabin, ready for the door to open and someone to bolt out shooting. He heard footsteps running toward him. A stout figure appeared around the cabin's corner on his left, and he swung his rifle around.

"What happened?" Mercy cried, eyes flashing in the wan light from the windows. She had her own rifle aimed out in front of her and was swinging it around, anticipating bushwhackers leaping out of the darkness at her.

Big Norm was running up behind her with his Sharps clenched in his big fists.

La Brie sidestepped toward the front door, which was the general direction Yukon's whimpering cries were coming from. The outlaw leader turned several complete circles, swinging his rifle around, then stopped when he saw the large black hole about six feet out from the front door.

More running footsteps sounded, then stopped suddenly nearby. Beaver Charlie stuck his hatted head out from the cabin's right corner, his long face pinched with alarm. "What the hell? Who's screamin' like that?"

As Yukon screeched once more, Beaver Charlie lowered his chin to peer down at the hole beside which La Brie had now dropped to one knee. La Brie stared down into the hole. There was just enough light from the windows and the rising moon to see that the pit — a bear or Indian trap — was about eight feet deep.

Several three-foot spikes stuck straight up out of it, the ends sharp as spearheads. Yukon lay on his back beside one of the spikes on the hole's far left side. The head of that spike glistened as though smeared with oil. Yukon threw his hatless head back as he screamed and clutched at his left leg impaled upon the spike.

"Help me, fer chrissakes, La Brie! My leg's all tore up!" Yukon panted and cursed. "Keee-riist, it hurts!"

La Brie looked at the cabin. Fury raked him. Gritting his teeth, he bolted forward and, setting his jaws against the pain in his head, rammed his left shoulder against the door. The door gave easily — it hadn't been latched — and La Brie bolted through it like a cannonball. His momentum carried him into the small kitchen and threw him across the stout eating table.

He piled up against the wall on the other side of the table, bellowing like a poleaxed bull, that little man in his head working on him with what now felt like a wood-splitting mallet. Amazed to see that he'd held on to his rifle, he swung it up and began firing into the lantern-lit shadows — levering and firing, levering and firing, cursing all the while . . .

Bullets hammered walls and shelves and the cabin's two crude wooden chairs and ricocheted off dusty pots and pans hanging from ceiling joists. They pinged off the stove and the stove's flue rising to the ceiling, and one shattered the hurricane lamp on a small table on the cabin's far side, sending burning kerosene licking up against the wall. The flames stretched up to the curtain.

They gave a *whoosh!* as they began consuming the dry brush of the ceiling.

La Brie looked around the cabin. No one here. Not even a goddamn mouse. He turned toward the door. Mercy and Big Norm stood just inside the cabin, wide-eyed, their eyes reflecting the light of the growing fire. Behind them, Yukon screamed shrilly, demanding help. Beaver Charlie stood beside the hole, staring sullenly down into it.

Mercy looked at La Brie, her tiny pig's

eyes sharp with rage. "I don't understand any o' this shit. I say we get the hell out of here and head to Mexico, brother." She glanced at Big Norm. "You, be damned!"

Big Norm snarled at her.

Mercy leaned her rifle against the front wall, then hurried around the table to La Brie.

"Come on, brother. Let's get you outta here before we add gettin' burned up to your list of miseries."

La Brie's jaw was set tightly. He let his sister drape his left arm over her neck and help him up off the floor. "Bastards led us here," he rasped. "They gotta be around here somewhere."

Big Norm stared around the cabin, the roof on the left side now almost entirely involved in the fire. He absently fingered one of his bear-tooth earrings. "They musta lit out after they set that old Injun trap for us."

"What about their horses?" La Brie said as Mercy helped him over to the door, nudging Big Norm out of the way.

"Maybe they got fresh ones here," Mercy opined. "Some rancher mighta been usin' the corral for his . . ."

She frowned as she stared out over the black, oval-shaped pit from which Yukon's wails were still rising. The bright orange flames inside the cabin showed through the windows on her left, making it hard to see into the darkness. But Mercy stared hard at the corral, noting that the gate looked open.

"What the hell's goin' on out here?" La Brie grumbled, stepping around the pit and slowly, methodically thumbing fresh cartridges into his Winchester's loading gate. "What in the name of . . . ?"

He frowned as he approached the corral. The gate stood wide. There was nothing inside but darkness. The musk of horses tainted the chill night air. Looking around, La Brie saw that the ground was freshly scuffed and chewed by the shod hooves of horses recently led out of the corral and led or ridden back toward the creek.

Just then he heard a distance-muffled *"Hoo-raww! Hooo-rawww, there — move, you mangy cayuses!"*

Mercy had moved up behind La Brie. She threw an arm out toward the creek. "They're gettin' our hosses, brother!"

La Brie broke into a sprint.

In the night's heavy silence, hooves thundered into the distance. Two men and a girl were yelling at the horses, their own voices dwindling as they galloped away across the valley.

La Brie, Mercy, Big Norm, and Beaver Charlie sprinted across the weed-grown ranch yard and bounded into the creek without slowing, water splashing silver in the moonlight. Beaver Charlie slipped on a rock and gave a yelp as he fell in the stream, his rifle clattering on the barely submerged stones.

La Brie continued through the aspens and knee-high grass, angling toward where they'd left the horses as though by magic he might still find them there. But all he saw as he came to a stop, breathing hard and wheezing, bending forward with his hands on his knees, was the cut picket line lying twisted in the brush.

The horses were gone.

Most important, the black horse carrying the gold was gone.

La Brie stared off across the valley, saw the black shapes of the gang's horses bounding to the right while three riders and a riderless horse — the one carrying the gold — angled off to the left, toward a jog of low hills tipped with silver by the rising powderhorn moon.

Rage threatening to detonate like a powder keg in the outlaw leader's head, La Brie dropped to a knee and started triggering lead toward the riders. He levered and fired the belching Winchester, hearing the whip-cracks boomeranging off across the pale purple valley, until his firing pin clicked, dead.

He stared through the acrid smoke wafting in front of him.

The riders had disappeared into the hills. His saddle horses were gone, as well, heading toward another, farther line of buttes to the southwest. No telling how far they'd travel before they'd stop.

"Oh, God!" Big Norm yelled, stopping somewhere off in the darkness to La Brie's right. "Oh, God — oh, *Christ!* Tell me that ain't our horses runnin' off out there!"

Mercy had been standing just behind La Brie, staring off across the valley in disbelief. Now she stepped forward and wordlessly placed a hand on her brother's shoulder.

Her thoughts were similar to La Brie's, all wrapped in the exasperation that, somehow, the deadliest gang in Wyoming and possibly even in the entire West including Canada at the moment, had been outwitted by one old man, a scar-faced kid, and a young squaw.

A savage, cunning young squaw, but a young squaw just the same.

Beaver Charlie was breathing hard and cursing as he tramped through the brush behind La Brie and Mercy, his wet boots squawking with every step.

La Brie lowered his rifle and slumped forward. He set his rifle down carefully in the grass before him, as though it were made of especially fine and fragile glass, and pressed his battered head against the ground in front of it.

"This just ain't been our day, brother," Mercy said.

"No." La Brie continued to press his head against the grass as if to drive out the pain and frustration. He swallowed, then said in an ominously quiet tone, "No, it ain't been our day. But tomorrow ain't gonna be theirs."

Behind him, on the other side of the creek, Yukon wept and sobbed like some slow-dying animal, begging for help.

Mercy turned to Big Norm and said quietly, "Norm, make yourself useful and put that annoying bastard out of his misery."

Big Norm looked at her dully. He still couldn't believe what had just happened. With a grunt he swung around and stomped back toward the cabin.

La Brie was still slumped against the earth, and Mercy was still standing beside him in contemplative silence when they heard Yukon's suddenly loud, desperate pleas cut short by three quick rifle shots.

CHAPTER 27

"All right, then," Spurr said as he pulled the needle from his sewing kit and held it over the burning brand that Pearl held up in front of him. "This is gonna hurt but probably no more than what you've gotten used to, Senor Farrow."

"Just do it and quit gassin'," Colter said, resting back against his saddle as Spurr dropped to both knees beside him.

"That's no way to talk to a seasoned medico, boy."

"You ain't no seasoned medico."

"Bullshit!" Spurr removed the cork on a whiskey bottle with his teeth, spat the cork out on Colter's bare belly. Pearl, kneeling on Colter's other side, grabbed the cork off the young man's belly and held it in her hand. "I was in the Injun Wars, amigo. There weren't enough medicos to go around up in Dakota in them days, and we soldier boys had to doctor not only each other but sometimes ourselves."

He tipped the bottle over the wound in Colter's side, which had opened up in spite of the drover's own self-doctoring with the cautering iron, and oozed a good pint of blood, judging from the good-sized stain on his shirt and coat and even over the left hip pocket of his duck pants.

Colter winced, sucked air through his teeth.

Spurr lowered his head without blocking the light of the fire they'd built at the base of the Rattlesnake Bluffs, six or seven miles from where they'd stolen the horses as well as the army loot from La Brie's bunch. Pinching up the edge of the wound with his left hand, he poked the needle through the purple, suppurating flesh with the other.

Colter groaned and clenched his fist. He was holding something warm. He looked down and saw that Pearl's hand was inside his, and he released the pressure.

"That's all right," she said, frowning down at him, her dark eyes glistening in the firelight emanting from behind Spurr. "Go ahead and squeeze. You can't hurt me."

Colter went ahead and tightened his grip as Spurr poked the needle through his skin once more, drawing the catgut tight. Pearl squeezed him back, as though trying to share her strength with him. She had it in spades. After being through what she'd been through with La Brie, staked out all night, hauled around like a sack of dry goods, then the spill from Colter's horse . . .

Colter looked up at her chiseled, aristocratic-Indian face with its high, clean cheekbones and full, dark lips, eyes like polished obsidian. She fairly radiated toughness.

Or was it hatred?

She glanced down at him as Spurr continued to work expertly at the wound, grunting a little from the strain of his position, and Pearl smiled reassuringly. The smile disappeared quickly as she lifted her head and stared into the purple night beyond the fire, toward the abandoned ranchstead where they'd set the trap — the pit had already been dug; they'd just covered it after Spurr had sharpened a few of the spikes — for the La Brie bunch.

Colter thought he could read her mind. She was hoping that it had not been La Brie whom they'd heard scream from the trap that the rancher — Spurr had said his name had been Flannagan — who'd built the ranchstead had originally dug for rampaging Indians.

She wanted the outlaw leader for herself,

to finish the job she'd started with the rock in the creek. With every fiber of her smoldering Sioux blood, she wanted revenge for what he'd done to Cimarron as well as to Shanley and Stretch Dawson. Not that the others in the gang weren't just as responsible as La Brie was, but La Brie was the leader.

He was the one who should pay the highest price.

She hadn't told Colter any of this, but he'd come to know her well enough to know what she was thinking. And he'd been through this all before himself   the all-consuming need to kill to somehow make right the killing of a person you'd loved.

She wouldn't know until La Brie was dead, however, that killing La Brie wouldn't bring Cimarron back. He'd still be dead, as Trace Cassidy was still dead even after Colter had exacted revenge on Chico Bannon and Bill Rondo. Pearl would find out just as Colter had found out, on her own, facing all the lonely years of having killed and having, likely, to continue killing in order to continue living.

Spurr drew the needle through the pinched skin once more, and looked up from his work at Pearl. He glanced over his shoulder.

"Don't worry, girl," he said, "they won't

show till after daylight tomorrow. First, they gotta run their horses down, and they won't be able to do that until dawn."

Pearl slid her dark gaze to Spurr, still squeezing Colter's taut fist in her own. He could feel her slow, insistent pulse through his skin. Her voice was a catlike purr: "I'm not worried."

Spurr stared at her. He, too, had read her mind. Pursing his thin, chapped lips, he nodded, sighed, and pinched the skin around Colter's wound and poked the needle through, sending a ripple of pain through the young drover's loins.

"There," he said, drawing the needle up in front of his face. There was only about a four-inch length of catgut trailing it from the sewn wound. He looked at Pearl. "Cut it, girl. My eyes are good at a distance, but close up . . ."

Pearl released Colter's slightly quivering hand, reached into the lawman's small leather sewing kit stamped with the emblem of the U.S. Cavalry, and removed the small, slightly rusty scissors. She leaned down over Colter's chest, her long hair feeling good as it brushed his belly, and snipped the thread just above the wound, which was so sensitive despite the whiskey that he could feel the cold metal of the scissors.

"How's your arm?" Spurr asked.

Colter glanced at his wrapped upper right arm. A little blood spotted the bandage, but the wound was closed. "That one's holding."

"I ain't gonna say you're good as new," Spurr said, turning toward the fire. "I don't like sewing a wound shut this late in the game. Invites infection. But if you keep a mud-and-whiskey pack on it, you'll likely live. Just stay away from easy women, high-stakes poker games, and tarantula juice sold by Indian agents."

Colter sat up, drawing his shirt around his shoulders. "What's that got to do with it?"

"I don't know," Spurr said, waving the needle through a burning branch to sterilize it, "but it's what sawbones always tell me, so I thought I'd share it. Never know, it might do you some good . . . if you listen to it. Me, I never did."

Spurr laughed as he packed up his sewing kit, thoroughly satisfied with himself and a little drunk, for he'd started taking short pulls from a bottle as soon as they'd pulled into the camp.

Pearl went back to the fire over which she was roasting a rabbit she'd shot with one of La Brie's two pistols just before they'd reached the base of the Rattlesnake Bluffs, on the far southern edge of the Cheyennes. She gave the meat a turn on her makeshift willow spit, and licked the juice off a finger.

"If you two are hungry," she said, "this rabbit's done."

"You younkers go ahead." Spurr hitched up his pants and picked up his bottle from beside the army saddlebags stuffed with the stolen loot. "I'm gonna take a little stroll, check on the horses and such."

When Spurr had gone, Colter and Pearl tore juicy chunks off the rabbit. Pearl sat back against a cottonwood on the far side of the fire from Colter, who leaned back against his saddle.

"He doesn't look good," Pearl said.

"Weak ticker."

"He's worried about it." She tore a chunk off the rabbit haunch and chewed. "He tries not to show it, but he's afraid to die. What makes it worse is that he suddenly found he enjoys living again. The hunt. He likes it. Knowing he will die soon makes it all the sweeter."

Colter chewed the rich meat hungrily but with a sad, pensive cast to his gaze, wiping his hands on his trousers. "He's an old raw-hider — I'll give him that. I've known a few like him in the Lunatics, but I don't think I've ever known one as tough. I figured he

362

was just a drunk and a whoremonger. Didn't think he'd make it three miles from Benbow's cabin."

Pearl set her plate down and reached for the coffeepot steaming on a rock in the fire. "He didn't, either." She held up the pot. "Coffee?"

When they finished, Colter took their plates down to a spring bubbling up from rocks to wash them. As he scrubbed the second one, he caught a whiff of tobacco smoke, and jerked to a standing position, grabbing his Remington. He looked off across the rocky slope, and saw a small pinprick of orange light making a slow arc in the darkness, near a hatted silhouette. The figure sat atop a boulder, facing the darkening plain under a vast sky of stars so thick they resembled snow streaked across velvet.

Colter stayed his hand. Spurr coughed, sniffed, and then the quirley rose once more to the old lawman's mouth.

Colter picked up the plates and tramped back to the fire. He stuffed the plates back into his saddlebags. Pearl sat on a rock, a blanket draped around her shoulders, facing away from the fire. She'd rolled a cigarette from Spurr's makings, and was smoking it slowly, thoughtfully, as Spurr was doing several yards away.

"What will you do when this is finished?" Colter asked her, sitting back down against his saddle.

She kept her head turned to the plain, and hiked a shoulder. "Go back to the ranch. It's all I have." She inhaled deeply on the cigarette, blew the gray smoke into the darkness, then turned to look at him over her shoulder. "What will you do?"

"Hell, I don't know." Colter hadn't really thought about it. He supposed he'd continue to drift, look for another job someplace, maybe farther north, even farther away from Sapinero.

"I still have a ranch, you know," Pearl said. "Just because Cimarron and the cabin are gone doesn't mean the ranch or the cattle are gone. Someone has to work the herds, bring them down to the winter pasture before the snow flies."

Colter looked at her.

"I'll need at least one man to help me through the winter," Pearl said.

Colter smiled. "I reckon you found him."

She kept her eyes on him as she took one more drag off the quirley, then stubbed it out beneath her moccasin and rose from the rock. She strolled slowly over to him, dropped to her knees beside him, and lay down as close to him as she could get. He wrapped an arm around her shoulders, felt her shiver as she pressed her cheek against his chest.

"It's gonna be cold tonight," he said.

"It's gonna be a cold winter."

"Not that cold."

She chuckled and snuggled her cheek against him, placing her hand on his belly.

They lay there for a long time in silence, sharing each other's warmth. The night got colder. The fire dwindled until Colter reached over and threw another log onto the flames. Then he lay back beside Pearl and she wrapped both her arms around him and sighed as if going to sleep.

Suddenly, she lifted her head and peered into the darkness beyond the fire's orange glow. "You don't think he died out there, do you?"

"Him? Hell, he'll wait now till he returns the gold." Colter shifted, making himself more comfortable and trying not to grieve his freshly stitched side. "If he did, I reckon it's as good a place as any."

Hooves scraped and thudded.

Colter opened his eyes and lifted his head from the wool underside of his saddle. Pearl, who'd slept curled against him all night, jerked awake also. She'd heard the horse, as well.

"What the hell . . . ?" she said as she and Colter sat up and looked around, blinking sleep from their eyes.

The sky was pale. The sun was a lemon splotch bleeding up behind them, casting a thick shadow out from the buttes and over the rocky slope rolling down away from them. Frost rimed the rocks and the short, spindly grass, melting only where the light touched it, sending steam tendrils skyward.

The fire ring was cold. Beyond it, only scuff marks where Spurr had thrown down his gear. The gear itself was gone.

No sign of the man himself.

Colter winced and clutched his painful side as he heaved first onto his knees, then his feet, looking around. "Where'd he go?"

Keeping her two wool blankets wrapped around her shoulders, Pearl shuffled across the campsite and stared down between two ragged cottonwoods. Hitching his shell belt around his waist, Colter did likewise.

A hundred yards out, Spurr was loping over the rippling slopes of the bluffs, drifting downward toward the slowly lightening plain and a distant river lined with turning cottonwoods and aspens beyond. As he rode out beyond the shadow of the Diamondback

Bluffs, the sun shone pale on the old lawman's hat crown and on the back of his ragged blanket coat, which bobbed with the roan's steady pitch.

"Damn his leathery old hide!" Colter turned and grabbed his saddle. "He's gonna try to take La Brie alone."

CHAPTER 28

Colter and Pearl were saddled and riding ten minutes after finding that Spurr had left the camp. A half hour after that, Colter reined up on the last of the hogbacks rippling out from the bluffs, and held up a hand for Pearl to do likewise.

He stared off across the sage-carpeted valley, where Spurr sat his own horse a good two hundred yards away, near the valley's center. The old lawman had taken his wool coat off and rolled it behind him, and he was holding his Winchester '66 across his right shoulder as he stared straight off across the valley, toward the pine-covered slope rising steeply on the other side of Diamondback Creek.

"There he is."

Colter batted his heels against Northwest's flanks but stopped when Pearl slapped his shoulder with the back of her hand, and jerked her head to indicate the pine-covered slope on the valley's far side.

Four riders were just now descending the ridge at an angle, moving among the sun-dappled pines. It was impossible to see them clearly from this distance of nearly a mile away, and sometimes Colter lost them among the trees, but there was little doubt who they were.

Colter heeled the blaze-faced coyote dun down the hogback and out onto the valley floor, Pearl loping the big black gelding just off his right stirrup. Colter kept an eye on the three riders descending the ridge beyond the river as he and Pearl closed the gap between them and Spurr, who, when they were within fifty yards, glanced over his right shoulder at them.

Colter saw the sour expression on the lawman's craggy face.

"Why'd you do that?" Pearl said, her voice pitched with anger as she and Colter drew up beside the old marshal. "We have just as much right to La Brie as you do."

"No, you don't, young lady." Spurr pursed his lips and narrowed an eye at her. "But I reckon you're here now, so you're in the fight." He slid his glance to Colter and said with warning to both of them, "You let me make the first move or so help me I'll see you both get a year in the federal pen."

Colter looked at Pearl. She kept her face tight, eyes on Spurr. "I have no argument with that. There's gonna be a fight no matter who starts it."

She reined her horse away from Spurr, sitting between him and Colter, who turned Northwest to face the river a half mile away. He slipped his rifle from the scabbard under his right thigh, and levered a fresh round into the chamber, leaving the hammer at full cock.

He, Spurr, and Pearl were each about ten yards apart. The four riders were crossing the stream, and Colter could see the water splashing up around their horses, reflecting the golden morning sunshine. There were three men and the yellow-haired woman, Mercy. As they bounded up out of the riverbank, they put their mounts into rocking lopes, heading straight toward Colter, Pearl, and Spurr.

Colter stared at them hard, moving his lips as he picked out La Brie on the far left, between the big man with the blue calico bandanna riding a beefy buckskin, and the cutthroat in the beaver coat straddling a stout-barreled grulla. Pearl had La Brie's pistols strapped around her waist, but La Brie had obviously found others; two black revolver grips jutted up in front of his tucked-behind duster flaps while a rifle angled up from his right thigh, the butt snugged against his hip.

The cutthroats came on grimly, the sun in their faces and reflecting off the conchos banding La Brie's hat. The sunlight made his sister's face look puffy and red beneath the narrow brim of her shabby bowler, all around which her curly yellow hair puffed.

As the group moved closer, Colter frowned slightly at the outlaw leader, trying to figure out why one eye looked white in the brash sunlight. Then he saw the three streaks of dried blood over and around that eye, and he glanced at Pearl, who sat straight in her saddle, shoulders back, breasts thrust forward, meeting the outlaw leader's gaze head-on.

The cutthroats stopped their horses about thirty yards away, holding their reins taut with one hand. The mounts snorted and chewed their bits.

La Brie and Pearl continued to glare at each other in the heavy silence.

"Ouch," she said with a tight smile.

La Brie's pale cheeks turned pink. "Where's the gold, you fuckin' bitch?"

"Safe and sound," Spurr told him.

The marshal loudly ratcheted back the hammer of his Winchester. "You four are under arrest." His voice had no conviction; he was just reciting the words because of the badge, because he had to.

Silence. The horses snorted, switched their tails, stomped in place. In the distance, Colter could hear the faint rush of the river.

His heart thudded but his hand wrapped around the neck of his cocked Tyler Henry was dry. He slowly flexed his other hand, ready to take his reins in his teeth and reach for the old Remy.

From left to right, La Brie, Big Norm, Beaver Charlie, and La Brie's sister, Mercy, stared hard at their opponents, dead-eyed.

Suddenly, Mercy bellowed, eyes flashing daggers of fury. She lifted both of her cocked Smith & Wessons, and triggered the one in her right hand.

Boom!

In the corner of his left eye, Colter saw Pearl flinch, then raise both her own pistols and aim them at the man she'd stolen them from. At the same time, Spurr brought his old Winchester up and drilled a slug through Mercy's left shoulder. The woman screamed. Her horse whinnied and pitched. But all that was in the periphery of Colter's awareness, because the rangy outlaw was bringing up his own rifle and drawing a bead on Colter.

He hadn't gotten the gun to his cheek before Colter's Tyler Henry roared. At the same time, Northwest pitched from the sudden racket, and Colter's slug punched through the rangy gunman's left shoulder instead of his heart where Colter had intended it. The gunman winced as blood spurted out behind him, glanced down at his shoulder, then brought his rifle up again.

To Colter's left, Spurr and the big man, Norm, exchanged rifle shots from their own pitching mounts, and Norm began bellowing like an enraged bruin.

Northwest was fiddle-footing too badly for an accurate shot, so, hearing Mercy add her own screams to Norm's, and Spurr and Pearl exchange shots with La Brie and his sister, Colter put the spurs to his dun. The horse rocketed forward. Beaver Charlie screamed, opening his mouth wide. Colter saw the maw of the man's rifle swing toward him. Its roar filled Colter's ears with a fierce ringing.

The bullet seared a line across Colter's right forearm a quarter second before he rammed the barrel of his Henry into the man's tight round gut.

The man regarded the Tyler Henry with a look of bald horror. *"No, you — !"*

Colter pulled the trigger just before

Northwest danced away from the rider's own pitching mount, and the rangy gunman jerked forward, dropping his rifle and wrapping an arm over his belly.

Colter jerked Northwest in a tight circle, swinging back toward where Spurr and Pearl, both still mounted, were exchanging shots with La Brie, who was also still mounted and bellowing curses, and his sister, who was down on both knees and shooting only one of her Smith & Wessons. Big Norm was on the ground on his hands and knees, bloody head lowered between his arms, bellowing and kicking his mule-eared boots.

Colter slipped out of his saddle. Enraged by the shooting, Northwest spun, and knocked Colter onto his back, probably saving his life, as a slug screamed through the air where his chest had been a quarter second before, nearly hitting the crow-hopping dun.

Pearl fired two shots at La Brie, missing the outlaw leader both times, as both their horses were dancing and prancing and shaking their heads too wildly for accurate shooting. La Brie fired at Spurr, who flinched and slid awkwardly down the side of his saddle, hitting the ground on his left shoulder, then, bellowing angrily, rolling onto his back and levering a fresh round into his rifle.

Colter brought up his own Henry. Big Norm lifted his head and cocked a pistol, looking around for someone to shoot. Colter swung his Henry at the man, aiming between his own upraised knees, and drilled a round through the man's chest, punching him straight back. He flopped around in the sage like a landed fish, arching his back and kicking his legs and triggering a round through his own left knee.

Colter racked a fresh round into the Henry's chamber but held fire as Pearl's black danced between him and Mercy, who just then fired at Pearl. The Indian girl groaned and flew straight back against her horse's rump, black hair flying.

"No!" Colter yelled, feeling his chest convulse.

He tried to swing wide of Pearl, to get a clear shot at Mercy, but then Pearl rose off her saddle's cantle to drill two quick rounds despite her herky-jerky ride into Mercy's chest and throat. Mercy instantly dropped her Smith & Wesson, both eyes bulging as she slapped both her hands to the blood welling from her neck.

Colter heaved himself to his feet and ran toward Pearl, but before he could grab her, the black flung its left shoulder into him, and he hit the ground hard on his left side. The horse gave his left ankle a painful kick, wheeled, and galloped away, shaking its head and screaming.

As Colter lifted his aching head from the ground, he heard Pearl scream. He blinked as though to clear his eyes, but it did no good. What he saw through drifting gun smoke and wafting dust was not a trick of his scrambled brains.

The black ran buck-kicking toward the creek. Pearl, her right foot caught in the stirrup, was dragged along behind, her arms flung straight up above her head and flopping over the rocks and sage. A tendril of dust lifted behind her.

Pearl!

Colter looked toward Spurr. The old lawman was on one knee, heaving himself up to his feet and grimacing at the blood welling from his upper right thigh.

La Brie was running away from the old lawman, cursing and bellowing and tripping over his own boot toes as he clamped an elbow over his side. The back of his shirt on that side was bloody.

Spurr remained on one knee, tossed his rifle into the sage, and palmed his Starr .44. He thumbed the hammer back, aimed, and fired. The slug plowed into the back of La Brie's left leg. La Brie screamed and dropped to his knees, panting and clutching the spurting wound.

As Colter heaved himself to his feet, he saw Spurr rise with a grunt and stumble over toward La Brie, holding his cocked .44 straight out in front of him. As the lawman approached him, La Brie swung around, bringing a long-barreled Dance Brothers revolver to bear. Before he could get it aimed at Spurr, the lawman slammed the barrel of his .44 against La Brie's left jaw.

La Brie's head snapped sideways. He dropped his gun, groaned, and, throwing his arms straight out to both sides, lids sagging over both eyes, slumped straight back in the dirt and lay still, his legs curled beneath his back.

Colter turned away from the two and, limping on his battered ankle that ached up into his knee, scrambled over to his horse standing a hundred feet away, near a lone cedar, twitching its ears and regarding the smoke-brushed shooting ground with large dark eyes. Colter had trained the horse well and, while the dun didn't come to Colter's whistle in the wake of so much shooting and the smell of freshly spilled blood, he stood there, ground-reined.

Colter swung up into the saddle, neck-reined the dun around quickly, and ground his spurs into Northwest's flanks. The horse lunged into an instant, ground-eating gallop, heading toward the line of turning cottonwoods and aspens along the river, following the scuffed ground across which the black horse had dragged Pearl.

Halfway across the stream, Colter saw the black horse standing facing him, about fifty yards beyond the opposite bank. Pearl lay on the ground about halfway between the bank and the horse, sort of twisted around, face in the dirt, hair tangled around her head.

Blood pounding in his temples, Colter gigged Northwest up the bank and slipped out of the saddle and limped over and knelt down beside Pearl, calling her name softly.

He grabbed her arm and turned her over. Her brown eyes were open, and her chest was rising and falling despite the ragged, bloody hole in her wet calico blouse. Colter's heart lightened.

She was alive. She would live. They'd head back to the Diamond Bar together, make a good run at the winter, and beyond that, who knew . . . ?

Cimarron's killers were dead.

"Pearl?" He smoothed her hair back away

from her face, saw her eyes move and her dazed expression change slightly. "Pearl? It's Colter. Everything's gonna be all right."

He gently lifted her head and shoulders onto one of his knees, sort of cradling her there and running the back of his left hand across her mud-splotched cheek.

Her eyes rolled upward and found his, gaining a tender cast. The corners of her mouth rose slightly. She lifted her right hand heavily, and with her index finger, gently, slowly traced the S brand on his left cheek.

Her eyes stared into his. Her finger was cold. It trembled against his knotted flesh.

When he felt her finger stop moving against his cheek, he reached up and grabbed her hand, squeezed it hard.

"Pearl . . ."

Tears rolled down his cheeks as he stared down at her face. Pearl's dark eyes rolled up. Her chest rose and fell slowly once more, and fell still.

Her hand went limp in his.

Vaguely, Colter heard hoof clomps and water splashing. When he finally turned his head away from Pearl, he saw Spurr sitting the big roan between him and the sunlit stream.

The old lawman, hatless and bloody,

leaned forward on his saddle horn. His eyes were bloodshot, grim. He gave a ragged sigh and lifted his gaze to the forested ridge from which a hawk's cry sounded, torn by the breeze.

EPILOGUE

Colter raised the flat fieldstone against the stout aspen tree, in front of the rock-mounded grave in which he'd buried Pearl.

He'd dug slowly, taking his time, feeling hollowed out and aching right down to the heels of his soul.

While he and Spurr and the badly beaten and wounded but still-kicking La Brie had lain up a day by the stream, Colter had chiseled the Indian girl's name into the fieldstone with a shoeing hammer and a nail.

It read simply PEARL PADILLA, DAUGHTER OF CIMARRON. KILLED HERE, 1878.

"Good on ya, boy." Spurr heaved himself up onto the big roan's back.

Colter stepped away from the grave, doffed his hat, and stared down at the rock mound in which Pearl lay, wrapped in a horse blanket. His throat was tight, his chest heavy. He felt the need to say something more over her than merely "The Lord's

Prayer," which he and Spurr had recited over the grave the day before, after they'd both laid her inside and covered her with dirt and rocks.

But if there were more words appropriate to the moment of his leaving her here, relinquished to eternity, he didn't have them. He merely set his hat down snug on his head and walked over to his saddled dun, grabbing the reins and swinging up into the saddle.

He looked around the sparkling river and the turning leaves of the aspens and cottonwoods, and his gaze settled on La Brie, who sat slumped in the saddle of his black-legged bay, half dead from three bullet wounds and Pearl's nasty tattoo on his temple.

La Brie was looking off, but he must have sensed Colter's eyes on him. He turned his head toward the young drover. His egg white eye was half shut, but the other glared at him while his lips lifted a mocking grin.

Colter's loins burned. He began sliding his left hand toward the handle of his Remy.

"Stand down, son," Spurr warned, reining the roan around and jerking La Brie's bay along behind him by a lead rope. "He'll pay for his sins all legal-like."

"I don't understand you, Spurr."

Colter glanced back at Pearl's grave, then, swallowing down that hard knot in his throat, heeled Northwest up beside the lawman as they began crossing the stream. His anger for La Brie was a wild, hot, living thing inside him.

"What's the damn point? You know what he done. What's the point of goin' to all the trouble of haulin' his mangy ass all the way back to Buffaloville to feed him and empty his slop bucket while you wait for the circuit judge?"

"It's real simple, Colter Farrow." Spurr looked down at the brown, clear water sliding over the rocks beneath him. "And it gets simpler the older you get."

"What's simple?"

Spurr put his horse up the opposite bank and checked it down under the rustling aspens, La Brie's mount stopping just off the roan's tail. La Brie sagged forward over his horn, half asleep.

The lawman looked at Colter, his eyes at once serious and sympathetic, as though he knew he was telling the younker something that Colter probably wouldn't understand for a while. "Because there's right and there's wrong. I've done both, so I know the difference. And haulin' this killer back for a judge and jury to decide his fate, no matter how either you or me feel about it, is the right thing to do."

He heeled the roan forward once more. "Now, let's get on down the trail before we're spendin' another night out here with this smelly son of a bitch."

La Brie grunted caustically in his saddle, but kept his eyes closed.

Colter glanced at the man once more, trying hard to repress his anger and sorrow, and heeled Northwest into a lope, headed east beside old Spurr.

Up and down the hills they rode, across a broad prairie peppered with cattle and through a jog of flat-topped bluffs before, late that afternoon, tired and dusty, they found the rough-hewn business buildings and tent shacks of Buffaloville pushing up around them.

Smoke drifted across the street, rife with the smell of supper fires. Saddle horses lazed at hitch racks fronting salloons, and a supply wagon was pulling out of town, heading for its headquarters before dark, its gray-mustached, windburned old driver looking none too happy about the long ride ahead of him.

A couple of bushy-tailed boys in ratty homsespuns ran out from under a porch to get a look at La Brie, then, as the outlaw cursed and spat at them like a caged bobcat, gave several frightened yells and ran off into an alley mouth.

Spurr reined the roan toward the street's left side, La Brie following and Colter bringing up the rear and looking around warily. Given his recent past, towns made him nervous. He'd just as soon have parted ways with Spurr back at Pearl's grave, but he didn't think he'd sleep through an entire night until he'd watched La Brie stretch some hemp.

Spurr had just passed a laundry tent run by several round-faced Chinese women in coulee hats, when he saw Abilene step out between the batwings of the Cheyenne Mountain Saloon, half a block up the main street, on its right side. The old lawman's tight chest opened, and all the bone-splintering fatigue he'd been feeling during the ride up from the Rattlesnake River melted away like spring snow in bright sunlight.

Abilene stepped down off the saloon's porch, hitching her green satin gown up her long legs, then pulling a wool, fur-trimmed shawl about her shoulders as she strolled toward him, a smile blossoming on her dark-eyed face. Her dark brown hair was gathered behind her head in a French braid.

As she approached the roan, Spurr turned the horse to face her, and leaned forward on his saddle horn. "You got a drink for a trail-blown law dog?"

She glanced skeptically at La Brie, then Colter before returning her gaze to Spurr. "I thought you were headed for Mexico."

"Ah, hell, they ain't got nothin' down there we ain't got up here."

A flush rose in Abilene's cheeks. She reached out and placed a hand on the big roan's wither.

Spurr sucked a deep breath, straightened his back, and looked around. "Besides, I figure I got another year of law doggin' in me."

"It went well, then?"

"No, it didn't." Spurr jerked a thumb over his shoulder, indicating Colter. "I want you to meet a friend of mine. Abilene, Colter Farrow. Colter, Abilene."

Colter pinched his hat brim to the woman, raking his incredulous gaze between her and the old lawman, neither one able to take his eyes off the other. Beyond Spurr, the jailhouse door creaked open, and a tall man in a string tie and funnel-brimmed Stetson limped out, leaning heavy on a cane. He was old and craggy-faced — even older than Spurr.

"Well, I'll be," the sheriff muttered, smoothing down his gray mustache with his gnarled left hand. Shaking his head, he shuffled out into the street, raking his eyes across the bunch gathered before him. "I thought for sure you was dancing with El Diablo, you old bastard. And here you are, makin' eyes with the purtiest gal in the whole damn territory."

Spurr raked his gaze from Abilene with effort. "Bill, this here's Skylar La Brie, a bad sort outta Canada. He's guilty of a whole lotta things, includin' federal robbery and murder over in Kansas, but I want him charged with murder right here in Grant County. He killed Cimarron Padilla, Cimarron's daughter, Pearl, and two men working out at the Diamond Bar. Can we wire the circuit judge and get him here *mas pronto?*"

The sheriff stared hard at La Brie sagging in his saddle but staring back at the local lawman with his cold, good eye and the grisly pale one. Wilden said, "I'll wire him just as soon as I can limp over to the Wells Fargo office, and first thing tomorrow I'll start Chester Phelps and his boys building a gallows."

"This is Colter Farrow," Spurr said, swinging down from his saddle. "Colter, Bill Wilden, sheriff of Grant County. Bill, this young man knows how to handle a gun, and he needs a job. I'll vouch that he's a right upstandin' citizen, as he done assisted me in running to ground the La Brie bunch and hauling its diabolical leader to justice. Would you be lookin' for a deputy?"

Wilden studied Colter, who jerked a skeptical glance at Spurr.

Wilden bunched his lips. "As a matter of fact, I would." He rapped his cane across his bad leg. "Don't get around near as well as I used to."

Colter opened his mouth to object, but before he could get any words out, Spurr said, "Now, boy, you was beggin' me to deputize you not two days ago!"

"Yeah, but that —"

"Deputy Farrow, please haul our prisoner's sorry ass into the sheriff's jail for us, will you? When you're sworn in and wearing a tin star, come on over to the Cheyenne Mountain, and I'll buy ya a drink to celebrate!"

"Hold on, now," Colter said, too weary to fully understand what he'd just been roped into. "Spurr!" the young drover called, swinging down from his own mount. "Hey, Spurr, hold on. I don't want no town job. Especially, no *law-doggin'* job!"

As the deputy U.S. marshal walked off

toward the Cheyenne Mountain, arm in arm with the lovely sporting girl, Abilene, he stopped only to say, "Oh, and stable my horse for me, will you?" He winked over his shoulder. "Age and seniority has its privileges!"

"I ain't no lawman!"

Spurr and Abilene, talking and laughing only between themselves, mounted the Cheyenne Mountain's covered veranda and disappeared through the batwings, leaving Colter standing on the street with the gimpy sheriff and La Brie. The outlaw grinned down at him from his bay's back.

La Brie hiked a shoulder. "Could just let me go . . . ?"

Colter looked at the sheriff, who arched a bushy silver eyebrow at him.

Colter slipped a knife from his scabbard and held it up in front of La Brie, just a few inches from the outlaw's throat. La Brie jerked back in his saddle, gritting his teeth and staring wide-eyed at the razor-edged blade.

Colter chuffed with disgust. He lowered the knife, cut the killer's hands free of the horn, and pulled him roughly down from his saddle.

"Get in there, La Brie."

ABOUT THE AUTHOR

Frank Leslie is the pseudonym of an acclaimed Western novelist who has written more than fifty novels and a comic book series. He divides his time between Colorado and Arizona, exploring the West in his pickup and travel trailer.